"Exciting . . . page-turning thrills." —*Booklist*

"A twist on the vampire novel. Fast-paced, nonstop action abounds." —*Romantic Times BOOKreviews*

Blood Retribution

"Pretty entertaining . . . hang on for the ride." —*The Times-Picayune* (New Orleans)

"Filled with plenty of excitement and intrigue." —*Booklist*

Second Sunrise

"Paced like a hundred-yard dash. Cross-genre entertainment at the top of its form." —*Kirkus Reviews*

"An entertaining start to a new mystery series." —*Locus*

Pale Death

A LEE NEZ NOVEL

DAVID & AIMÉE THURLO

A Tom Doherty Associates Book / New York

This is a work of fiction. All of the characters, organizations, and events portrayed in this novel are either products of the author's imagination or are used fictitiously.

PALE DEATH

Copyright © 2006 by David and Aimée Thurlo

All rights reserved, including the right to reproduce this book, or portions thereof, in any form.

A Tor Book
Published by Tom Doherty Associates, LLC
175 Fifth Avenue
New York, NY 10010

www.tor.com

Tor® is a registered trademark of Tom Doherty Associates, LLC.

ISBN-13: 978-0-7653-5256-9
ISBN-10: 0-7653-5256-7

First Edition: October 2005
First Mass Market Edition: September 2007

Printed in the United States of America

0 9 8 7 6 5 4 3 2 1

To Melissa, Jodi, Natasha,
and, of course, Tom for believing in Lee Nez

ACKNOWLEDGMENTS

To Judy and Jack, from the Albuquerque Police Department, for their friendship and technical assistance

Pale Death

To a vampire, expertly applied sunblock could literally mean the difference between life and death. For New Mexico state police officer Lee Nez, a half vampire—night walker in Navajo terms—it meant he could venture out into the sun for a while, though it was always risky. What if his FBI-style wraparound sunglasses were knocked off, or he'd missed a spot?

That thought on his mind, Lee considered pulling off the road before he reached Bloomfield and adding another layer to the thick, SPF forty-five goo that made harmful wavelengths of light manageable to the sunlight-impaired.

Lee's own clothing provided excellent protection. The dark gray New Mexico state police uniform covered him well, and with the billed cap, his head was safe from harm. Thank goodness Navajos were rarely bald; though due to his own extremely slow aging process, it would still take a few more hundred years to reach middle age. If he'd been a full vampire, he wouldn't have aged at all, but thanks to the help of a medicine man back in '45, Lee was only partially afflicted with the rare condition.

Dawn was only an hour away, but his shift would be ending soon and by the time the sun rose he'd be safely inside a motel room in Farmington. There, he could clean up a shift's worth of sweat and replace the sunblock. But sleep was still not on the schedule. In three hours he was scheduled to meet with a federal forensics expert, Dr. Victor Wayne.

The Justice Department employee wanted to interview Lee concerning several human-shaped outlines made of ashes that had been found in the forest near Fort Wingate during one of Lee's previous cases. Wayne suspected there was a connection between that incident and another, more recent death in Albuquerque involving a former CIA agent. This person had experienced a vampire's worst nightmare—full New Mexico sunlight.

Lee knew there was a connection and an explanation, but in order to avoid disclosing something that would jeopardize the life he'd made for himself, he'd have to come up with a spin on the truth. It was going to be a sticky morning, and the only way he'd be able to duck the issue altogether was if a time-consuming emergency call came through.

He took a deep breath and pushed the thought from his mind. Navajo beliefs told him that to talk or think about something dangerous or undesirable might serve to bring it on. He reached down and grabbed the small leather medicine bag he carried in his left-hand pocket. Inside the pouch, which was definitely not regulation for a New Mexico cop, was a sliver of flint, blessed corn pollen, a quartz crystal, and a carved turquoise bear with arrowhead attached—his personal hunting fetish. The contents of the *jish,* the pouch, had been provided by a friend, a medicine man named John Buck who knew his secret.

Lee checked the rearview mirror, saw no lights behind, and decided to pull off onto the shoulder of the highway. There was little traffic at this hour, though it wouldn't be long before oil and gas workers and truck drivers took to the roads, heading south out of the small New Mexico community beside the San Juan River.

"PD 16 Adam." It was the state police dispatcher out of the Farmington office. Lee forgot about the sunblock and reached for the mike.

"16 Adam. Go ahead," Lee replied.

"16 Adam, are you 10-6?"

Lee shook his head, despite being more than thirty miles from the dispatcher. No, he wasn't busy. But no doubt he was about to be. Fifteen minutes earlier he'd overheard a 10-76 call for a SWAT team to a Kirtland location, but that was clear across the county. It was a homicide, and perhaps because SWAT had been called, there was a standoff. Maybe more troops were being called in. "Negative. 10-8."

"16 Adam. 10-65 east of Bloomfield on 64, approximately seven miles. Assist local deputies on the scene. Code 3. Stay safe, Officer Hawk."

"10-4," Lee replied, acknowledging the call and hanging up the mike. These days he was known as Leo Hawk. Lee Nez had officially died in 1945, but only two people on earth knew that, and neither of them were around tonight. He reached over and turned on the siren and emergency lights, then accelerated immediately. A 10-65 was a hostage situation, and with one SWAT team already working another call, he might be heading into a bottom-of-the-barrel personnel situation. It was near the end of the shift for most officers on call. They'd be tired and irritable, to say nothing of the demeanor of whoever was holding a weapon to someone else's head at the moment.

High-speed travel in a vehicle was easy to manage with his agility and night vision, but there was always the possibility that some half-awake idiot would pull out in front of him. The section of highway he was entering now curved back and forth off a high mesa into the river valley, and he had to focus to keep his unit in the lane while taking fifty-mph-rated curves winding up and down the foothills. The black-and-white cruiser roared as he crossed the long bridge across the wash at Kutz Canyon, and he peaked the hill above Bloomfield at eighty-five, slowing quickly as he remembered there were businesses just ahead, and the turnoff to the gas facility.

Four minutes later he was across the river, through the big highway junction, and hauling ass east out of Bloomfield on Highway 64. Trees and mailboxes flew by, and he had to let off the gas to avoid rear-ending a county sheriff unit he'd come upon that was also running emergency to the 10-65, no doubt.

It didn't take long before Lee saw stationary flashing red and blue lights ahead, apparently at the site of the hostage situation. As he got closer he could make out an isolated two-story wooden home nestled up against a bluff to the right of the highway.

A county sheriff's white unit was parked twenty feet from the front porch, headlight beams directed at the front door. A deputy was standing beside the open driver's side door, shotgun or rifle in hand. The officer had the common sense to angle his unit so that the engine block was between him and the house. If he'd been smarter, he would have lowered his own profile by about two feet.

Lee picked up the mike and confirmed his location to Dispatch, then followed the lead vehicle up a gravel driveway lined with rosebushes. The property was well landscaped, and the house appeared to be in fine condition for a structure that must have been at least sixty years old.

As Lee swung his vehicle around to take a position beside the second county vehicle, he noticed the cargo bed of a black Dodge pickup sticking out from the rear corner of the house. There was a two-car garage, but the only vehicle in sight other than his and those of the deputies was that pickup.

It was very dark around the back of the house, at least to normal human eyes. On the rear bumper of the pickup Lee noted the NM license plate—a personalized tag that read "CMartin." It could easily belong to a Cathy instead of a Charles, though. After all, this was New Mexico, and a lot of women owned or drove trucks. Whoever it was had parked around the back. Why, when there'd been so much room out front?

Lee called Dispatch for the vanity plate name and registration as he pulled up and parked parallel to the second deputy's unit. The man was already out of his cruiser, fiddling around with his shotgun. Lee kept an eye on the windows and doors of the house as he slipped out the door of his state police car. The dome light was always turned off, of course, so it wouldn't highlight him inside or close by. It didn't matter too much, at least for those inside the house. The three officers were behind the blinding beams of their vehicle headlights, all directed toward the structure.

"What's the situation?" Lee shouted at the first deputy. When the officer turned, Lee could see the deputy was a woman in her early twenties. Her pale green eyes were almost invisible against her face, and her expression said young and inexperienced. She was directing a handheld spotlight at the second-story windows of the house, looking for anyone inside the darkened interior.

"Officer . . . Hawk, is it?" The woman's voice was high, but she sounded in control. Not that he doubted the law enforcement capabilities of a woman. They usually worked twice as hard at the job anyway.

"Yes, ma'am."

"I'm Gorman, and that's Deputy Lucero," the blonde replied. "Dispatch said the woman resident, Brenda Martin, called on her cell phone and reported that her ex had shown up drunk, with a gun. Then the call ended, like the husband grabbed the phone. Dispatch said there are two children inside—two and three years old."

"What's gone down so far?" Deputy Lucero asked, looking back and forth between them. He was older than Gorman, and a bit pudgy. His voice was surprisingly deep—like that guy from the Righteous Brothers—the tall one.

"Not much, I hope." Gorman shrugged, not taking her eye off the house. "I arrived maybe five minutes ago, and there was a light on in the front room. When I pulled up, the light went out and a woman yelled—well, screamed a name—Chuck—I think. Or maybe it was a curse."

"There's a Dodge pickup out back, with a vanity tag—CMartin. Might be Chuck," Lee said just as Dispatch broke through on the radio with the information he'd requested. The big truck was registered to Charles Martin, and the address was the same as on the mailbox he'd passed beside the driveway.

"It's Chuck's pickup," Lee called out. "I'm assuming he's the ex. Any intel on the weapon?"

"No," Gorman answered. "But I'm hoping it's not a rifle. I'd hate to ruin my new vest." She managed a weak smile as she patted the front of her tan uniform shirt, which barely concealed the specially woven material that traded femininity for a better opportunity at survival.

"Doesn't look like we're getting any more backup," Lucero said, looking back toward the highway.

"Guess we need to try and open a dialogue," Deputy Gorman said, reaching onto the floorboard of the passenger side of her unit and bringing out a bullhorn. "I hate this domestic disturbance crap. Even the battered wife turns on us when we cuff her husband. Maybe this'll drag on till dawn and then we'll at least be able to see what's going on."

Lee, who could do without the light, didn't comment on that possibility. "I'll cover the back entrance—just in case Mr. Martin decides to sneak away with one of the kids." He had a lot more experience than both the deputies put together. Maybe he could make an entry while the deputies distracted Chuck, and end this before sunup. "Just get Mr. Martin talking and focus on getting the children released. Okay with that, '74?"

Officer Lucero's eyebrows went up, then he realized Lee was referring to the ten code for a tactical plan. "'4."

At Lee's suggestion they all switched over to the same tactical frequency. Lee knew he'd be turning the volume way down on his handheld radio, however. He wouldn't be taking any calls where he was headed.

Just then, a woman dressed in jeans and torn sweatshirt

appeared at the front door of the house. She was pushed a step, then kicked in the rear, hard. She yelped and fell forward onto the sidewalk. "You bastard, let the kids go!" she screamed back at the man in the doorway as she struggled to stand up. She was dazed, drunk, or both.

"Go to hell, bitch!" he yelled back, then slammed the door shut.

"Cover me," Lee said, running out from behind his unit and toward the porch. He moved quickly, but not unnaturally so, scooping up the woman before she could climb back onto the porch. She struggled, but he tightened his grip until she grunted from the pressure. She reeked of booze, and he thought for a moment she might throw up on him.

"Hang on, lady," Lee said, carrying her toward the vehicles. He didn't relish the idea of being shot in the back, but if it came to that, the woman was more likely to suffer permanent damage from a bullet than he would. Besides, the sooner he got her to safety and set her down, the less likely it was that he'd be wearing her stomach contents.

When he reached the vehicles, Gorman opened the rear door to her unit, and Lee placed the woman inside. Before she'd even sat up, the door was closed.

"Good work, Officer Hawk," Gorman said, then gestured toward the woman slumped over on the bench. "Think she's injured?"

"No, but you may have to hose out your unit later. She's loaded to the gills." Lee regretted using that particular wording immediately. It really dated him.

"Great. Next time, pick Lucero's vehicle."

"Now I'm going to cover the back. Stay low and see if the woman can tell you anything about the kids—and find out about the gun," Lee added. When Gorman nodded, he turned and sprinted around in a wide circle, leaving the area illuminated by the glow of the headlights, and heading toward the bluff that ran along just behind the house.

Lee found an easy way up, taking big leaps now that he knew nobody was watching. Once he reached the top of the bluff, which was about twenty feet higher than the crown of the pitched roof of the house, he moved along the summit, watching the back door below and the four windows facing his direction for signs of activity and movement. A figure passed by a ground-floor window, carrying a flashlight, and Lee froze in place. That person was carrying a rifle or shotgun, but he'd walked by too fast for Lee to note any more details.

Glancing down at the pickup, which had been driven up onto a flagstone patio and through a garden patch—not a normal parking spot, obviously—Lee noticed a Ducks Unlimited sticker on the tailgate. There was the standard-issue New Mexico gun rack beside the rear window of the cab, and it was empty. Charles probably had a shotgun, which was deadly up close, but at least might not penetrate more than one interior wall—or an officer's vest.

Lee stepped back from the edge of the bluff and clicked the mike button. "Just saw the perp pass by a ground-floor window at the rear of the house. He has a rifle or shotgun, and a flashlight."

There were two answering clicks of the mike, then Gorman spoke. "Two kids inside—and it's a shotgun. That's all Mrs. Martin could give me."

Lee clicked to acknowledge, then moved closer to the edge of the bluff to check out the details of the house. The rear door looked solid, and was probably locked, so he'd have to pick it. Forcing it would make too much noise.

He looked for an easier point of entry. One of the upper-story windows was full length, opening out onto a small porch or sundeck. He could jump the twenty feet or so from the bluff to the deck, but it would make too much noise when he landed, so Lee rejected the idea.

He scanned the roof, but there were no skylights, and the chimney . . . not an option unless you were a squirrel. Unless he could pick the back door lock, he'd have to go through a window on the ground floor, or climb up that balcony. Suddenly he heard a woman's booming voice. It was Deputy Gorman, calling for Chuck Martin on the bullhorn.

Lee glanced down and saw a big object moving in front of one of the downstairs windows. It was a dresser or bookcase. Charles was blocking the ground-floor windows.

Knowing he had to act quickly, Lee looked for a place to jump down, and found a shrub of some kind growing up the cliff on a wooden trellis. Lee took a quick look at the house, then swung out over the edge. He hit the shrub directly in its center, and it broke his fall with a soft crunch.

Thanking God it hadn't been a rose, Lee squirmed out of the mashed plant and sprinted to the wall, ducking down low between the two ground-floor windows. There was a loud thump, and he saw what looked like a child's bed being propped up against the wall, mattress and all, blocking the window completely.

He was running out of options. The horizon would be lightening up within a half hour or less. Darkness was his ally, and if he was going to make use of it, the time to act was now.

"Charles Martin. Talk to me, please. We need to make sure you and your children are safe." Deputy Gorman's amplified voice echoed off the side of the bluff and onto the exterior wall.

Lee heard someone inside the house curse loudly. A half beat later came the sound of running footsteps, followed by the sound of breaking glass and the blast of a shotgun. "Get the hell off my land, cop, or somebody's going to die. I'd rather see my kids dead than living with that drunken slut."

Lee clicked his mike, and got two clicks back. The deputies were still okay, but it was obvious Charles Martin wasn't going to be reasonable.

"Mr. Martin. We want your children to be safe as much as you do. Let's talk this out. We want to make sure nobody gets hurt today," Gorman said through the bullhorn. She'd begun in a shaky voice, but had finished strong. *Good for you,* Lee cheered silently.

He inched over beneath the balcony, which was at least sixteen feet off the ground, and rose to his full height. Looking up, he gauged his jump, crouched, and, focusing his strength, leaped up. Powerful legs and the fluid motion of his hips and upper body propelled Lee to the wooden floor of the balcony, where he grabbed on to the bottom of the support rails. The wood creaked, but the balcony was well constructed and remained intact, holding his nearly two hundred pounds. Lee did a chin-up, and looked inside through an opening in the full-length curtains. The window was really a sliding-glass door that led into a large bedroom. The covers were messed up, and he could see a whiskey bottle on its side atop the carpet. Next to it was a child's doll. Other than the typical bedroom dresser and lamps, the room was empty.

Lee pulled himself up easily, slipped over the rail, and took two steps across the wooden deck to the sliding-glass door, his regulation Smith & Wesson .45 semi-auto in hand. He checked the latch, knowing he could lift the door off the track and defeat the lock, but it wasn't fastened. When he moved the handle it slid open easily. It figured. Nobody could get up here without a long ladder.

Lee opened the door just enough to step inside onto the carpet, then listened, his eyes directed toward the open door that led into a hall. A child was crying somewhere in the distance, but he couldn't detect any footsteps or activity within the house.

Then Officer Gorman started another round with the bullhorn. If he timed it right, her speech would cover his movements. He stepped across the room quickly, crouched, then peered down the hall. Several wheeled children's toys and a folding gate were scattered along the passage, perhaps placed there by Chuck to trip up an intruder. Either that, or the parents were lousy housekeepers.

Chuck's flashlight beam streaked past the stair railing on the ground floor. Inching closer, Lee took a quick glance over the rail. A baby crib had been inverted in the middle of the spacious, sunken living room, and two children were lying on a quilt inside the hastily improvised jail. They had stuffed toys with them and their faces were tear-streaked, but although visibly upset, they appeared unharmed. At least he didn't have to worry about them getting in the way or stepped on.

The beam of the flashlight swung around toward the stairs and Lee flattened against the wall of the landing, barely avoiding a plastic dump truck. Meanwhile, Deputy Gorman's litany continued, calling for Mr. Martin to come out, unarmed, and turn himself in to protect his children.

"Yeah, right. Give them back to that drunk?" the man mumbled to himself. Then he shouted again. "These are *my* children, and I know what's best for them. Leave us alone."

Lee finally located Charles Martin as he moved across the room. A big man—no, make that an enormous man, Chuck looked like a walk-in freezer with a head. He reminded Lee of that ex-UNM Lobo All-American that now played pro ball for Chicago, only half again as large. Chuck stood beside the curtain, peering out, shotgun in his right hand.

Lee felt the reassuring weight of the Smith in his own grip, and knew he could take out the man right now with a head shot and end the danger to the kids once and for all. But that wouldn't solve the real problem here.

One of the kids called "Daddy" and Mr. Martin turned to look, directing his flashlight beam toward the crib. "It's okay, JJ. Daddy's here," the man whispered softly, crouching down on one knee to greet his son eye to eye. When the man placed his shotgun down on the rug for a second to wipe away a tear, that's when Lee decided to strike.

Easing his .45 back into its holster, Lee jumped up and swung over the top of the stair railing, directing the leap with his left hand as he cleared the banister by two feet.

Charles must have heard the wood creak, because he looked up just as Lee arrived. Lee landed with a thud just a foot away from the shotgun, and barely another foot from Mr. Martin, whose jaw had dropped a foot as he tried to decide what the hell was going on.

In one fluid motion, Lee slid the shotgun across the carpet in the opposite direction, then, using the heel of his other hand, leaned forward and propelled Chuck toward the front door with a thump in the middle of his chest.

Chuck gasped and slammed into the carved wooden door so hard that it cracked right down the center. The stricken man collapsed to the floor, landing hard onto his butt. Gasping, Chuck fumbled at his chest, trying to catch his breath. He was dazed and disoriented, his eyes wide with fear from the shock and speed of the assault.

"Stay down, Mr. Martin. I'm a state police officer, and you're now in my custody." Lee reached over and turned on both wall switches. A table lamp came on, as well as the outside porch light.

Charles Martin groaned, clutching his chest, but he was unable to take his eyes off Lee. "I'm twice your size. How *in the hell* . . ."

"Stay where you are or you're going to find out, Mr. Martin." Lee reached over and clicked on his mike. "This is Hawk. Mr. Martin is in custody and the children are safe. Come on in."

Lee ended the call, then brought out his handcuffs. "Turn around with your back to me, Mr. Martin, slowly. And make sure I can see your hands. Please don't try anything else in front of your children, or I'll bounce your head off the fireplace."

CHAPTER 2

P rocessing the scene, plus the paperwork and logistics—waiting for the agency people to take custody of the children and all that—took a couple of hours. By then the sun was up. Lee had managed to remain inside the house for most of his stay, and when he was outside, he stood in the shade of one of the old house's big cottonwood trees.

He'd covered up his ability to leap onto the second-story balcony by making it look like he'd entered through a rear, ground-floor window. All that had required was repositioning a piece of furniture and unlocking a window before either of the deputies looked around. Lee doubted that Charles Martin would bring up what he'd seen, having to put all his efforts to avoid extended jail time. But Chuck would undoubtedly wonder what had really happened for the rest of his life.

Leaving the scene, Lee drove quickly to his temporary quarters in Farmington, the largest city in the area, about thirteen miles west of Bloomfield. He'd have to hurry to make that meeting with Dr. Wayne, but now it didn't seem like such a bad day. Lives had been saved.

Lee was just stepping through the doorway to his motel on Farmington's east side when the phone rang. "Officer Hawk," Lee answered automatically, closing the door and locking it. Security, even from sunlight itself, was second nature to him now.

"Officer Hawk. I'm Sergeant Rodriguez—with FPD. Dr. Victor Wayne asked me to let you know that he's been forced to cancel this morning's meeting. He'll be contacting you later to reschedule."

Lee thanked the Farmington police officer, then hung up, relieved. Here was his chance to take a leisurely shower and grab some breakfast. He didn't need much sleep, but food was essential for someone with his metabolic rate. Unlike the myths of the undead, vampires burned a lot of energy, especially when repairing body damage or after really intense physical effort—like leaping tall buildings with a single bound. He chuckled at the thought. Superman was the invention of his generation—when comic books and Saturday matinees had been a boy's most popular indoor pastimes.

After a long, relaxing shower and fresh application of sunblock, Lee dressed in dark slacks and a long-sleeved knit T-shirt. He normally also wore a baseball cap—without any logo or slogan—and high-top boots, which concealed the long commando dagger in an ankle holster. His off-duty weapon was a sixteen-round 9mm Beretta Model 92—purchased before the limit of ten-round magazines became law, and he carried a six-round semi-auto backup .45 in his pocket.

Overkill was needed sometimes—there were dangers out there much worse than angry ex-tackles toting shotguns. Fortunately, for the past year he'd often had a highly skilled ally covering his back, FBI Agent Lopez.

Diane. Lee and she were getting along quite well, going out to dinner or a movie whenever their paths crossed, making time at least once a month or so to see each other even when it was inconvenient. They weren't lovers yet, but their friendship had advanced well beyond mutual trust and respect. Diane joked with him about being old-fashioned, but it was a gentle tease, especially because from what he knew about Diane, she'd also been raised in a very traditional family.

His transfer to the Four Corners area two months ago—the department had a shortage of officers who spoke Navajo—kept them apart nowadays. Neither had actually voiced the "L" word, but Diane was the only woman in his life, and she'd made it clear that he was the only man in hers outside required Bureau assignments.

Taking one more look around the room, Lee patted the small bottle of backup sunblock in his light-weave sports jacket pocket, put on his bad-ass sunglasses, then opened the door and glanced outside. The sun was still low in the east and the porch overhang wasn't providing any shade yet, so Lee worked quickly, locking the door behind him. A minute later he was seated inside the motel's coffee shop.

The food wasn't bad, for a motel eatery, and coffee was swirling into his cup before he could even open his laminated menu. "Good morning, Officer Hawk. Busy night?"

Lena—a cute, chubby Navajo girl around nineteen—gave him the biggest smile he'd seen since, well, yesterday morning about this time.

"The usual. Speeding tickets, fender benders. Stuff like that." Though he was really ninety-two or so, Lee looked twenty-five and seemed to get his share of womanly attention. It was something he didn't want to encourage, though. Friendships were difficult for half vampires.

"Guess you missed out on all the excitement, then. I heard they found some bodies over by Kirtland when the sun came up. Two or three Anglo people dead." Lena shook her head. "It's terrible."

The girl was obviously not a traditional Navajo since she was so willing to speak of the dead. Then, as he took a big sip of coffee, Lee thought about Dr. Wayne's cancellation. "Not an accident, then?"

Lena shrugged. "It was down by the river, so I don't think so.

My cousin works for the tribal police, and his wife watches my two boys. She told me his shift was extended and he might be getting some good overtime. That's all I know. It was too late to make this morning's papers."

"Well, I guess we'll find out more about it eventually. Okay if I order breakfast now?" Lee's stomach was beginning to grumble.

"Ooops, you're right. What'll you have, officer, a jumbo Southwest Sunrise, with extra green?"

Lee nodded, looking forward to the pile of scrambled eggs topped with Hatch green chile, steaming, crispy hash browns, and a half-dozen thick slices of bacon. The toast was homemade, thick sliced, and smeared with real butter. "And keep the coffee coming."

"Gotcha. Where do you put it all, handsome?"

"I'm a bottomless pit, what can I say?"

Lena giggled. "Then I'd better get this into the kitchen before you starve to death." The young woman winked, then hurried off.

A half hour later Lee was munching on his last piece of toast when his cell phone started to vibrate. He picked up the device and looked at the sender's number.

He recognized the caller and pressed the receive button. "Good morning."

"Lee, it's me." Special Agent Diane Lopez's sexy, slightly gravelly voice was quite distinctive. "I need your presence, officially, at a crime scene just west of Kirtland. We have three homicide victims, and based upon what I've seen so far, you're *extremely* qualified to deal with this situation."

"Extremely?" Lee looked around to make sure none of the other breakfast crowd could hear him.

"Yeah, I'd say that—for sure. We're just north of the San Juan, a few hundred yards east of the bridge at Fruitland. An officer will lead you from the highway to the site. How soon . . . can you get here?" Her voice nearly broke, then finished strong.

"Within a half hour." Lee checked his watch. "I'll call back once I get on the road. Hey, you okay?"

"Yeah, I'm fine. And, Lee, there's a fed here we've met before. That forensics expert from the Justice Department—Dr. Wayne."

"I'm not surprised. Is this scene going to remind him of Fort Wingate?" Lee said, standing and leaving a few dollars beside his plate. He'd paid when the meal was served, a good strategy when he sometimes had to eat and run.

"Not exactly, but you might want to bring a wooden stake or two, just in case."

Lee heard Diane yell something to someone else. "Sorry, Officer Hawk. Gotta hang up now. See you in thirty." Her tone had changed, which meant someone had moved within listening range at her end.

Lee jammed the cell phone back into his pocket and hurried out the entrance to the coffee shop.

T wenty-five minutes later Lee was directed toward a sandy spot beneath a stand of cottonwood trees. There was dust in the still air, and it was obvious what had stirred it up. Several other vehicles, most of them patrol units like his own but from the sheriff's department and the Navajo tribe, were in various locations between this place and the river. The cold, usually shallow San Juan River was visible beyond the willows and grass, a hundred yards farther south.

A generic federal sedan, which he surmised was assigned to Diane though it wasn't her usual vehicle, was about fifty feet from his. The Navajo officer that had led him to this parking area in the bosque—the closest thing to a desert forest at this elevation—climbed out of his own vehicle and motioned with his head toward a group of officers among the rim of willows and grass in the flood plain beside the river, which wasn't really much of a barrier this late in the summer.

"Thanks," Lee said, stepping away from his own black-and-white. The officer walked on ahead of Lee until reaching a yellow crime-scene tape, which roughly encircled a section of red and green willows, damp sand, and river-bottom boulders leading to the sun-drenched river.

There were several officers standing at various distances from three blanket-draped figures sprawled atop the moist sand only a few feet from the water. The tribal officers were together in one group, watching silently, and three county deputies were occupied taking photos and placing wire flags next to various traces of evidence.

Two men in civilian clothes, one wearing a suit and the other in jeans and an OMI jacket, were crouched beside one of the bodies. The blanket had been drawn back to the waist, revealing a bloody shirt. The victim had been impaled with a piece of wood. The OMI man was taking notes on a clipboard.

Lee took a quick glance around, spotting Diane, alone and wearing a dark nylon jacket, walking in his direction from the west. One of the deputies working the crime scene stopped to study her form. His companion nudged him none too gently, and the deputy got back to work immediately.

Diane was a hard-nosed law enforcement professional, but she could be a heart-stopper too. Twenty-seven years old, Agent Lopez was a fair-skinned Hispanic beauty with light brown hair and haunting amber eyes. She wore lightweight boots that added about an inch and a half to her short stature, and was in very good shape, a fact that she often tried to conceal with sensible slacks and a loose-fitting jacket. Right now, she could have been a runway model for the business professional, if it wasn't for the 9mm Glock at her belt and the radio.

"Officer Hawk." Diane nodded as she spoke, showing her

professional respect in front of the others. She also knew not to shake his hand—a Navajo taboo among traditionalists. "I'll brief you while the OMI and Dr. Wayne complete their preliminary examination."

She continued her walk downstream, and Lee joined her, matching strides. Diane seemed quite pale, even when considering the morning light, and he wondered just how bad the victims had been mutilated to bring out this reaction in a veteran like her. He kept quiet, letting her continue at her own pace.

"Glad you were in the area, Lee. I was at the Albuquerque Sunport interviewing on an unrelated case when I got the call to check this out. The Bureau flew me to Farmington, and I drove from there. Dr. Wayne, unfortunately, was at the Farmington station at the same time, and decided to join me since he'd heard the buzz."

"Buzz? We've got three murder victims, right? I know you suggested that I bring a wooden stake and I saw the one that had been impaled. Is another vampire on the loose?" Lee knew that even a multiple homicide probably wouldn't have attracted the attention of a special Justice Department forensics specialist—not unless there'd been something unique about the crimes. But although Diane knew about vampires, Lee couldn't believe Dr. Wayne would buy into such a possibility unless one jumped out and actually bit him on the ass.

"The superficial evidence is there. It looks to me like the victims, three Anglos, were killed by either a Hollywood-style vampire, or possibly someone playing a sick game. The victims all lost a lot of blood, had wooden stakes jammed into their chests, and, get this, have what looks like bite marks on their necks. All three, and in the same place . . . like a vampire drained them, then staked the bodies so they couldn't turn."

"But you and I know"—Lee glanced around to make sure no one could hear him or read his lips—"that real vampires aren't neck nibblers. It's way too inefficient—and messy."

"But, Lee, those people over there on the riverbed were armed with wooden stakes—I found three being carried in jacket pockets—and they obviously fought hard for their lives. The two men looked relatively strong and healthy, and I know the woman was young and fit . . ." Her voice broke slightly again and she looked away for a second.

"What's up, Diane? This isn't just a nasty crime scene to you. There's more." Though he'd tried to sound sympathetic, it came out more like an order. His feelings were sincere, but he was a little out of practice.

"I know . . . knew the woman," she said, her voice unsteady. "Her name was Lynette Alderete and we grew up in the same neighborhood in Albuquerque. I even dated her brother a few times."

That explained the falter in her voice when she'd first called. "What's she doing here at the edge of the Navajo nation?"

"I have no idea. She's a dermatologist, and last I heard, she was teaching at the UNM Medical School. Maybe she was in the area to give a seminar to local physicians or something like that. We've been out of touch for nearly a year now, I guess."

"Anything on the male victims? Are they doctors too, maybe specializing in biochemistry or radiology?" Lee was starting to see the light, and light wasn't always a good thing. He glanced over at the Navajo officers, who seemed more interested in them than in the medical examiners, and urged Diane closer to the cold, clear water. From there, they'd prevent their words reaching the others—even via lip reading. "Maybe the feds have gotten past the ridiculous notion of demons and the undead and are taking a closer look at vampires from a strictly scientific point of view. That might explain Dr. Wayne's interest. I'd better take a closer look."

"I'll talk to the deputies and see what they've got." Diane went to join the deputy photographing footprints leading from the river to the crime scene, and Lee walked toward the bodies.

Lee recognized Arthur Cooper from the Office of the Medical Investigators, a member of New Mexico's statewide network of investigators. OMI people went to the scene of any suspicious death, and sent bodies to Albuquerque for autopsies at their UNM Hospital facility. Cooper looked up at Lee and nodded, handing him two pairs of latex gloves to wear.

The man worked the Four Corners, and knew most Navajos didn't like to touch the dead, or anything that had touched the dead—hence two pairs of gloves, one over the other. "State Patrolman Hawk, this is Dr. Wayne. He works with the Justice Department criminal forensics division."

"We've met. Victor," Lee acknowledged the tall, slender man in his early sixties. He had sharp eyes and a firm jaw that reminded Lee of a bulldog. Wayne was an expert on all forensics matters—at least he thought he was—and wasn't slow to express his views.

Dr. Wayne had insisted at their first meeting, about a year ago, that Lee call him Victor. It was all part of the good ole boy strategy Wayne used to get any additional information, gossip, or off-the-cuff remarks that might help him on the case. It worked for the fictional TV cop, Columbo, but not for Victor—at least not when dealing with him or Diane.

Victor smiled, despite the presence of a cold, pale, attractive, and very dead young woman on the rocky ground just three feet away. Lee took one glance at Lynette Alderete's face, then couldn't help sneaking a look at Diane.

"Ah, you notice the resemblance too, Officer Hawk. They could have been sisters. And Special Agent Lopez knew the victim, she tell you that?" Dr. Wayne said offhandedly, enjoying the expression on Lee's face. "Coincidence?"

Lee refused to let Victor get to him. The man had bugged him and Diane for weeks following the deaths of those vampires near Fort Wingate last year, and called on them again after those incidents in Albuquerque. He fought the urge to pull the doctor aside and treat him to a vivid show-and-tell about vampires. That might have shut Victor up and gotten him out of their hair permanently.

"Why don't you take a look at the victims and tell me what you think did this or, to be more precise, what kind of person, Officer Hawk," Dr. Wayne said, standing. "Meanwhile, Arthur, maybe you should start making some calls and getting the authorizations for me. I want to begin autopsies on these victims *this* afternoon."

Cooper turned toward Lee so the fed couldn't see, and rolled his eyes. "I'll get started right away, Dr. Wayne."

Lee worked hard not to smile as he nodded to both men and walked away. The Navajo officers had moved farther away, and were now walking toward the bridge in the distance. Maybe they were going to search the far bank—their turf.

He stepped closer to the body, making sure not to touch any of the splattered blood on the rocks, stooped down, and moved the blanket off the victim completely. Directing his gaze at the feet, he noticed the woman's shoes. The leather pumps were dirty and badly scuffed—months of wear put in them probably within a few hours of harsh use. They were still moist from the water. Her ankles had been rubbed raw, probably from running across the desert in street shoes.

Bruises and scrapes ran up her body, and her slacks and blouse had been torn. In places, pieces of branches and brush had snagged and remained. Enormous black and blue marks on her upper arm indicated she'd been grabbed with an iron grip. In the center of the bruises bones protruded through broken flesh. Whoever had killed her had also broken her arm with two hands, snapping the bones like a twig.

Lee felt Dr. Wayne was watching him, so he showed no emotion as he conceded silently that Ms. Alderete *had* been killed by someone incredibly strong. Maybe a vampire. Of course, the holes in her neck encouraged such speculation, as did the wooden stake that pinned her to the ground through the left side of her chest. But the wounds on her neck were pure theatrics. His guess was that the holes by her jugular had been made with either a nail or a piece of wire.

Lee covered the body back up carefully, then stood and stared right at Dr. Wayne, who couldn't see his eyes anyway through the dark glasses. "She ran, and was hunted down after being pursued for some distance. She either entered the water here and came back out, or maybe she crossed to this point from the opposite bank just before being attacked. Either way, she was killed at this spot by someone very strong and brutal. Her arm was broken before she died. Hopefully, she'd already passed out before the wood splinter finished her off."

"Stake. She was killed by a wooden stake. And with the marks on the neck as well, what does that suggest to you?" Dr. Wayne asked. His tone suggested that he wanted Lee to be the one to bring up the obvious.

"Halloween isn't for a few months, so don't expect any *X-Files*-flavored speculation, Victor. We have a very strong, angry person with a propensity for mass murder. You know as well as I do that everything here has been staged. Special Agent Lopez will have access to any profiling that might lead to the appropriate terminology. Mutilating victims is the kind of thing sick people do to get attention. Fifteen minutes of fame—at somebody else's expense."

Lee turned to the OMI man, Cooper. "Are the two other victims like this?"

Cooper nodded. "They're impaled by similar wooden stakes, and they have the same kind of wounds on their necks—not really bite marks, though." He glanced over at Dr. Wayne, who shrugged.

Cooper continued. "Their shoes are wet and their pant legs are damp, indicating they'd all gone into the river, though only to a depth of about two feet. It's very shallow around here, so they might have come all the way across. They either decided to make a stand here, or whoever was chasing them finally caught up. They had the crap beaten out of them too. There are lots of defensive wounds, bruises, scratches, minor cuts, broken fingernails—like that. The men were pinned to the ground, like the woman. Whether they were already dead by then, well, that's not my call. The stakes were the last touch, though."

Cooper was very matter of fact about it. Working in the Four Corners, where murders were often the result of beatings, he'd probably seen worse.

"What about IDs?" Lee asked. "Agent Lopez knew the woman. She's a physician and her last-known position was as an instructor at the UNM medical school. Were these men scientists or doctors too? Coworkers of hers?"

"We'll move the bodies in a few minutes and check their wallets," Cooper said. "We were able to search their front pockets, and found coins, ChapStick, chewing gum, and two sets of vehicle keys. One is to a Beemer, the other a Dodge. Both keys look new, so these guys must have been making good money. And Agent Lopez found a set of keys in the woman's pocket. There are officers checking for any abandoned vehicles in the area. The older deputy over there has the details," Cooper added.

Diane was talking to the younger deputy, but looked up just as Lee turned in her direction. When she diverted her eyes to check something behind him, he followed her gaze. The Navajo officers who'd gone down the river had crossed over and were starting to look for tracks and evidence on the far bank. One of the officers shouted something in Navajo that Lee recognized. Tracks. He'd expected as much.

He looked back at Diane and she nodded, so Lee got the OMI man's attention once more. "Arthur, let me know if there's anything else. Agent Lopez and I are going to try and backtrack from here."

Cooper nodded.

"Let me—us—know what you find, Officer Hawk," Dr. Wayne asked. It was more like an order, though, not that Lee cared. Wayne had no authority over him.

"Sure," Lee replied, wondering why Dr. Wayne was involved and what kind of interference he could expect from the man. With any luck, Wayne would be on his way back to Washington within a day or two.

Noticing Diane was already halfway to the bridge, Lee had to jog to catch up to her. With no traffic on the rural bridge at the moment, they walked across quickly, then reversed their direction and angled back toward where the Navajo officers were scrutinizing the ground beside the river.

"Well?" Diane whispered loudly.

"Well, what?"

"Come on. Did a vampire do this?"

"If it wasn't for the corny horror touches, I'd say yes, almost certainly. Taking on three adults at night after running them to ground, beating them all to death at about the same time in hand-to-hand combat, breaking arms like sticks, then pinning each one to the ground . . . very few human fighters could do that. But for a vampire, it would be relatively simple, especially if none of his opponents had been trained in hand-to-hand."

"Of the vampires I've met, some were good and some were bad. Ultimately, it's their character that determines how they choose to use their abilities. Could we be dealing with one who's insane, despite an ability to self-heal? A vampire mass murderer or serial killer could be extremely hard to catch—and destroy." Diane watched his face carefully. He'd begun to open up to her a lot more emotionally, and she could read him quite well now.

"I think you've already made up your mind, or you wouldn't have called me this morning, Diane. But for what it's worth, I think you're probably right. By the way, who discovered the bodies?"

"An old Mexican man who works at a farm near here. Apparently he was looking for a horse that got out, saw the bodies, and ran all the way back home. He called the sheriff and told the deputy I spoke with that a *chupacabra* had killed these people. Some kind of goat creature from Mexican folk stories. The old man looked like he was having a heart attack, so the EMTs took him away."

"I've heard the stories of *chupacabra*. Goat sucker, I think is a close translation. Wonder if we're about to find out about another kind of vampire—whether we like it or not," Lee said.

They were getting close to where the Navajo officers were crouched, checking footprints or signs, so she whispered, "Got enough sunblock?"

Lee nodded. "I hope so."

"Officer Hawk," one of the Navajo officers, clad in the tribe's tan uniform, said, nodding to Lee. "Ma'am," he added, glancing at Diane. He then pointed to the ground beside the waterline, which had receded slightly since earlier that morning.

"Please tell me what you think happened over here," Diane said, trusting the officers to know their field craft as well as her and Lee. It would save time.

The two other Navajo cops looked up almost in unison. Maybe they weren't used to being asked for help from other agencies—other than with crowd control or traffic.

"Those three died over there, but they crossed the river here first." He pointed to three sets of prints, one smaller than the others and obviously belonging to Dr. Alderete. "The length of stride tells us they were running."

Diane nodded, but Lee got down on his knees to check out a particular set of prints—boots, it looked like.

"There was one person chasing them—the one wearing the boots." The short, barrel-chested officer crossed his arms in front of him. "He cut them off before they could reach the bridge, forcing them to turn and enter the water."

Lee turned and looked in the opposite direction. A bluff ran along the river valley for miles, and few buildings were visible, even to him. Who had they been running from, and what had happened to put them in the path of the killer? Lee looked toward an arroyo not far from the river that led up to the cliff side. He thought he could see skid marks where they'd slid down a steep spot.

The officer saw where Lee was looking. "Good eye. That's where we plan to look next. It looks like they came down the bluff, then to the river farther downstream and hid there for a while. One of my officers found a place where they stood behind some willows not far from here. But they must have been seen or heard by the one after them, because they broke cover and ran to this spot."

The tracks showed the three had stuck together, probably not a good idea because it made them easier to track—and catch. If their hunter was a vampire, they'd have been better off scattering and hope he or she couldn't get them all before daylight. Darkness itself wouldn't have helped, only good, solid cover, and there wasn't much of it around here south of the river.

The distance between individual boot prints revealed that the person tracking the three also was running, keeping the three from reaching the bridge by cutting them off and herding them toward the river, as the officer had said.

They were already up on the bluff, moving toward several low hills beyond when Lee noticed a sand-colored, one-story stucco building constructed into one of the hillsides. The tracks weren't leading in that direction at the moment, but he suspected that was probably only due to the terrain.

The Navajo officer in the lead stopped, seeing what was ahead as well. He turned and waited for the other Navajo officers to catch up. They spoke in Navajo, their voices low, but Lee could hear what they were saying despite being fifty yards away.

The building was some kind of federal agency structure, and the locals were kept away by private, uniformed guards. Five vehicles were in a small parking area, and though Lee noticed there were outside security lights, there was no tall fence with the usual strands of barbed wire at the top.

"What's that building?" Diane asked the officers. She was closer to them, and he'd kept back, not wanting to challenge their authority on the Navajo Nation though he was a state police officer with jurisdiction here as well.

"The sign says it's a federal air quality research center," the spokesperson for the Navajo policemen said. "The tribe leaves them alone, and the staff comes and goes at all hours. I don't know any more than that."

Lee looked at a set of instruments on the roof that might be sensors. "Kind of a big building—out here all by itself. Where's the security fence? The feds—no offense, Agent Lopez—usually have a big one with barbed wire."

"There are guards here, at least three at a time, so I hear," the Navajo cop replied. "But they rarely come outside. They're big guys. But no guns, right?" He looked at one of the other Navajo cops, who shrugged.

Lee looked at Diane. Usually security guards protected the outside from intruders. What would they be guarding that kept them mostly inside? He could see Diane was curious too.

"Well, let's find out if the murder victims came from here, or if anyone who works in there might have seen or heard something," Diane said.

"Go ahead, ma'am," the first cop said. "We'll keep following the trail."

Lee stuck with Diane, and they quickly arrived at the front entrance. There were no windows in the flat-roofed, sturdy structure, which looked more like a bunker than a lab. It reminded Lee of that Albuquerque base where the nukes had been stored.

The sign on the steel door confirmed the facility as an air quality research center, but the locks were state of the art, electronic, and solid-looking, with a keypad to enter a code number. "Why go to all that trouble with security, then stick a rock in the door to keep it open?" Lee pointed to the baseball-sized rock wedged at the bottom.

"Yeah, and it's dark inside," Diane said, looking through the opening. "Hello. FBI. I have some questions."

She reached for the handle, but Lee grabbed her hand. "Hold on. This doesn't look right. There's water all over the floor in there, and I see exposed wires in the way." Lee took a closer look. "Those are bare wires. It might be a booby trap."

Diane reached into her pocket and brought out a small, powerful flashlight and directed it to shine through the three-inch-wide opening.

"The wires run up to the door, but from this angle, I can't see where they're connected." She looked down on the floor again. "But there must be a half inch of water on the floor. There's a lot of glass too. Looks like somebody broke one of those big drinking water dispensers."

"Water—bare wires—broken glass. Let's back up a step and think about this. What's the address here, anyway?" Lee wondered, looking around for a mailbox.

"Post office box something, I'd guess, unless there's a mailbox down at the highway. Thinking of giving them a call?" She brought out her cell phone.

"Check and see if you can get a number. If someone's alive inside, they might be able to reach a phone. If they're not inside now . . ."

"Then some of the cars in that parking lot belong to the dead people down at the river," Diane said, finishing his thought. She noticed one of the Navajo officers standing in the parking lot. "Could you start running the tags on those vehicles and get the owners' names for us?" she shouted.

The officer nodded, then grabbed the radio off his belt and started to work.

"Good idea," Lee said, glancing at Diane potting a small tree limb on the ground that still had a fork where a branch had been, Lee fashioned it into a crude hook. "Diane, got a latex glove I can borrow?"

"I see what you have in mind." She tossed him a glove, he slipped it on, then took hold of the branch. "Stand way back, in case there's more to this we can't see."

Lee hooked the notch in the branch to the door edge, then used the piece of wood to pull the door open. As the door swung back, wires taped to the inside of the door were yanked loose and dropped to the floor, landing in the water. There were sparks, a loud buzz, then the acrid smell of burning rubber and insulation filled the air.

Lee held the door open and looked inside. The room, more of a foyer with a second, closed door leading farther into the building, was spartan, with a coat rack, a stand for the water bottle, a calendar on the wall, and a hand-lettered sign that said "Security Is *Your* Responsibility."

On the inside of the exterior door above the handle was an electronic lock with another keypad. Apparently, employees had to enter a code number to get out as well. This "to hell with fire codes" attitude reminded him more of a prison than a research facility. But maybe it all depended on the kind of research being done. If it was an air quality research center, then the equipment being used must have been priceless.

The hot wires were from an outlet, and had been literally ripped from the wall, creating a long, jagged hole in the sheetrock. Diane handed him the rock, and he used it to prop the door wide open so she could see inside as well. He stretched out his arm, grabbed the two wires, then, making sure he didn't handle them where the insulation was missing, touched them against the metal in the wall outlet box. Nothing happened. "The circuit breaker has been tripped now, so we don't have to worry about getting fried." He bent the wires up and out of the way.

"Before anyone messes with the main panel, remind me to have something done with those bare wires," Diane said.

"Ma'am?" It was the Navajo officer who'd been in the parking lot.

Diane turned. "Got an ID?"

"The red Mercedes out there belongs to the dead woman. And all the vehicles have been vandalized. There are ignition wires and modules scattered about. None can be started, even with the keys, until they're repaired."

"All three victims must have worked here," Lee said. "Can you check out the names of the other vehicle owners, then see if any match with the IDs the OMI got from those other bodies?" Lee said to the officer, then turned to Diane. "Okay with that?"

Diane nodded her approval to the Navajo officer, but as he turned, she suddenly called out, "Wait!"

The officer looked back.

"Be very careful what you touch. We've already found a hot wire—a booby trap left by someone, probably the killer—and there may be more," Diane added.

"Thanks. I'll tell the others." The officer hurried back out toward the parking area, looking around for his own people.

Diane joined Lee, who was examining the interior door without touching it. "Locked?"

"No. I tried the handle. I was just wondering, before we went any farther, what happened to the other three people here—the guards, I imagine."

"I counted five vehicles too. Well, I guess we're about to find out." She stood back, aiming her light, as Lee opened the door.

CHAPTER 3

The building appeared to be unoccupied by the living or dead, though there were various security and other unique modifications to the structure that would have puzzled anyone *not* thinking about vampires. A room serving as a laboratory contained light sources that would allow researchers to select a wide spectrum of wavelengths for illumination. Some of the sources, unlike normal artificial lighting, would be dangerous or lethal to a vampire.

In one hallway they found signs of a violent struggle, with blood splattered along the floor and up the walls. In several places large dents and holes in the wall suggested that someone in the struggle had bounced off the wall so hard they broke through the surface. They even found drag marks through the blood, but still no bodies—other than those already found, a few miles away, down by the river.

Locked strongboxes were found attached to the walls in the office area that had the word "Emergency" written on them, but the containers couldn't be forced open without tools, even by Lee. One box, however, *had* been opened, and two wooden stakes, exactly like those found in the victims' chests, were still inside the box. There was also a dart pistol, and two loaded darts containing a knockout drug Lee recognized was used for sedating large animals.

After groping around in the dark with her small flashlight for about fifteen minutes, Diane finally had enough. "Dammit, Lee, you can see in the dark, but having to use this flashlight is a pain in the ass. We haven't found any more live wires, so let's check the main panel and see if we can get the power back on."

Lee managed to find some electrical supplies in a small toolbox in the lab, and tied off the exposed wires in the foyer with a screw-on wire nut. Meanwhile, Diane had located a closet containing the main panel. When they were ready, she started flipping the breakers.

"Hey, turn that last one back off!" Lee yelled, ducking out of the foyer. He could feel the heat on his fingers.

Diane came to see what had happened and found him applying sunblock to his upper arms and hands. "The light in the foyer?"

"Would have fried a full vampire without sunblock. Got me on my fingers where the protection was starting to wear thin. With that light on, no unprotected vampire could stay here more than a few seconds before they started to cook."

"It could just be a coincidence. What if our suspicions are wrong and these people were some kind of natural light health nuts trying to enhance their creative karma?"

"For that we'd have to ignore everything else we've seen. Diane, I think we have a vampire situation here," Lee said, then clamped his mouth shut, a terrible thought suddenly occurring to him. He whipped out his pocket notebook and scribbled Diane a note. "Hope this place isn't bugged."

"Let's assume it is, Lee," she answered aloud, nodding her head. "And let's go into all these other rooms very carefully."

Fortunately none of the other rooms had lighting that was hazardous to a vampire's health, except for the lab area. Diane was trying to decide if she wanted to start going through desks when she got a phone call. She spoke for a few moments, then hung up and turned to Lee.

"Cooper and Dr. Wayne have IDs on the other victims now, and are trying to contact their next of kin. The men were MDs, one named Prescott, the other Krause. Their vehicles are among those outside. The tribal cops are going over the cars now, but I got the feeling they're not too eager to come into this facility. Could it have something to do with that Navajo belief in the *chindi,* the bad part of a person that's left behind when they die?"

"Could be, though the spot where they actually died is the most dangerous place to be," Lee answered. "But maybe they're worried that there are more bodies in here someplace."

"That's a real possibility. The blood we found in the hall might not be from the victims beside the river. Maybe we'd better give this place a real going over. There were supposed to be security guards, right?" Diane said. "Let's check out every closet and behind every cabinet—and in them."

He and Diane checked every obvious spot, then Lee thought of something they'd been overlooking. "There's no blood around the foyer—the only way out—but blood is all over the hallway where a kick-ass struggle took place. Chances are, it doesn't belong to those found outside, so take a closer look at the blood trail and see if we can find the source."

They went back to the hall, which continued in a big L across the center of the building. Though most of the blood spills were near the hall where it dead-ended, they managed to find a few drops farther down. The trail led to a big closet that housed a heating unit, one they'd looked inside earlier while searching for more victims. The metal box was resting on a big plywood sheet, and had a big electric cord leading to a wall socket. Lee looked at the connection closely.

"This doesn't look right, somehow," Diane commented, shining the light around the enclosure. "There's a power cord, but there aren't any ducts at the top to transfer the hot air." She stepped into the closet and looked around the back of the unit.

"There aren't any coming out the rear of the unit, or the bottom, either. How could this heat anything except the closet?"

"It couldn't. So either it's a boondoggle or a dummy unit. But why?" He looked around the enclosure and noticed a light switch inside. But there was no light fixture or bulb, nor was there a thermostat or heater switch anywhere, inside or along the hall. "Let's see what happens."

He flipped the switch, and the floor began to move. Diane stepped back, and they both watched the heating unit rotate to the left, into an opening that appeared as a hinged section of the wall recessed farther back to accept the unit. Where the heater had been there was an entrance to a short hall that extended another eight feet, then disappeared to the right. Lee studied the light in the ceiling of the passage.

"I don't trust that light. See the color?" Lee pointed out. "It's one of those natural bulbs—vampire-proof." He stepped into the closet, trying to see around the next corner. "I hear something. Yelling, I think."

She listened for a moment. "Must be your sensitive ears. I'm getting nothing."

"It's coming from farther ahead," Lee whispered. "Somebody's still alive."

"I'll go first," Diane said brusquely, pushing her way past him, "just in case there's another vampire-resistant spot."

Lee followed her into the narrow hall, then into a small room with a massive, barred steel door on the opposite side. Overhead were three high-wattage lamps and no wall switch to turn them off. The bulbs were intense, and shielded behind thick glass or plastic, and a heavy wire frame.

"Definitely vampire-resistant. Nothing a vamp could do to avoid getting fried unless he was covered up. For a full vampire, any sunblock wouldn't last long. And that voice. It's louder now," he said.

"Step back into the hall while I check out the door," Diane suggested, then she stopped talking. "I can hear it now. A voice."

Lee nodded. "I can smell blood too, lots of it. Behind the door." He stepped over quickly and swung up the heavy metal brace that kept the door from being forced from the other side. "No need for locks, not if you're keeping a dangerous animal behind this door."

"Or a vampire as a prisoner," she added. They both brought out their weapons, and Lee pulled the heavy door open as she kept her sights on the opening. A flight of stairs led down to a darkened room with a bare concrete floor. Diane directed her flashlight and found a light switch just inside. She flipped it on. "Oh, shit."

"The guards?" Lee asked, joining her as she rushed down the steps. The lighting was a normal, fluorescent fixture in the concrete box of a room. A bed, sink, and simple toilet were all that occupied the cell-like room—except for the pools of blood, two battered, motionless men on the floor, and a naked, beaten man curled up on the bed in a fetal position.

The one on the bed reacted to the light, a good sign of consciousness. His face was swollen, and from the bruises on his body, he probably had some broken bones as well.

"Thank God you heard me," the man on the bed managed. "My voice . . ."

Lee started to take off his jacket to cover the man up and save him any more embarrassment, but Diane held up her hand. "Let me do this."

Because you'll be needing yours for light protection, Lee knew. Diane didn't have to speak the words out loud for him to understand. And she was right.

He checked the men on the floor for signs of life. "They're both dead." They'd been pummeled with an iron fist, like Lynette Alderete, and their heads were askew.

"Broken necks," Lee added, taking a quick glance around the room to confirm his thoughts. Whoever was being kept here, in an obvious cell, hadn't been given any covers. There were no blankets and not even a sheet on the mattress.

The absence of one set of clothes, taken from the guard that was closest to the right size, suggested that the prisoner had been naked. It made sense. If a vampire had been held here, they would have wanted him to have no way of covering himself up and keeping the light from burning his skin if he somehow managed to get past the gate. The guard's clothing size had saved his life. The killer hadn't wanted to wear a bloody outfit.

Diane pulled out her cell phone, then realized she wasn't getting a signal. "I need to call for medical help, but it'll have to be from another location. See if our friend here can tell you what happened, Officer Hawk."

Diane hurried up the steps, and Lee moved over to the officer, who seemed a bit more relaxed with the center of his body covered by the jacket. He found a paper cup, filled it with water from the sink, and held it to the man's lip so he could drink.

"I'm State Police Officer Hawk," Lee introduced himself. He decided to make the first question an easy one. "What's your name, friend?"

The man finished the water. "Gus Mendez." His voice was raspy, almost gone now despite the drink.

"Call me Lee. What happened here, Gus, and who did this to you?"

"The others. Did they get away?" The man's eyes were starting to well with tears.

Lee had to shake his head. "I'm sorry. They made it as far as the river, then the man wearing the boots caught up to them. Three are dead. Were there more?" Lee wondered why Gus was still alive. He looked to be smaller than the other two guards, though he was still at least six feet tall.

"He got all . . . except me."

"He—who? The man who was being kept in this cage— prison—cell—whatever the hell this is?" Lee wanted to know everything Gus knew. All the evidence so far added up to a vampire being kept prisoner here.

"He took my clothes. Stewart. Sunlight causes terrible burns on his skin. Drives him crazy. Had to be locked up."

"Stewart was the prisoner, right? Kept naked?"

The man sobbed silently for a moment. "See what he did to Ralph and Leo? He's insane. Took my boots, clothes, wallet. Bastard. Probably took my pickup too."

"The big white Dodge?"

"Still outside? Must have stolen someone else's." Gus was whispering now, but Lee needed to know as much as possible.

"How many vehicles should be out there?"

Gus thought about it for a few seconds. "Five. They rode together." He tried to gesture toward the bodies on the floor, paying for the movement with a groan of pain.

Diane came back into the room just then. "EMTs are on their way from the fire station at Kirtland. Should be here in ten minutes or so." She smiled at the badly injured man. "How you doing . . . ?"

"Gus. Feel like shit. Take me outside. This room . . . secret."

"No way," Diane said firmly.

"Need my job. Nobody is supposed to know about . . ."

"The work here has just ended, Gus. The patient *won't* be coming back," Lee said. "Just stay put. We need you alive to tell us what happened so we can catch this guy—Stewart."

"Stewart? Last name or first?" Diane asked.

Gus shrugged, then grimaced.

"What triggered the violence?" Lee prodded. Once the EMTs arrived, some questions might be tricky to ask. And if Gus needed to be sedated, they'd lose even more time. The only thing Lee knew for certain was that if the "patient" was a vampire, he'd be holed up now inside a vehicle, dwelling, or somewhere out of direct sunlight. "What happened, Gus?" he repeated.

"Lightning. Power went out. Taking Stewart back to his cell.

Handcuffs didn't stop him. He found us in the dark, somehow. I got knocked out. Woke up here on the floor. Crawled to door. No good, locked. Quiet. Afraid he'd come back if he heard. Finally decided—fuck it. Started yelling."

"Gus, we've got a killer to catch, so we're going to need all the help we can get," Diane said. "I need to find out all I can about this patient—Stewart. Where are the keys needed to get into the desks and files around here?"

"Key in phony electrical outlet in break room. Gets you into Prescott's file cabinet. More there." Gus started coughing, and Lee got him more water from the sink.

Diane looked at her watch. "I'll go find that key. Officer Hawk, you stay here. Officer Toledo said he'd find us once the EMTs arrived, and they should be here anytime. Make sure everyone's got gloves on before they come in here, because we're going to need to dust this cell for Stewart's fingerprints. We need to know who we're dealing with."

Lee nodded. If Stewart could do all this damage in one night, they couldn't afford to give him another.

CHAPTER 4

T wo hours later, with the bodies removed and Gus Mendez in the emergency room at the Regional Medical Center in Farmington, Lee and Diane had the laboratory to themselves.

A quick dusting of Stewart's cell had turned up several fingerprints. According to Gus, only the guards and Stewart ever entered the cell, and the guards' fingerprints were on file and quickly identified. A search hadn't turned up a match on the unknowns, so they were forced to look elsewhere for a lead on Stewart's identity.

Prescott's file cabinet had contained a folder with duplicate keys for all the other locks and a list of the current access codes to the computers—and the main entrance keypads. At least they now had all they needed to get into every room in the lab.

The entire facility was being treated as the crime scene, so no one was allowed to enter without Diane's permission. Navajo officers had processed all the evidence they could find outside, on the grounds, turned what they had over to Diane, then left, not eager to stick around.

Diane had gone through channels and given all other local agencies Security Officer Mendez's description of the missing patient—Stewart—and a copy of his fingerprints.

Law enforcement officers in four states were keeping a eye out for the mass murderer, possibly dressed in a gray security guard's uniform, and Lee and Diane were going through records trying to find a photograph of Stewart, as well as any other pertinent information.

Diane was using Lynette Alderete's computer, reading the reports of experiments conducted on "Patient Beta," exposing him to various wavelengths, intensity, and duration of light. Also recorded was the practical effectiveness of several materials, including glass, fabric, and sunscreen, in preventing changes on Patient Beta's skin. Anecdotes followed that related his quick healing after each episode where he suffered skin damage.

Lee was searching Dr. Prescott's desk and work area, trying to discover where he'd hidden the combination to the heavy safe attached to the floor. After going through several drawers, and even looking under the desk pad, Lee sat back and tried to think of places to hide a password or combination. Where could someone conceal it, yet insure it was always available in case the user forgot it? Lee knew people, and most would have had it somewhere nearby. Hopefully it hadn't been in the doctor's wallet, because that, along with the other evidence recovered from the victims, was locked up in the evidence room at Farmington's main police station.

Lee scooted the chair back, got down on the floor, and looked at the bottom of the desk drawer. A piece of tape was stuck there and written on it in ink, a number.

With a satisfied smile Lee tried the sequence on the safe's combination dial. When the safe failed to open, Lee tried it again, reversing the direction he'd spun the dial at the beginning. No good. Finally he reversed the number sequence and tried it one more time. The safe unlocked, and he opened the door.

"Got the safe!" Lee told Diane, then poked his head out from behind the partition that defined one of the three workstations in the office.

"Great. Maybe we can finally put a face to Stewart's name. There've got to be visual records somewhere. I'll tell you one thing,

Lee. Based upon what I've already seen in Lynette's files, these people *were* using a vampire as a guinea pig. I'd have never thought Lynette could do something like that."

"Maybe they convinced themselves that the end justifies the means . . . a monumental discovery in medicine in exchange for a life. Spin can be placed on almost every shady operation, especially a government project. Or maybe their motive was the old-fashioned garden-variety type. That Mercedes of hers in the parking lot must have cost a bundle," Lee reminded her.

"Yeah, well. She paid the ultimate price for it." Diane looked away, avoiding his gaze.

Five minutes later, with the access codes to Prescott's encrypted files from the safe, along with the CDs where he'd stored them, they were able to identify and play back visual recordings of Stewart—listed only as Patient Beta in the records. Lee stared at the "before" images on the computer screen. The "after" ones always showed Stewart in varying levels of sunburn, some very painful-looking.

There was no audio track, but it was obvious that Stewart had often been in agony. In some recordings he'd been screaming—in others he had shown no reaction other than contempt or anger.

"The man is a lean, mean Arnold Schwarzenegger type—the Arnie after he shed his bodybuilder image. Pale skin, with light, almost spooky eyes. Dangerous, as if he was nursing his hatred and biding his time. A hunter with infinite patience."

Diane was close behind, peeking over his shoulder. It felt good to be working with her again, even on something as serious as this case.

"I see what you mean about the resemblance, Lee. Being that pale, he must have been avoiding the sun for years. Does your skin continue to get lighter the longer you're a vampire?"

"Being a Navajo, I'm not that familiar with deep tans—though

I can darken even more, of course. I think it all depends on your genetic makeup. How pale you can become without a tan."

Diane smiled. "We'll have to figure out who Stewart really is. If he hasn't been a vampire for too many years he should have a file somewhere in a database or government agency, even though he doesn't seem to have a fingerprint record. And they called him Stewart for a reason. That might be his first or last name. Maybe we'll get lucky after going through these files." She motioned toward a stack of twenty-seven CDs.

Selecting two of the images of Stewart's face, Lee printed them out on the office's color laser printer, then faxed them to the county sheriff and every municipal police force within two hundred miles. Diane sent copies to her Albuquerque FBI office as well, with instructions to disseminate the photo and run the image through any recognition programs that might provide a hit. They still didn't have a positive ID on the man, though it was probably somewhere here in the records.

"Well, Stewart's a vampire, at least we know that. I wonder how he ended up in this place? We need to uncover what agency is behind this piece-of-crap operation," Lee said to Diane.

"I'll need to find out who pays the bills."

She remained silent for a moment, and Lee, seeing she was struggling to keep her emotions under control, looked back at the computer monitor.

"I should call Lynette's parents," she finally said. "The sheriff's department has already asked one of their people to notify them about her death, but I want to speak with them too, and see if they can give me any information that'll help. I sure wish I had time to do this personally instead of over the phone, though."

"Did she have a boyfriend? Or girlfriend? Maybe they could tell us something?"

"I don't think she was having a serious relationship with anyone. She lived alone, and has been married to her career since college. Last time we spoke—her last birthday, I think—Lynette told me she wanted to get herself established in her field, then find herself a good man and start raising kids by the time she was thirty. She joked about being way behind schedule."

"People always think they'll have time," Lee said.

She looked at him curiously, then cleared her throat. "Well, anyway, her paychecks had to come from somewhere. I'll use the Bureau sources to backtrack."

"While you're doing that, I'll search the lab for the hidden camcorders. Maybe we'll get a clue if they were recording Stewart in the lab last night before it happened."

Diane reached over and touched Lee's arm. "Look for tissue samples in their laboratory storage, the refrigerator and whatever. If you find any, destroy them. I don't want vampire blood in the hands of whoever takes over this place."

"I thought of that when we did a quick look earlier, and came up with a disposal method. I'll just aim one of those all-spectrum lamps at the samples. If they happen to go toasty, then so be it."

Lee was back in ten minutes with three camcorders, which he'd placed in a plastic washtub to make them easy to transport. Diane looked up and he nodded. "Nothing was on the camcorders. The CDs are blank, so either they are newly replaced or else they didn't record anything last night."

"Any tissue or blood samples?"

"Yeah. There were fifty blood and tissue samples in storage. All but ten turned to ash when I aimed the lamp at them. The unaffected ones, according to their labels, came from the staff."

"Probably the 'controls' in their nasty little experiments," Diane said. Then her cell phone rang. She spoke for about three minutes, then ended the call.

"Lee, we've got a positive ID on the suspect—Patient Beta. His name is Stewart Tanner. One of our agents out of the Albuquerque office recognized the photo we sent. Tanner dropped out of sight about seven or so months ago. Gossip was that he'd supposedly decided on the spur of the moment to take an around-the-world trip. Nobody has seen him since then."

"How did the Bureau guy know him?"

"Tanner owned the Night Owl restaurant in Albuquerque. He was the master chef there as well, and the place specialized in game animal cuisine. He was popular among the late-night dining crowd. That's how the agent came to know of him. Then, about six months ago, Tanner suddenly failed to show up for work. A relative—cousin, supposedly—took over the restaurant, claiming that Tanner had become bored and gone back to his true love, hunting and adventuring. His disappearance didn't cause any stir—he wasn't married and didn't have any kids or close relatives, so that was that," Diane added.

"Well, he didn't volunteer to become a prisoner, so some event must have brought him to the attention of whatever agency is funding this lab. And they must have had enough influence to do something to the guy that is obviously illegal—not to mention unconscionable," Lee said.

"If a government agency, big or small, knows about the existence of vampires, and is willing and capable of doing something like this to them, then your life is in real danger, Lee."

"Tell me something I don't know. And if the people here drove Tanner insane and turned him into a killer, anyone out there who knows about night walkers but not about the months of pure torture Tanner endured is going to conclude we're all a menace to society. Just more reason to believe I'm really screwed. And there's something that's been bugging me about the designation, Patient Beta," Lee added.

"There must have been a Patient Alpha?"

"Exactly. But I've haven't found any mention of other guinea pigs, have you?"

"No, at least not yet. But we'll have to keep our eyes open. Maybe there's another lab like this somewhere else."

"That's what worries me," Lee said. "By the way, how'd it go with Lynette's parents?"

Diane summarized the conversation. Lynette's mother was heartbroken, having already learned about the death of her daughter, and it took a while for Diane to learn that Lynette had mentioned that she worked for OSHA and was doing research on improving safety standards for outdoor workers. Something about skin cancer, her mother thought.

"Not a bad cover story, Diane," Lee concluded when she was done. "It does offer an explanation why a dermatologist might be working out here, and everyone knows that New Mexico is a high-risk state because of the altitude and solar radiation."

"There's got to be a file in here somewhere that will tell us what happened and how this operation and any others got started. We live in a bureaucracy," Diane said, pointing out the obvious. "The paperwork's in here somewhere."

"There's a lot of 'somewhere' here." Lee waved toward the stack of CDs, each of which could contain thousands of pages. "Plus, we still have another computer to check out, and every file in this file cabinet. At least there's only the one office."

She nodded, then looked down at her watch. "It's already past one, but I'm not in the mood to eat anything right now. Let's skip lunch and keep searching. The truth has got to be here somewhere."

"Look everywhere. Meanwhile, think outside the box. If I were working here I'd be in a constant state of paranoia. I'd know that if anything went wrong—like what happened here last night—and I happened to survive, my ass would still be on the line. I'd be keeping my own set of records, just to ensure I wouldn't be left to take the blame alone. Someone was responsible for initiating this project, and my guess is that it wasn't the doctors who were working here. We need to follow the trail back to the beginning and find out who the real boss is."

"Once I'm sure the families of the victims have been notified,

I'm going to have deputies interview everyone that might have come in contact with the victims. Let's find out what Prescott and the others, including the security guards, were telling their families about their work here. I've already got agents in Albuquerque checking Tanner, his friends and coworkers, and that relative of his."

"Sounds thorough enough." Lee sat back. "If I had been Prescott, I wouldn't have kept my trump card here. He could have been denied access to the building if things got sticky, or it could have been found and taken from him."

"Maybe he has it stashed at home—or in his car. No, forget the car, that's too easily stolen. How about a safety deposit box?" Diane offered.

"Too predictable, and access is limited to bank hours. If Prescott was smart he'd have settled on home, or somewhere close by his home. I'd also doubt he'd leave it with a relative who might decide to take a look, or be vulnerable to outside pressure."

"So let's lock up this place, get the Navajo police to keep everyone out, and go search Prescott's home. I've got the address—it's in Farmington. Prescott lived alone, but Cooper, the OMI man, should have left his keys in the FPD evidence room."

"Don't go signing them out, not right now," Lee said with a hint of a smile. "We'll manage."

"Now that's a scary concept. Next time I'm hooked up to a polygraph, my career is over." Diane shook her head.

"You don't have to ask, see, or tell. If there's anything illegal to do, I'll do it when your back is turned."

By the time they'd locked up the lab, returned to the riverside crime scene to retrieve their vehicles, and touched bases with the Navajo officers assigned to watch the facility, it was late afternoon. Taking Diane's Bureau car and leaving Lee's black-and-white at the lab, they drove east.

Diane's hunger finally caught up with her, so en route to Farmington they stopped in Kirtland at a fast food place and stocked up on green chile cheeseburgers, french fries, and large colas. By the time they reached Prescott's home, a large ranch-style home on the western outskirts of Farmington and up the La Plata highway, they'd already eaten their lunch/dinner.

"I swear, since I met you, Lee, I've been eating like a pig. At least it hasn't started to show . . . or has it?" Diane stepped out of the car and looked down at her hips.

"I've never seen you look more . . . fit," Lee said, coming around to her side of the car, then walking toward the wooden gate that granted access into the big yard. The lawn was so green it looked artificial, and well manicured.

"Wise choice of words." Diane opened the gate and walked up the flagstone path. "Big house for one man. Must have four bedrooms and a den."

"Lots of places to hide a computer disk or a notebook," Lee said. "And if he stashed his secrets under one of those flagstones, we have, what, fifty to look under?"

"Let's check the house first. Maybe he picked an easy spot, like with the safe combination you discovered." Diane glanced down the graveled lane, noting that the closest house was several hundred yards away. There were horses in a pasture just on the other side of a tall fence, grazing on the tall grass closest to the wire.

Following her gaze, he shook his head. "Nobody is going to see us, Diane, unless they have a friggin' telescope. Don't start getting paranoid."

"I've been paranoid for years. It's what keeps me alive."

"Come to think of it, after what they did to Tanner, maybe paranoia's a good thing." He stopped, visualizing the lab images of the vampire for the fiftieth time in the last hour, then saw Diane watching him closely.

"We'll make sure it never happens to you," she said somberly, reaching out to touch his arm.

"Thanks." He placed his hand over hers, then awkwardly

removed it again. "Wanna go up onto the front porch for a moment? I'm going to see if the back door is unlocked."

"That's okay, Lee. Go ahead and pick the lock. It's for the public good, and SAC Logan doesn't have to know I've actually become very skilled at avoiding questions I don't want to answer."

"Don't let him hear you saying that," Lee teased. "Lieutenant Richardson already knows I'm a sneaky guy, so he never asks for details he suspects he won't want to hear."

"Just pick the damned lock," Diane grumbled, grabbing his sleeve and pulling him around the flagstone path to the back of the house.

They put on latex gloves, then searched in all the likely hiding places first. They checked under drawers, inside the refrigerator, boxes in the back of the closets, and in plain sight among diskettes and DVDs beside an inexpensive entertainment center and small desktop computer, but couldn't find any lab-related files. Everything had a commercial label and looked genuine.

Diane was checking under the furniture, and Lee was searching for stash places behind outlets and heating registers, when Lee had a moment of inspiration. He walked back over to the CDs and DVDs in the small rack, and began going through, reading the labels again.

"Hey, Diane?"

She walked back into the living room from the hall. "Find something?"

"Maybe." He turned on the television set, then picked up the remote, trying to figure out how to turn on the DVD player.

"Nothing to do, so you decide to watch a movie?" She walked over to see what he was really doing.

"I was thinking. Dr. Prescott had some good movie selections here. Good oldies, like *The Great Escape*, *Indiana Jones*, and a few new ones like *Master and Commander* and the *Lord of the Rings* trilogy."

"So?"

"If you broke in and wanted to steal them, which ones *wouldn't* you take." Lee held up a DVD, hiding the label.

"You're serious."

"Absolutely." Lee stuck the DVD into the player, thumbed a button on the remote, but got nothing but a blue screen. "Doesn't work, just as I suspected." He held up the laser disk, and she could see the label.

"*Golf Legends of the PGA.*" Diane chuckled. "Call me disappointed."

"We didn't find any golf clubs in the house. Maybe it's not really a DVD." He booted up the computer, inserted the laser disk into the CD drive, and several seconds later they were looking at scanned documents from the research lab.

On the typed documents, which were directed to Dr. Prescott, the laboratory employees were told that their establishment, listed under two cover agency levels, was a classified medical research operation and that they could be arrested if they ever spoke to anyone who hadn't already been cleared by the director about their work.

The facility had been created solely to study a unique individual, Stewart Tanner, who'd demonstrated an unusual immunity to disease and infections, the ability to heal and regenerate damaged tissue, and who was, at the same time, highly vulnerable to natural sunlight and certain wavelengths of radiation.

The lab was tasked to quantify Tanner's physical and biochemical nature, conduct experiments to determine the nature of his extraordinary healing capacity, and to try and isolate those elements in his body chemistry responsible for his unique abilities.

The doctors were being asked to find a way to make Tanner resistant to damaging radiation so that the elements responsible for his healing abilities could be used to manufacture the ultimate medication without making the patient vulnerable to sunlight as well. The name given the funded research was, fittingly, Project Lazarus.

Several documents setting up the operation and security procedures, avenues of research, and other details were stored on the CD. They also found a lengthy document prepared by Prescott which stated that Stewart Tanner had been brought to their hastily prepared facility as a uncooperative prisoner, and had been very difficult to deal with because of his extreme physical capabilities.

Prescott had stated that Tanner had to be kept bound and sedated most of the time in order to keep him from overpowering his handlers, and that if the man ever got the upper hand, people would die. Prescott pointed out that Tanner had become increasingly enraged and violent, and if he ever managed to escape the facility, he could be counted upon to take out his anger on virtually anyone.

After a half-hour survey of the information on the CD, Diane sat back in the chair she'd placed beside Lee and the computer monitor. "This pretty much confirms what we already know, though I'm almost relieved that there's no mention of a Patient Alpha. To most people this will probably be as credible as the Blair Witch Project. Anyone reading this will seriously doubt Dr. Prescott's mental state."

"I'm sure Prescott realized that too. But it was the only way to protect himself and the others if things went south. Who's more to blame, Tanner, or the people who tortured him? I also notice that Prescott didn't name his superiors—like this vague 'director.' I wonder why?" Lee took the CD from the computer, then turned off the machine. "What do you want to do with this?"

She brought out the jewel case, Lee inserted the CD, and handed it to her. "He might have been more afraid of his boss than he was of Tanner," Diane said. "I'm going to mail this to my Albuquerque home address. Until we learn which feds are behind this, we won't know who to trust." Diane stuck the case into her jacket pocket.

"In the meantime, Tanner is out there somewhere and we need to put a stop to him. What next? Any suggestions?" Lee glanced around the living room. It was dark outside now, and he wouldn't have to freshen up his sunblock before they left.

She turned out the lamp beside the computer, making the room very dark. "We'll use the radio in my unit to contact all the other agencies and see how the search for Tanner is going. We'll have to stick to the obvious facts—the man escaped from the laboratory, killed five people, and is extremely strong and dangerous." Diane started to move across the living room and bumped into a chair.

"Take my hand," Lee offered, reaching out for her. "It's not a man-woman thing, it's because I can see and you can't."

She grabbed his hand firmly, then accompanied him into the kitchen. "That the only reason?" she asked quietly.

"Of course not." Lee opened the back door, then stopped, turning the button in the knob so it would lock when he closed it.

"Good." Diane went ahead of him, letting go of his hand after giving it a squeeze.

Lee closed the door, turned, then noticed Diane had frozen in place, watching a shape at the far end of the house. Then the shape moved. The sun was down, but there was still enough light to reveal Stewart Tanner, wearing a hooded sweatshirt.

"Stay here and don't let him get close," Lee whispered harshly, pulling out his pistol.

The vampire disappeared around the corner of the house, so Lee holstered his pistol and followed—indirectly. He jumped up, grabbing on to the top of the porch, then swung onto the roof. He ran up to the crown of the house and looked down onto the yard, trying to determine if Stewart had moved away from the building.

Not seeing anyone except Diane in the backyard, Lee knew that the vampire was staying beneath the eaves of the house. Out of view, the vampire could have run around to the front of the house or be waiting just around the corner at the end where he'd seen him first.

Lee ran to his left and jumped to the ground at the opposite end of the rectangular structure, hugging the wall and looking to his right. Lee knew Stewart couldn't be around back, or Diane would be making some 9mm noise by now. That still left the front or far end.

Lee heard a loud crunch, like snapping timbers. "Tanner's in the house," he yelled, fearing that the vampire was going to run through the building, burst out the back door, and take Diane by surprise.

CHAPTER 5

Diane had jumped away from the porch and was covering the back door. Spotting motion to her left, she swerved around, her pistol ready.

"It's me, don't shoot," he said, quickly ducking back.

"Damn. Don't *do* that," Diane cursed, lowering her weapon.

He stepped into sight and waved her toward him. Together they moved away from the house, her covering the back door, and him the front. Then Lee heard the whinny of a horse. He looked out into the pasture beyond the fence in the front of the house, and saw a running figure.

"Crap," Lee yelled. "He faked us out. Get the car."

Diane turned and ran toward their vehicle while Lee took up the chase. Tanner was already more than a hundred yards away, sprinting at a speed Lee knew he couldn't hope to match. Vampires had it over half vampires in every Olympic event except thinking.

Gamely Lee followed, hoping to keep the fugitive in sight, but Stewart raced to the highway, jumped into an old pickup parked by itself on the shoulder, and pulled away in a cloud of dust before Lee could get close enough to read the tag.

A minute later Diane came up in her vehicle and Lee jumped inside. "He had an old pickup parked by the road. He's heading for Farmington. *Now* we can equal his speed. Catch his ass while I call it in."

Diane nodded, and accelerated down the highway at pursuit speed. Lee buckled his seat belt, then grabbed the radio mike. Within thirty seconds, every law enforcement unit on Farmington streets knew about the older model silver Ford F-150 Tanner was driving.

"That bastard can run faster than the Bionic Man, Diane. If we had any doubts he's a full vampire, they're gone now. Tanner must have been looking for the same thing we were after—confirmation of what was really going on over at that lab."

"What's the point now—for him? Even if he can prove they were torturing him, that won't get him off the hook for killing Lynette and the others," Diane argued, not taking her eyes off the road, though she'd slowed a bit after entering the city limits.

"Yeah. Things might have been different for him if he'd escaped and *not* hunted them down."

Diane was quiet as they searched the western section of the city, which spread up from the river into the mesas and foothills along the valley. Once in a while, a call would come from a Farmington patrolman or a San Juan county deputy, pulling over a vehicle that fit the general description. But each time, it turned out to be a false alarm. After a half hour, the calls slowed and she pulled off the road in a residential area and parked. A small apartment complex occupied that section of the block, and they could see every vehicle. None was a potential match.

"Do you suppose Tanner will stop killing now that he's taken care of those who were responsible for what happened to him?" Diane asked.

"Tanner knows how he revealed his vampire nature to the feds, and that the list of those who know about him exceed those employed at the facility. I'm sure he's trying to find more names and addresses—not only for revenge, but so he can ensure his own survival."

Diane nodded. "Makes sense. And because of that, we have to find out who's responsible for turning his life into a living hell before they either end up dead or engineer the mother of all cover-ups."

"There's something else they have to do—get Tanner back, or get him dead—before the secret gets out to the public, or even worse, to whatever government agency they're competing with for power and resources."

"You don't suppose the Bureau is responsible for these vampire experiments?" Diane turned to Lee, her voice low.

"You *were* the one called to deal with it," Lee said with a shrug. "But no, I don't think so. Whoever did this is probably concealed by layers of cover, much more than we saw in Prescott's home files. We know it's very unlikely that the CDC or a health agency would come up with this. Just the suggestion that they believe in vampires would destroy their reputations. That's always been my best fallback story, you know. The truth about something like this cannot be taken seriously."

"So that leaves an organization with a lot of resources—one that's perfectly willing to do something that sounds stupid," Diane replied. "That narrows it down quite a bit."

"Yeah. It's either a major television network, the current presidential administration, or the CIA. They'd be my first choice, based upon the unbelievable stories I've heard about them from the Cold War."

"How do we establish any of this? Our only recent contact with 'The Company' is very dead. And amazingly enough, a vampire was the one responsible for that one too."

"Let's think outside the box, and come up with possible scenarios of how Tanner gave himself away. Once we have a few of those, we can use the Bureau resources and the Internet to check out our theories. In order for a vampire to be discovered, somebody with federal connections must have seen Tanner do a vampire thing—then been able to provide enough evidence to get others to take action." Lee lapsed into silence as he thought about it for a moment.

"Okay, let's brainstorm, and while we're doing that, we can drive around some more and look for that silver pickup." Diane started the engine, and eased back onto the road.

They turned into one of the older neighborhoods, a boulevard with big, overhanging willow trees along a central median, and drove slowly down the block. Diane used the vehicle's spotlight to check out the left side, but Lee didn't need the extra help.

They'd passed several houses and were nearing the next intersection when Lee heard the roar of an engine somewhere close. "I don't see anyone." Diane glanced back in the rearview mirror, then slowed and looked to both sides.

When the sound continued to grow, Lee looked in the side mirror. A pickup was bearing down on them at high speed, its headlights out.

"Turn!" Lee lunged to the left and grabbed the steering wheel, yanking it hard and throwing them into an unsettling two-wheeled slide.

"What the hell?" Diane yelled, trying to regain control as the car spun around to her left. There was an explosive crunch as the speeding pickup clipped the left rear fender, and the car was jerked so hard they were thrown sideways. Lee scraped the top of his head on the window frame of the door as his head was thrown where the glass would have been if his window had been rolled up.

"Whoa!" Diane yelled, her voice drowned in the squeal as the tires fought to keep traction. They continued to slide backward, and finally stopped with an abrupt thud against the curb. Their heads bounced off the seat headrests like crash dummies, then the engine died.

Rubbing his head, Lee turned, looking for the pickup. It was already halfway to the next intersection.

Diane looked over, shaken. "You okay, Lee?"

"Scraped my noggin, but otherwise fit. How about you?"

"I'm going to have some major bruises in places where it won't show, but yeah, I'm okay."

"Then let's get that bastard." Lee grabbed the radio while Diane started the engine. She had to turn left to get into the intersection, then after another hard left, they raced down the boulevard in pursuit.

"He was stalking us with his lights out," Diane said. "Somewhere along the way he let us pass him, then he started following us. With his lights out, we—I—couldn't see him, and you were too busy looking ahead. If you'd been driving, you'd have seen him coming, considering the way your vision works." Diane shook her head. "Ow. That was stupid. Now I've got a headache too."

"You need to have a doctor look at that?" He glanced over at her, concerned.

"No. Just keep your seat belt on."

Lee sent out a bulletin on the hit-and-run, and it wasn't long before they got a call. The pickup had been located, abandoned, in the parking lot of the old library just north of downtown.

"Tanner must be holed up somewhere now, and with his athletic ability, he's going to be hard to find. There are enough backyards and homes with trees and gardens that he could avoid detection for days," Diane finally said, pulling to the side of the road again, this time into a church parking lot.

"Yeah, but he'll have to be out of the sun by morning, and it's nearly midnight," Lee said.

"I'm going to have officers take his photo into every late-night business that sells sunblock, and every other potential source as soon as they open tomorrow morning," Diane said. "Even if he's already shoplifted a bottle or two, maybe we'll get lucky and it'll show up as missing on inventory." Diane picked up her cell phone. "And his photo should be in tomorrow's newspapers. I asked for cooperation from the press."

"The more people looking out for the guy, the quicker we'll find him."

"I just hope no more people die confronting Tanner. Problem is, I'm not sure how to warn the officers helping in the search. If anyone *does* manage to put him down—and it's not with a real destructive head shot, or to the heart—he'd get right back up again in a few minutes and be *really* pissed off."

"Tell everyone you enlist exactly what he did to that young woman doctor—breaking her bones, stake in the chest and all, then let them know exactly how he killed two security guards and disabled a third—while unarmed and in handcuffs. Hint that he's all hopped up, like on drugs, so *extreme* force is needed. None of his victims' relatives will be complaining if Tanner gets blown to pieces," Lee reminded.

"And that's what it's going to take, isn't it," Diane said, reaching down to her waist and touching the butt of her pistol.

Lee and Diane spent the next few hours meeting with local law enforcement officers and setting up a command center. Then, around four in the morning, they decided to return to the laboratory near Kirtland to continue searching through the remaining files and CDs for anything on either Tanner or the agency behind the operation.

Lee was driving now, and Diane was catnapping, having been up almost twenty-four hours straight as well as being drained emotionally by the loss of an old friend. Lee had been awake even longer, but he didn't need much sleep anyway, only occasional rest from physical exertion—and a bite to eat. Calf or pig blood would be particularly tasty and nutritious right now, but with vampire talk everywhere, just having blood in his possession would raise too many eyebrows.

He'd left the window open so he could hear, and was traveling slowly, keeping one eye in the rearview mirror, and another on the road ahead, looking for the turnoff that led, in a circuitous route, to the laboratory on the mesa to the south.

Finally he saw the narrow gravel road, which ran between two apple orchards. Several old, traditional farms were in the area, though a lot of the old fields in the small communities of Waterflow, Fruitland, and Kirtland had succumbed to ugly, urbanlike sprawl and relentless developers. Even the Navajo Nation was littered with housing in this area, though much of it was substandard.

The sun would be coming up in a few hours. Lee thought for a moment where he'd been yesterday about this time. It seemed like years ago now, but at least nobody had died in that incident.

He looked at the gnarled, gray trunks and branches of the old apple trees, and the few windfalls still on the ground. It had been a decent year for apples, but these trees looked old and neglected. At least the cottontails he saw hunkered down beneath the overhanging branches would be supplied with fall bounty.

Lee slowed to cross an irrigation ditch. A culvert ran beneath the road, but the track was humped up into a small ridge that required care to avoid jostling.

"We there yet?" Diane said with a mumble, opening her eyes and sitting up. "Sorry I dozed off."

"A mile or so to go," Lee said, smiling. "You needed the rest, so don't apologize."

Ahead, Lee could see a white SUV in the road, taillights on and all four doors open, but nobody was within view and he couldn't see anyone inside either. There were no orchards this close to the river and the vegetation on both sides were typical trees and brush of the bosque. The closed-in nature made it a perfect place for an ambush, and suddenly his heart started beating a little faster.

"What do you see?" Diane squinted. "Wish I had some low-light goggles."

Lee slowed the vehicle, then came to a stop, leaving the motor running. "You don't suppose the criminal actually returned to the scene of the crime?"

"Tanner? He went to Dr. Prescott's home, didn't he? But we got there first." Diane picked up the vehicle's radio mike and called Dispatch, asking them to connect her to the Navajo officers still on duty outside the lab. They'd been warned to increase their vigilance, and firepower, after what had happened earlier in the evening.

She spoke for a moment, then ended the call. "The tribal cops heard gunfire in this direction about fifteen minutes ago, but stayed at their posts, fearing it was a diversion. They've already put in a call for more tribal backup, but their officers had to come from Window Rock and they're still at least a half hour away."

"Then who's in the SUV?" Lee squinted, shifted his POV, then saw something on the ground. "Looks like somebody's down."

"We need to make a move, Lee. Tanner is probably behind this as well. He's a cocky—bloodsucker. No offense."

"None taken. But let's try and even the odds a bit. I'm going to add a little more light to the scene." Lee turned to the right slightly, directing the headlights into the brush and undergrowth beyond the white vehicle. Then he turned on the spotlight, aiming the beam to the left. Now the area ahead and to both sides of the SUV were being illuminated to any non-vampires still alive.

"Stay to the right of the road, I'll take the left." Lee reached behind the seat, pulled out Diane's shotgun, then handed it to her as they met in front of the vehicle.

"Thanks. I'll watch your back and provide cover," Diane said, clipping her flashlight onto the shotgun, turning it on, then working the pump to rack a shell into the chamber.

"Okay. Here goes."

Lee moved quickly and quietly, his .45 Smith out. Diane followed, staying in the headlight beams from their own vehicle. She'd be silhouetted, of course, but anyone looking at her from farther down the road would have their night vision destroyed as well. Vampires could be blinded by the light just like regular people, even when the wavelengths weren't harmful to them.

Someone rose out of a low irrigation ditch on the driver's side and fired a pistol twice into the brush farther down. Then two more men jumped out of the ditch at the same spot as the first one and sprinted toward Lee and Diane. The man with the pistol moved to the SUV, putting it at his back, and stood still, watching but not firing.

"One of the men coming this way looks like Dr. Wayne," Diane said to Lee. "What's he doing here?"

"I can guess." Lee ran forward.

"Tanner's back," Dr. Wayne said breathlessly as he approached Lee. "He tricked us into stopping, then ambushed the federal marshals. Two are down, and they look dead to me."

"How's Tanner armed?" Lee asked the other man, who was carrying what looked like a Browning Hi-Power semi-auto. He looked over at Lee, fear instead of cockiness showing in his eyes.

"A big knife, no gun. But he's silent and quick, with eyes like a cat in the dark. Don't let him get close to you," he said, his words tumbling out quickly.

"Go with Hawk, Arnsworth," Dr. Wayne ordered. "He'll need more backup."

Arnsworth had to think about it a second. "Okay. Lead the way, Officer Hawk."

Diane intervened, seeing a wound on the man's left hand dripping blood through a hastily contrived handkerchief bandage. "No, you stay with Dr. Wayne, here. I'll back up Officer Hawk."

Arnsworth was relieved. "Good idea, you've got a shotgun."

Dr. Wayne looked annoyed, but Arnsworth glanced away, scanning their perimeter and avoiding eye contact with the doctor.

Lee and Diane jogged down the road toward the remaining marshal, who was slowly turning, his pistol ready, as if an attack could come from any direction. His upper arm was badly slashed and blood was soaking his jacket.

"The bastard's a devil. He yelled out like a loon, said he's going to kill every fed he can find. I believe it. If you see him, shoot . . . and keep shooting," the short stocky man in his early fifties said with a growl, pointing down the road. "He took off when he saw your lights, running faster than anyone I've ever seen. You'll never catch up to him without a car. He's gone."

Lee looked over at the SUV, and saw the body of a tall, muscular black man in a sports jacket. Blood was everywhere, though, because his head had been nearly severed. There was no way he could be alive, yet Lee had to make sure. As he was feeling unsuccessfully for a pulse, Lee saw a pistol on the road beside the dead man, and beyond, a few steps, a shattered night-vision device. Two of the vehicle tires were flat from large punctures in their sidewalls, and the headlights were broken. A big rock lay on the road among the shattered glass.

"Got a first aid kit in your unit?" Lee asked, keeping his gaze scanning the area. Tanner wasn't going to make another sneak attack from darkness with him around.

"In the front seat, under the passenger's seat," the man said.

"I'll get it." Diane hurried around the SUV, keeping her eye on the bosque beyond in case the vampire had circled around. After confirming that a second, blood-covered agent on the side of the road was dead, she stepped over to the vehicle, reached in, and switched on the interior lights, which had been kept off for normal tactical reasons. No officer wanted to open the door and turn himself into a spotlighted target.

Finding the first aid box, she returned to where Lee and the wounded man were. Taking the flashlight from her shotgun, she located a compress and placed it over the man's wound. "Just hold this in place until we can move to a safer location and bandage you up right."

"Yeah, okay. Let's get out of here." The man grimaced as he covered his wound. He was reluctant to let go of his pistol, and trying to hold on to both was a struggle.

"Want me to carry your weapon?" Lee offered, but the man shook his head.

"No way." He put the pistol in his jacket pocket.

"I understand completely." Lee knew what it meant being unarmed and pursued by a vampire. That was how he'd become what he was today.

"How'd it go down?" Diane asked as they hurried away, Lee taking up the rear and guarding their backs as they walked up the road.

"All kinds of bad shit happened. I stopped the Chevy after nearly running into what appeared to be a drunk passed out in the road. He was facedown and there was a bottle by his hand. He played us for suckers. We all got out and never saw it coming. It was Tanner, of course. He took out Bruce, the black guy over there, first. Damn near decapitated him, and smashed the night scope in his hand. Then he broke the headlights out with that rock. We couldn't see shit in the dark, couldn't risk shooting each other, and Tanner kept away from the taillights. He kept pouncing out of the bushes like a friggin' panther, slashing, then ducking back out of sight. All he had was a knife, but he was so fast we couldn't get our pistols around in time. He took out Steinberg next, luring him off the road on the passenger side. Gutted him like a fish. We made it to the ditch, but meanwhile, Tanner cut the tires so we couldn't drive away either. None of us had a handheld, and we couldn't raise anyone closer than Farmington on a cell phone."

The man continued, his voice stronger now that it appeared they were out of danger. "We tried to duck into the SUV twice, but he came over the top of the vehicle from the blind side. I thought I hit him solid, but he kept coming. Finally we got down, back to back in the ditch so he couldn't sneak up on us. Glad you came along when you did."

"Didn't he grab a pistol from one of his victims?" Diane asked.

"No, and that was a welcome surprise," the man said.

"Panther doesn't need a gun," Lee said under his breath.

When they reached Diane's unit, Dr. Wayne was using the radio while Arnsworth anxiously kept watch. He'd grabbed Diane's big flashlight from her car, and was constantly aiming it into the brush on both sides of the road.

"Any more help is still about ten minutes away," Dr. Wayne said to Diane as she came up to the window.

"Tanner has a death wish, coming back at us like this," Lee said, looking at Diane, not Wayne. "We'd better make sure he hasn't reached the lab and made a move on the officers there."

"I called them already," Dr. Wayne said. "They've taken up a defensive position beside the front entrance with their backs to the building, and they've got flashlights."

"He took on all of you with a knife. They're not safe either," Diane argued. "Pile in. We're going over there right now."

$\mathbf{D}$iane drove, with Lee keeping watch and Dr. Wayne patching up the wounded driver, whose name was Chase. Lee wanted the man functional in case they had another encounter with Tanner tonight. Arnsworth's nerves seemed shot so his usefulness was questionable, and Dr. Wayne, supposedly, was a physician, not a hired gun. But at least Wayne was armed, and hadn't been completely unnerved yet.

"Want me to check in with the tribal cops?" Lee offered, gesturing toward the radio.

"Not the two at the lab. They need to concentrate on keeping alive. Think I'll let them know—and Tanner too, if he's still close by—that we're nearly there." She reached over and turned on the siren and emergency lights.

Within four minutes they arrived at the lab, tires sliding in the loose gravel of the parking lot as Diane quickly braked to a stop. The disabled vehicles from yesterday were still in their spaces, and the white tribal unit was nearly on the sidewalk. Lee's state police vehicle was where he'd parked it earlier in the day.

Lee looked toward the entrance to the building, where a battery-powered lantern was sitting on the sidewalk about fifty feet from the entrance. Beyond, barely visible, were two Navajo officers standing side by side beneath the porch overhang. They both held shotguns.

"Good strategy. Tanner would have to go through that circle of light to approach the officers," Diane said, climbing out and turning around to view the entire area. Arnsworth and Dr. Wayne followed.

"Unless Tanner had come over the roof from above and behind and dropped down right in their faces," Lee said, moving forward quickly, his eyes scanning the roofline of the laboratory. It seemed clear of vampires. With daylight not far away, Lee knew that Tanner had probably shot his wad for the night. He'd have to get behind shelter—at least a vehicle with good windows, since ordinary glass screened out the wavelengths of light deadly to vampires.

Sirens could be heard in the distance, closing in from the highway. Reinforcements would soon arrive. "Thank God," Arnsworth said, his eyes still searching the parking lot.

Lee turned and nodded to the tribal cops, who hadn't moved from their protected positions. One of the men motioned to Lee with his hand.

Lee caught Diane's attention. "I'm going to speak to the officers for a minute, but don't let your guard down. Tanner's unpredictable. He may be out there among those vehicles right now, waiting to take out one more person before calling it a night."

"Daylight's coming. He's not worried about us. He has to go into hiding someplace soon," Dr. Wayne said confidently. "Once the sun's up, we'll have the advantage and can start looking for him again."

Lee nodded, then walked down the sidewalk to the Navajo officer who'd signaled him. The officer pointed up toward the roofline, where there was a chipped-off section of stucco right on the edge.

"He tried to come at you from up there?" Lee asked. "Good thinking, getting back under the overhang so he'd have to show his face."

"We both fired. Almost got him too. Pale face, that Anglo. White as a ghost."

"Pale as death," the other officer mumbled. "What in the hell is going on at this place? It's no weather station—more like a nuthouse. That man on the roof was . . . strange."

The first officer shook his head. "Don't talk about evil. You'll draw it back."

"Just between the three of us," Lee said, his voice low, "he's not going to stop killing. Supposedly, he said he's after feds, but I'm sure not taking his word on that. Don't go looking for him alone, always have someone to watch your back. Tanner'll have to hide in full shade during the daytime. The sun causes his skin to burn very quickly. But he'll be hunting again tomorrow night— count on it. Make sure that the other tribal officers understand the danger. If they corner Tanner, they should shoot him in the head and heart. Nobody should try to take him alive. Insanity increases his strength and resistance to pain."

The officers nodded. These men had already seen what Tanner could do. Lee knew the message would get out.

What is Dr. Wayne up to now?" Lee looked up from the late Dr. Krause's computer terminal. Diane and he were alone in the office section of the research laboratory.

"I think he finally decided to leave. He and the OMI finished examining the bodies of the two dead marshals. Afterward, they walked around, studying the facility for a while, although Wayne looked beat. He got a little pissed off when he found the destroyed blood and tissue samples in the lab, but blamed that on Tanner. Then, weird as it sounds, Victor, as he insists I call him, actually invited me to breakfast," Diane said, looking exhausted.

"He's got an agenda. I've been watching him and he seems to know his way around this place pretty well for a man who claims he never heard of the facility, much less been here."

"I noticed that too." She looked at the big paper bag sitting on the desk. "What is that wonderful smell?"

"I think you must have charmed the tribal officers we dealt with last night. They gave these to me when their relief arrived. They're called *naniscaadas,* homemade tortillas filled with diced hash browns, ground beef, green chile—stuff like that. No cheese or rice, like with Mexican food. All very fattening and incredibly good."

They ate greedily for the next ten minutes, then finally Diane looked up from a bite. "I didn't get the chance to ask. What did you tell those tribal officers last night when we came here looking for Tanner? They looked so relieved to see us, and they pulled you aside more than once later."

"There was some stuff they didn't feel comfortable telling Dr. Wayne and what was left of his entourage. I don't know what's going to show up in the reports they file with the tribe in Shiprock, but Tanner *did* beat us back here last night. The tribal officers were grateful we'd warned them. They were ready, and almost took his head off when he looked down for them from atop the roof."

"So that's why I saw one of them pointing at the roof. Do you suppose Tanner was after them specifically, or that he'd just come back for a quick look around the lab?"

"Probably the latter, but we beat him to the punch at Prescott's home, then here as well. Whatever he's looking for has got to be worth a lot for him to take risks like that."

"I think it's the history behind his situation—how he got exposed as a vampire, and why he ended up here."

"That's likely. Add who's *really* behind the operation here—and that's all the press and public will need to nail those responsible for imprisoning and torturing a civilian."

"So if we don't find whatever it is, you think Tanner will be back, regardless of the risks?"

Lee nodded. "I'd count on it, if he's really out for revenge.

What arrangements have you made for stepping up the search for Tanner?"

"Agencies in the area are on full alert—BIA cops, tribes, counties, municipalities, even the sheriff's posse. Roadblocks are in several locations, teams are working the neighborhoods between Farmington and Shiprock, inclusive, and every report of a stolen car is being run down aggressively. We still don't know how Tanner left this location the second time, if, indeed, he did. All we know is that it wasn't in the pickup he used to try and take us out. Once the sun came up it was found in somebody's field two miles from here."

"The tribal cops got my message about the need for overwhelming force, and you've been pumping up the other agencies,". Lee said. "But I don't think we'll find Tanner before dark without a good lead. He's holed up again, and the man is one crafty son of a bitch."

"The sheriff has got a bloodhound team trying to pick up a trail now, and two helos from Albuquerque will also be helping us tonight. They're equipped with low-light devices. It could make the difference if he gets into open country. There's not much cover once you leave the bosque." Diane yawned, and took a swallow of coffee. They'd raided the snack room and brewed a pot hours ago.

"Better get some rest, partner. There's that big padded table in the laboratory, and two fire blankets you can use for a pillow."

"Hell if I'm going to use that table for a bed. You've seen the array of lights overhead. That was the toaster oven for Tanner. Tell me where the blankets are and I'll curl up in Lynette's chair."

"There's a red metal box in the snack room, and another one in the lab. They're just wool blankets, not mylar, so you don't have to worry the TV dinner look."

"Don't you need to catch some zzzzzzs?"

"Maybe tomorrow. I'm good again once I've stuffed my belly.

Meanwhile, I can screen the rest of the records and see if I can find what Tanner's after besides government employees."

It was nearly noon when Lee finally made a breakthrough in his search, though the information was on a single sheet of paper stuck in a dusty medical dictionary among a hundred other equally entertaining volumes.

Krause had typed a short note on his word processor, printed it out, then either erased the information on his computer or else hid it among thousands of other files.

According to Krause, they had been contracted by a federal employee—ostensibly from the CDC—to set up a research facility. Their sole mission had been to study and conduct tests on a civilian who'd been discovered to have miraculous abilities to heal himself—as well as other unique physical attributes and a few potentially lethal afflictions.

"No shit," Lee mumbled, then heard movement and saw that Diane had sat up, and was looking at him through sleepy eyes.

"No shit what, Lee? You find something?" She stood, wearing the blanket like a poncho, and walked over to see what he was reading.

He handed her the note, and a spark jumped between their fingers as they touched. "Ow," she exclaimed, then looked down at the wool she'd been wrapped in for the past two hours. "Guess I'd better get rid of this before I damage some computer hardware."

She tossed the blanket over the back of a chair, then reached down and touched the metal static strip on the table. There was another snap and a small spark. "Okay. Now I'm discharged. Where'd you find the note?"

"Krause stuck it inside a book few people would be interested in browsing through. It was the fifth book I'd looked through, fortunately, not the sixty-fifth."

Diane held the paper up so she could read it. Then she spoke. "Okay, this confirms that this facility was created to put Stewart Tanner under the lights, inside the test tube, and whatever else they could think to do. And his abilities were discovered accidentally by someone with federal connections and an overdose of curiosity. Everything they're doing here is probably a violation of Tanner's rights as an American and a human being. No surprise there, though, according to Krause, they'd been told the project was sanctioned by the executive branch of the government and classified as Top Secret."

"Notice that nobody wants to use the 'V' word, even in their private, hidden notes?" Lee commented. "These guys are smart, sticking just to the facts as they did what they could to cover their asses."

"Lee, this is page one, according to the number in the right-hand corner. Shouldn't there be a page two, then?"

He looked at her blankly. "Didn't notice the page number. Guess we'd better keep looking." He looked up at the metal bookshelves. "Damn. How many books are here?"

"A lot. You started from the top, left-hand side, right?"

He shook his head. "No, I just grabbed the five books in the middle of the bookcase. I was trying to psyche the guy out. Anyone starting systematically from the beginning or end might have given up after the first shelf or two. So I started in the center of the search area, so to speak."

"So check more books from the center."

He brought out two books to the left of the five he'd removed, and a couple more to the right of those volumes. "You check two, I'll check two."

She took the books he handed her. "Bingo!" she said, even before he could open his first book. "Page two."

"Read it aloud."

She began immediately. "Our employer—nature of research—and community cover are all fantasy, as anyone can immediately determine just by entering this facility and having a cursory look around. Our real supervisor—listed only as a consultant in our reports—classified as Top Secret—is Dr. Victor Wayne, supposedly from the forensics office of the Justice Department. Dr. Wayne plays the perfect devil's advocate, constantly trying to poke holes in our work and refute our conclusions, especially the evidence we've been compiling that proves Stewart Tanner is a miraculous human being with capabilities well beyond documented biological traits. All our test results, official notes, and observations are delivered to Dr. Wayne via encrypted files. Victor's visits are frequent but unscheduled, and we are forbidden to discuss any of our work with any individual outside this office except for Dr. Wayne. Our research team believes that Dr. Wayne knows the potential applications of our studies and is keeping that from us. If any harm comes to Drs. Alderete, Prescott, or myself, investigators should first question our patient, Stewart Tanner (officially known as Patient Beta), or Dr. Wayne. Either may be ultimately responsible for our injury, death, or disappearance."

They sat there for a while, digesting the new information.

Lee was the first to speak. "That explains why Dr. Wayne has been so interested in these murders from the very beginning, and seemed to know his way around this place so well. His meeting with me was probably just an excuse for his real visit—to this facility. If he'd have come here a half day earlier, he might have been one of those killed as well."

"Just Tanner's bad luck. You know if he'd found these slips of paper, he would have gone for Dr. Wayne, especially if he's after those who put him here."

"Partner, it's time for a confrontation with Victor," Lee said.

Diane looked at her watch. "It'll be four or five hours before Tanner can go outside again. Let's do it now."

CHAPTER 7

Diane's Bureau unit had been dropped by an auto shop in Farmington to undergo repairs after last night's collision with Tanner, so they were using Lee's state police black-and-white. He drove while she made a steady stream of calls, checking for news.

Still officially in charge of the original investigation, Diane had turned over most of the logistics of the search to the San Juan County sheriff and the Farmington Police Department, wanting to remain in the field rather than sit across the desk and issue commands. Still, she'd managed to stay in touch with the heads of every agency.

Diane hung up from her latest call and glanced at Lee. "Dr. Wayne is at the local federal office."

Lee nodded. "I know where that is. I patrolled this area at one time, remember?"

"How can I forget? Which reminds me. Have you picked up any rumors of Navajo witch activity in the county?"

"No. Skinwalkers seem to be off the radar at the moment. There haven't even been any awkward silences about suspicious neighbors on the NM side of the Rez."

Diane knew that Navajos wouldn't speak publicly about the presence of skinwalkers, Navajo witches capable of shape-shifting into wolves and other predatory animals, but Lee had a sixth sense about them. He'd become very good at rooting their dens out, and had made them his special targets for several decades now.

Diane had learned about skinwalkers the hard way—even before discovering Lee was a night walker. She'd lost her first partner to a shape-shifted Navajo in the guise of a black jaguar.

The small Bureau office was at the rear of a local federal building. And, within minutes, they entered the bustling lobby of the four-story structure. News of a vicious serial killer had been everywhere, and it seemed to be the sole object of discussion behind every counter—that is, until Lee and Diane entered.

"Everyone is watching us, Lee. Do I have my bra on backward or something?" Diane whispered.

"Naw, it must be the newspaper articles." Lee pointed over at a front-page report tacked to a big bulletin board. The headlines read "Serial Killer On Rampage" and below were other related stories, one titled "FBI Agent Attacked." A recent photo of Diane was included.

"They knew we were coming too," Diane said, seeing Dr. Wayne standing halfway down a hallway that extended from the lobby to offices beyond.

"Diane, we need to talk." The voice came from their left. A muscular-looking Hispanic man in his early thirties stood up from one of the visitors' benches and stepped forward.

"Charles? I'm so sorry about Lynette," Diane said. After a long hug, the man stepped back and stared at Diane, moisture in his eyes.

"We need to catch this bastard, Diane, before he kills someone else's sister."

Lee studied the man before them. Like his late sister, Charles was tall and fit, with handsome features and dark brown eyes. Dressed in a loose-fitting blue jacket and tan slacks, Charles looked military, all the way down to the buzz cut and ramrod stance. He was also carrying a handgun in a shoulder holster. If he'd gone ten feet farther into the room, past the metal detector, the man would have set off the alarm.

"I've got a meeting to attend, Charles, but I need to ask you a few questions about your sister and her work." She looked out of the corner of her eye and noticed Dr. Wayne had disappeared, apparently into his temporary office. "Want to do that now?"

"Sooner the better. But not inside here, okay?" Charles looked over at Lee, gauging how he measured up, as some aggressive men tended to do. He couldn't see Lee's eyes because of the light-protecting sunglasses. "Just you, Diane."

"Sorry, Charles, but this is my partner on this case, State Policeman Leo Hawk, and we work together. I trust him completely, and so should you. Let's take a walk across the street to that little park. We can speak freely there."

Charles shrugged. "If that's my only choice."

They walked back out into the street, Diane leading the way and Charles a half step behind her. Lee followed to Charles's right, not taking his eyes off the man with the gun.

"Mr. Alderete, we need anything and everything you know about your sister and her work at that research lab. Tanner has to be taken down," Lee said as they proceeded to the crosswalk.

"Not just taken down—destroyed," Charles said, letting his emotions show. "I'll tell you what I know and why I'm here. Then either you do your job . . . or I'll do it for you."

Nobody spoke again until they'd crossed the street and were standing in the center of the small, grassy square. A big, black two-faced clock stood atop an old iron streetlight pole.

Lee watched Charles Alderete. The man was tightly coiled, but had the confident stride of an athlete who believed he was a winner. If he was afraid, it didn't show.

"You still own the gun shop in Albuquerque, Charles?" Diane asked casually. "And I trust you have a permit for that pistol in the shoulder holster?"

"Yes, and yes. You can check my wallet if it'll make you

happy. I'm a legitimate firearms dealer, and that makes me a potential target for thieves. I've gotten into the habit of carrying concealed protection when I travel or pass through rough neighborhoods," Charles said casually.

"You just lost your sister, Charles, and I understand why you're eager to even the score. But that's an extremely dangerous idea—on every count," Lee pointed out. If Charles was thinking of hunting down Tanner, chances were he'd end up facedown no matter how much confidence he had.

"Hawk, most cops like you have never even fired your weapon outside the target range. You'd piss your pants just hearing what I went through in Iraq. *I* know what it's like to hunt down another human being." Charles crossed his arms across his chest and waited for Lee to react.

Diane couldn't suppress a smile.

Charles stood there a moment, then his face started to turn red. "What's so amusing?"

"Chuckie, *I* can beat the crap out of you. And if you knew what Officer Hawk has experienced in *his* lifetime you'd faint dead away. A man who knows his own capabilities doesn't have to posture or strut around."

Lee had remained expressionless up to now, but he finally cracked a smile as well. "Charles, I appreciate the fact that you placed your life on the line serving in our country's military. But this is our job now, not yours. What we need from you is information that'll help us bring down Tanner."

Alderete's bluster finally faded and he nodded. "Lynette told me that they were working with a really dangerous man whose name was Stewart Tanner. She was terrified that if he ever got half a chance he'd murder all of them. Lynette said that they kept him in leg irons and handcuffs, and three guards went with him every time he stepped out of his cell. But she said that she could feel him just biding his time. She was right, judging from the way things went down."

"Two of those three guards died," Diane said softly. "What did Lynette find out about Stewart Tanner anyway? Where did he come from, why was he so special, and why all the secrecy?"

"According to what she discovered—and I wasn't supposed to tell *anyone*—Tanner was a civilian, a chef and restaurant owner from Albuquerque. When she told me his name I remembered reading an article about him in the lifestyle section of the morning paper. Tanner was very outgoing and popular with some of the late-night crowd. Apparently he had a phobia about sunlight due to a skin condition. Before he'd come down with that, Tanner had done a lot of hunting and shooting, but his skin condition pretty much ended that. So he made his restaurant into a night owl place. Lynette says some fed agency kidnapped him—all illegal as hell—after they got a tip that he wasn't 'normal.' Tanner, according to Lynette, has remarkable healing abilities—like a cut would seal up and close within a few hours—bizarre stuff like that."

He looked at Diane, and Lee knew from his delivery and from the way he avoided meeting her eyes directly that Charles was holding back. Lynette had to have known a lot more than Charles was telling them, and Lee was guessing that she'd told him everything, maybe even the vampire angle.

"What else did she tell you?" Lee asked, just to confirm his suspicions.

Charles tried to challenge Lee by staring him down, but all the man saw was his own reflection in Lee's shades. "That's pretty much it," he said, glancing away.

Diane looked at Lee, letting him know that she knew Charles was holding out on them. "Okay. If you think of anything that might help us find this guy, call me." She handed him her card. "Lynette and I were close once, Charles. Let me do this for her, okay?"

Charles nodded, then placed the card in his jacket pocket. "You have a cell phone, right?"

"That's the second number on the card," she said. "Right now we've got to go meet with one of the federal honchos, but we *will* track down Tanner. He's our *only* job until it's done. Assure your parents of that when you see them again."

Charles nodded. "Thanks for taking time to see me. Now that we've spoken, I'll be heading back to Albuquerque." He started to walk away, then turned back. "Diane, be *very* careful with this guy. Don't let Tanner get close enough to get his hands on you. A double tap in the head might not be enough. Empty your frigging gun into his face, then reload and do it again." Charles turned and walked toward the street, leaving them standing there.

"Well, that cinches it. Lynette told him *everything* about Tanner," Diane whispered.

Lee nodded. "Unfortunately, Charles Alderete still has no idea what he's really up against. Let's hope he doesn't get the chance to find out."

Dr. Victor Wayne shrugged. "You're right, I've known about the basic research taking place at the lab—from the beginning. But I had no reason to believe that Tanner might be capable of overpowering his guards and assaulting his physicians like this—much less killing them." Victor leaned forward in his chair—the brown leather executive model behind the oak desk with somebody else's name on the coordinating nameplate.

"So to you, Stewart Tanner was just a disturbed patient, undergoing treatment?" Diane countered.

"Let's not be naïve about this, Agent Lopez," Victor replied. "Patient Beta—Tanner—is criminally insane. He required confinement under very close supervision. Yet, due to his obvious physical capabilities and unusual ailments he's somehow managed to convince a handful of federal officials—and the late staff of the lab—that he's some kind of . . . superhuman monster."

"You seemed a little *less* relaxed last night when the armed professionals around you were being sliced and diced rather handily by Tanner. He was outnumbered four to one, and he didn't even have a pistol," Lee pointed out.

"Hell, Officer Hawk, I *know* the man is a skilled fighter—an assassin type like one of those movie ninjas. But to insist he's like some kind of . . . vampire? That's a real load of crap, and you know it." Victor stood, leaning forward with his hands on the borrowed desk for emphasis.

"I don't buy that notion either, Dr. Wayne. He's just another out-of-control human with some unfortunately lethal skills," Diane said. "But if you knew Tanner was so dangerous, why didn't you pull the plug and shut down the lab months ago? You could have placed Tanner into a maximum security prison."

"The vampire thing was fantasy and a non-issue. But there were still questions about his quick healing abilities. What if Tanner had some antibodies or mutated genes that will lead the way to a breakthrough in the treatment of trauma patients, surgical healing, skin cancer, or any of a number of other possibilities? That's the only reason why I've kept from, as you say, pulling the plug."

"But now Tanner has pulled it for you," Lee countered. "And it looks like he's going to keep everyone in this county awake at night until we get him back into custody. That's what should really concern—and not to mention frighten—you and everyone else involved in this hunt."

Diane nodded. "Tell me what you know about Tanner's alleged reaction to sunlight. I understand it's a rare condition. I saw something about that on a news show once, and read about it in a couple of popular novels."

"Tanner is *extremely* vulnerable to sunlight, according to the data I've seen." Victor sat back down again.

"I saw the videos of some of the experiments, but those could be faked. What physical proof does the lab have?" Lee pressed. "No proof?"

"*Nobody* is supposed to know what's been going on there, so the paper trail is very slim—just numbers and scientific jargon. There were the camcorders, but the recordings are kept in the safe and unavailable. Cell phones weren't allowed into the facility because some now take images. The project needed some kind of plausible deniability in case of bad publicity. We're probably lucky that Tanner decided to destroy all the tissue samples. At least they can't come back to haunt us."

"So, officially, we're not having this conversation?" Diane asked.

"What conversation?" Wayne said with a shrug. "All we're doing is coordinating our interagency tactics in order to apprehend a psychologically disturbed mass murderer."

"One more question. Who are *you* working for?" Diane asked.

Lee and Diane waited, knowing that Victor Wayne wasn't likely to answer. Admitting to anything came as unnaturally to him as sunbathing did to Tanner. And the only evidence they had was secondhand—unofficial.

Silence stretched out. Finally Lee, who'd been in his normal position, standing with his back to the wall where he could watch the door and the interior at the same time, nodded to Diane. "Let's get to it."

"Right. Dr. Wayne . . . will you be returning to Washington—Atlanta—Virginia?" Diane asked as she reached the door and joined Lee.

Victor smiled, again ignoring the implication. "No, I'm going to be working at the lab—cataloging research and removing all classified information and equipment, even the destroyed biological samples. You two already know not to reveal any sensitive information to the press and public. I also insist that you restrict your written and oral reports to the facts as you've seen them."

Wayne was very cordial, but it was clear he was sending them a warning. Maybe he was with some branch of Homeland

Security, perhaps a subagency deeply buried within the new, bigger than ever federal government. If he'd been Bureau-connected, Diane would have already heard.

"I can only speak for myself, but except for very clear warnings of the danger Stewart Tanner presents to the public, I'm not going to be doing any speculating concerning what has been discussed and learned over the past two days regarding this case," Diane said flatly.

Lee shrugged. "Sounds reasonable to me."

"Good hunting, then," Dr. Wayne added, and reached for the phone.

Diane and Lee didn't speak again until they were on the sidewalk outside, walking toward his unit. "Suppose those men with Victor last night are really federal marshals? They acted more like military than law enforcement."

"A lot of law enforcement people are ex-military, but I was thinking the same thing. If it wasn't for jurisdictional issues, I'd have concluded that Victor Wayne is more CIA than Justice Department—or working with the CDC. Or maybe he's attached to another intelligence operation we don't know about—yet."

"Whatever he is, he isn't just a forensics expert. Let's continue to be very careful about what we say, and *never* volunteer any information," Lee advised.

Diane waited at the passenger door of Lee's state police car while he slid across the seat and undid the lock.

The dusty oranges and reds of a beautiful New Mexico sunset announced the upcoming activity of bats, owls, and, unfortunately, a vampire or two. Not that vampires could really fly—except for the vampire bats from Mexico and farther south—but night walkers could easily leap three or four times their height.

Lee and Diane didn't have any idea where Tanner would strike next, only that such an attack was extremely likely, and that the vampire intended—if his words were to be believed—to kill only federal employees. Since agents in Albuquerque were already checking his old haunts and contacts in central New Mexico, they'd remained in the Four Corners area to keep watch on potential federal targets. A day-long search had turned up no new leads.

Several heavily armed Navajo police officers, along with four new federal marshals accompanying Dr. Wayne, were now at the research lab. Temporary floodlights had been added, taking away the advantage of darkness for Stewart Tanner, if he decided to return, and night-vision devices had been supplied to several officers out in the field. The residences of the deceased lab employees were also being guarded, along with the surviving guard's home and hospital room.

Every available law enforcement officer in the county, including some borrowed from adjacent communities, were in four-officer groups, patrolling the community, especially watching government offices that could have been identified via phone books and other resources Tanner might have had available.

Lee and Diane were parked in the outside lot of a Farmington hotel, which contained the most likely targets for Tanner if he was thinking of striking back against images of federal authority. A judiciary conference—really not much more than a four-hour workshop—had been scheduled at this hotel and the county courthouse in Aztec, for months. Though Diane had tried to get it postponed or relocated, she'd been turned down, and conference publicity had been on the front page of the local newspaper. Even the schedule had been given, so Tanner could easily know all he needed. The Farmington police chief, also a woman, had bristled at the idea that she couldn't provide adequate security, and convinced those putting on the conference to continue as planned.

"We have federal judges attending from five states, and the

guest speaker is U.S. District Court Judge Ronald Baca, from Albuquerque," Diane told Lee. "So, if Tanner has decided to take out another federal employee, he'll strike here, or at the courthouse session in Aztec."

"Or while the judges are in transit. If Tanner's after headlines, he's going to try and take out a federal judge or two, not just some postal worker," Lee said, looking closely at any vehicles that entered the parking area. With binoculars and his unique eyesight, he could see into every vehicle and check out the passengers, despite the darkness.

"Cable TV, local radio, and the *Daily Tribune* sure gave him center stage. Even the Albuquerque papers and network affiliates have reporters roaming the county looking for a story. Once word got out that the suspect was an enigmatic Albuquerque businessman that had mysteriously disappeared months ago, there was no stopping the coverage."

"Yeah, but tagging him as 'the vampire chef' was bushleague journalism. It makes Tanner sound like a bad joke, and people might downplay the danger. Damn whoever mentioned those wooden stakes to a reporter."

"Think all this vampire talk could make it more difficult for you?" Diane asked.

Lee shrugged. "I just want to get Tanner, then make sure Victor Wayne leaves town. He's got an agenda, though I doubt he had anything to do with Tanner's breakout."

Diane nodded, then glanced down at her watch. "Well, in another ten minutes the conference people will be boarding the bus for the trip to Aztec. The courthouse there is crawling with city and county cops, and the guests all have escorts, even for the short bus ride. We may have picked the wrong target."

"There's no higher-ranking fed in the Four Corners, not one that we know about, anyway. And if we don't know, neither does Tanner," Lee reminded. "All he's had access to is the local media."

"Unless Tanner's already eluded the roadblocks and is halfway to New Orleans," Diane said. "Supposed to be a real vampire hangout."

"Must be the nightlife. I wouldn't know," Lee replied.

Diane groaned. "Here comes the bus," she said, suddenly wide awake.

An hour and a half later, very close to schedule, the same chartered bus left its parking space and pulled up adjacent to the courthouse steps. The conference attendees boarded quickly, then, led by a police car, the bus pulled out. Another vehicle, this one an unmarked SUV containing four heavily armed deputies, followed right behind.

"Let's stick close to the bus," Diane suggested, starting the engine. They were in an unmarked unit, one borrowed locally. "Once everyone is safely tucked away for the evening, we'll check with Dr. Wayne and see how things are going over on the Rez. You know, if Tanner ever finds out that Victor Wayne was overseeing his captivity, that'll make our mystery doctor the next target. But I doubt Tanner knows that yet. And I just can't see joining Victor's already significant security team and leaving these other targets protected only by people who don't really have a clue how dangerous Tanner is."

"Tanner has more than eight hours of darkness left, and vampires don't get sleepy. He could wait until everyone is dead on their feet, then make his move. Most of the best raids are conducted in the very early morning hours," Lee reminded.

"If nothing's gone down by three A.M., I'm going to start making calls and getting everyone stirred up again." Diane looked over at him, smiling.

"Just because you're good-looking doesn't mean you can't be a hard-ass, right?"

"Damn straight," Diane shot back.

Lee already knew his partner was tough and smart, but thank God she also had a sense of humor.

The bus trip back to Farmington took less than twenty minutes with the accompanying escort making certain no stoplights slowed them down. The route was simple and the well-maintained road allowed for a fast transit.

"Tanner could strike when they start getting off the bus," Diane said, "though he'd have to force his way past security unless he has a rifle now."

She parked their vehicle in a slot away from the entrance and they walked up to the rear of the big vehicle before the passengers started to disembark.

Lee watched the roofs and higher floors of surrounding buildings, and she kept an eye on the parked vehicles closest to the entrance, but everyone from the bus made it into the hotel lobby without incident.

"Judge Baca's room is on the top floor, so the only way Tanner could get past the inside security is by coming down from the roof," Lee reminded. "He could start at ground level, then climb up in steps, balcony to balcony."

"That's still four stories. But how would he know which room is Baca's?" Diane countered. "That information is being kept from the public."

"The judge was in his room for a few hours earlier. If he happened to pass in front of his window, someone in the right position could have seen him. And Baca's photo was in this morning's paper. Tanner could identify him from that."

"Okay, Lee. If *you* wanted to check out the hotel rooms, where would you position yourself to watch from the outside without being seen?"

"There's only one other building more than two stories high within visual range—that old brick office building across the street. An upper-story office or the roof would work."

"If Tanner is planning on striking at the judge later tonight, he might be watching right now."

"Didn't the police chief place an officer on that roof? Someone from the local SWAT?"

Diane nodded. "Yeah, you're right. Let me see if I can get a call through to that officer." She picked up her handheld radio and contacted the local Dispatch. Lee listened as she struggled through the protocols, then finally spoke to the officer on the roof. After a minute, she ended the transmission.

"You probably got the gist of it. The officer is one of the SWAT snipers, and he's been in position on the roof since six P.M., when the last tenant left the building. He's got a low-light scope, and he hasn't seen any suspicious activity around the hotel. Judge Baca is on the top floor, second window from the right."

"Did FPD officers check out the brick building when the sniper moved in?"

"Yes, according to Dispatch."

"Let's go check it out again. Maybe Tanner came in later from the back or sides. He could be watching us right now." Lee turned and looked up at the office building, an old structure probably dating from the thirties, based upon the design and condition of the bricks. On the parapet of the roof, which was decorated in zia sun symbols, Lee could see the rifle barrel and big lens of the sniper's scope. The officer was wearing a baseball cap, the bill backward.

Lee and Diane returned to their vehicle, and three minutes later parked in the alley a half block from the rear of the office building.

Lee led the way up the alley, staying to the side so they could see the rear of the building and as high as possible as they approached. "The sniper could be compromised if Tanner came up the fire-escape ladder," Lee said.

"You think Tanner would use the rifle? He's supposed to be a skilled hunter and a good shot."

Lee shrugged, looking up. The only rear windows were on the

east end, linked to the fire escape. That would be Tanner's only way up from the back. "He could have taken a pistol the other night, but didn't. He's unpredictable. Let's go to the roof, checking the building on the way up."

The back was locked, and so was the front, and the quality of the locks was good enough to make picking them a chore. "Tanner probably has locksmith skills, and even a vampire would have difficulty forcing the doors," Lee said, finally. "Let's just warn the sniper to cover his butt."

Diane nodded.

Lee picked the big brass lock at the rear entrance beside the loading dock within a minute. He'd been a vampire long enough to know the danger of being denied access by a locked door, especially when going indoors could be a matter of life and death. He'd maintained locksmith skills for decades, keeping up with the times, and could even defeat most of the modern electronic security devices.

Working their way around the rooms in the basement, they confirmed that anyone inside, like them, would have to pick room locks to get beyond the halls and stairwells. The only unlocked facility was a small bathroom. The single elevator was blocked by a metal security door and was unaccessible.

They walked quietly up the stairs to the second floor, signaling each other rather than speaking, and working together, covering one another with their weapons as they moved. The rooms on the back side of the building were all locked, so they moved next to the hallway that gave access to the four offices that faced toward the street and the hotel beyond.

The hall was dim, illuminated only by the exit light just before the stairwell door, and Diane used a small flashlight, directing it away from doorways so it couldn't be seen from inside a room through a glass panel or at the bottom.

The first office, leased by a bookkeeper, had two locks and no glass panel in the door. The second, just ahead, belonged to a lawyer, according to the raised brass lettering on the wall that read "Henry Blackburn, Attorney at Law."

Diane covered Lee as he stood sideways and reached down to check the knob. The door moved. It was unlocked and open.

Lee listened for any sound within. He could hear a ticking clock and a bubbling sound—probably an aquarium or one of those desk fountains. He swung the door open, pistol ready, and came in low and quick. He saw two desks, a broken chair with a missing leg, filing cabinets, and a big credenza with an aquarium and light, tasteful Southwest art on the wall. There was also a man, faceup on the pale gold carpet. He had the missing wooden chair leg extending from his chest. The blood had stopped pumping, but it hadn't caked up much yet, and the bright color suggested he hadn't been dead for very long.

The blinds were open, and through a large window Lee could see the hotel across the street. Judge Baca was standing at his room window, a phone in his hand.

Out of the corner of his eye, Lee saw Diane moving into the room. "Shit. He was here, all right, not long ago. Where is he now?"

The phone on the desk rang, and Lee suddenly had a good idea. He watched across the street as Diane grabbed the phone. "Hello?" She turned to Lee. "It's Tanner," she mouthed.

Lee saw a man in Baca's room across the way, waving. "He's in the judge's room. Get someone there, now!"

Diane dropped the phone and reached for her radio as Lee ran for the door. He heard a gunshot from somewhere above, and realized the SWAT officer must have finally realized what was going on. Maybe they'd be lucky and Tanner had stayed in view a second too long.

Lee went down two flights of stairs in two steps, then sprinted for the front entrance. He hit it full force and it sprung open, jarring his shoulder heavily. Sprinting across the road, Lee heard brakes squeal, but knew the car would miss. By the time it reached that spot, Lee would already be on the sidewalk.

Where to go? Lee wondered. Tanner wasn't going to stick around the hotel much longer—if he was still on his feet. Lee knew that a jump off the roof was unlikely. The fall would break the vampire's legs—for a while at least, and render him immobile.

Officers were moving now, some coming out to watch the exterior. Diane must have already made contact. He turned to look back up at the sniper. "I missed him," the officer yelled, looking down from beside his rifle. "I'll watch the front and sides."

That left the rear. Lee circled the rectangular structure to the left, thinking the interior would be swarming with officers, and Diane would be watching the street. Dodging past the rows of vehicles in the parking lot, Lee sprinted past a side door, noting the backs of two officers. Good, they were watching in the right direction—inside.

Lee reached the back corner of the structure and looked up. A rope dangled from an upper-floor window, and was still swaying back and forth. "He ran into the park," he heard a woman shouting.

Lee saw a woman in a blue FPD uniform holding a handheld radio and looking toward a small park comprised of several pine trees, shrubs, and a bench or two. She had her weapon out, and was advancing slowly.

Beyond the park, down a steep hill, was a street. Lee heard screeching tires, a curse and a thud, then the sound of a slamming door. He ran toward the woman officer, who was intent on looking ahead, but less motivated to advance any faster. Before he got close, Lee shouted, "I'm a police officer!"

She turned to look as he came up, but didn't aim her weapon at him because of his warning.

"It was Tanner. I saw him just as he dropped off the rope at the bottom. I think he's already made it to the street," she said, pointing ahead.

"Cover me." He didn't wait for an answer, instead jumping down the twenty feet to the pavement in two strides. A speeding pickup was just turning the corner at the next intersection. It disappeared, but in the street a man in denim coveralls was on his hands and knees, struggling to stand up.

The old guy, in his sixties at least, judging from his white hair, was clenching his fists, and his glasses were halfway down his nose. "Get that punk bastard, son. He stole my pickup. Wish I'd have run him over."

Diane broke in with a radio call as Lee was helping the man to his feet. "Tanner just drove by real casually in a red pickup—like he was sightseeing. Meet you at the car," she said.

On the move quickly, Lee was already there, waiting but taking calls from various officers in the area by the time Diane ran up, out of breath. "You're too damned fast for me, Lee," she managed, opening the door and jumping in. "Judge Baca is dead, according to the officers now in his room. Pretty gruesome, apparently. All I was able to get so far is that the judge had been impaled with a wooden chair leg."

"How original," Lee responded as Diane pulled the unit out into traffic. "Where are we going?"

"Tanner was going west. I doubt he'll be checking into the hotel again anytime soon, so I thought he might have another go at the targets he was unable to finish off last night."

"Dr. Victor Wayne and his entourage?"

"Or us." Diane checked the rearview mirror. "Keep an eye on our tail. And heaven help us if he decides to start using a firearm. With his physical abilities, he'd be really hard to stop, working at long range as a sniper. I can't shake the feeling that it's all a crazy game to him now," Diane added.

"It's payback time. So far he's only gone after the people who tried to harm him. Or, in the case of Judge Baca—someone he can identify as a federal honcho."

"New Mexico has a lot of federal employees," she warned. "But what about the lawyer?"

"Wrong place, wrong time. And it also establishes that Tanner will kill *anyone* who gets in his way."

Ten minutes went by before they received a call from a team of county deputies on patrol. The vehicle Tanner had stolen from the old man had been found across the street from the police station. Diane turned to Lee. "Everyone there is now looking over their shoulders. Suppose Tanner plans on killing some police officers?"

Lee shook his head. "Too much firepower, and he'd have a hard time blending in. My guess is that he wants to read about his big *cojones* in tomorrow morning's paper. He obviously reads the news."

"Then where did he go from the pickup, and did he walk, or steal another vehicle?" Diane picked up the mike and placed a call to the police station. Within a few minutes, she had officers checking the video from cameras that monitored the area around the station. Like banks and most big businesses, the local government had decided years ago, after the Oklahoma City attack, that it would be a good thing to keep an eye on their own front yards. It also cut down on vandalism to police units.

Then a call came through on Diane's cell phone. She spoke for a moment, then ended the call. "That was Victor. He's confident that if Tanner decides to make a move on him or the lab, they can deal with him."

"Dr. Wayne must have a small army up at that lab. But no way he called just to reassure us about his safety. What did he really want?" Lee asked.

"He'd like for us to check out Baca's hotel room. We wants us to figure out how Tanner got in. I agreed to take a look. Okay with you?"

Lee shrugged. "Until we get some idea where Tanner has gone, we might as well. He has a habit of making return visits, so maybe he'll go for some of the other judicial targets at the hotel. People have a way of relaxing their security, sometimes too much, when they think they've already dodged the bullet."

They gave up their search pattern, which had been directed to the west, and returned to the hotel. Lee had taken the wheel while Diane contacted the officers at the hotel, warning them to continue tight security. The reminder that he'd returned to the scene of his last murder got their attention, she told him when she broke contact.

Lee parked across the street in a fire lane, noting that officers were visible at each outside corner of the building. A crime-scene tape had been placed across the entrance, and two officers were stationed there, shotguns out and ready.

"Who's working the scene?" Lee asked as they crossed the street. He looked all around, high and low, hoping to verify that Tanner had not returned. Traffic was being diverted around the hotel, so no vehicles except those belonging to emergency units were in front.

"FPD detectives, two OMI techs, and whoever else they can find. Dr. Wayne—Victor—instructed them not to move anything until we had a look," Diane said, holding up her gold shield for a tall, angry-looking uniformed FPD sergeant who was blocking the hotel entrance.

Lee, in plainclothes, also had his gold state police badge out. He recognized the sergeant from previous encounters—mostly traffic accidents—and nodded.

"Ma'am. Officer Hawk. I think you're going to Room 412. The elevator on the east side is reserved for official traffic."

"Thanks, Sergeant . . . Braun." She noted the photo ID on his pocket, which was at her eye level, then looked around the lobby, now empty of guests. A doorman stood glumly by the main desk, watching them.

"Sergeant, do you happen to know if SWAT is still watching from the roof across the street?"

"Somebody is there," Lee answered before Braun. "I saw a cap and shoulder when we crossed the street."

The big cop nodded. "We're keeping in touch on a tactical frequency. The sniper tracks everyone coming in the front and sides. Three officers are now in the back lot."

"Stay sharp, Sergeant," Lee said. "Tanner might decide to come back."

"Let him come," Braun said, his voice a low growl.

They didn't have to look hard for Baca's hotel room. A woman FPD officer was standing in the doorway, holding a clipboard. The room across the hall and facing the rear of the hotel was sealed with yellow crime-scene tape. The door was ajar, and from the damage on the door itself and the lock, it had been kicked in. Tanner had descended to the parking lot from there after killing the judge.

Diane had clipped her badge to her belt, beside her pancake holster, and Lee had fastened his to a shirt pocket, but the officer at the victim's door, a tall black woman, insisted they wait until she checked their names on a list.

"If you think you might puke, do it out here," the officer—hard-looking and in her early fifties—warned. Her name tag identified her as Officer Johnston.

Diane frowned. "I've already seen the victim across the street, Officer Johnston."

"I haven't," Johnston said. "But this scene's gotta be worse."

Lee caught Officer Johnston's attention as Diane stepped into the room. "Trust me, kid," she whispered to Lee.

Lee was used to a person who looked physically much older than he was believing he was young, and it didn't faze him anymore, so he just nodded.

As he came into the room, Lee noticed Diane had stopped, and he looked past her. Judge Baca was looking toward the door. At least his head was positioned in that direction from its resting place on the backrest of a small sofa.

The judge's decapitated body was ten feet away, on the floor to the left, a spindle from a damaged wooden desk chair jammed into his chest. Blood was splattered everywhere, but the biggest pool came from where the neck had been severed. On the soaked carpet was a black-handled machete and a bloody white jacket like those worn by room service.

On the far side of the room, next to the open window, stood two men in OMI jackets and a couple of police detectives in suit coats. They looked at him too, but only briefly before all four sets of eyes returned to Diane.

"Ma'am. The room where the perp used the rope to climb down was vacant—no vic. We'll get to it next. We were instructed to stop our work until you and Officer Hawk had the opportunity to survey the scene," the shorter of the two detectives said, not bothering to introduce himself.

Diane nodded. "We appreciate the courtesy. Who was the first officer on the scene?"

"Christine," the short detective said. "Officer Johnston."

"How'd she get in?" Lee asked.

"Officer Johnston found a key card on the floor outside the door."

Diane and Lee took a quick look around, noting that the machete looked new and still had the price tag from a local hardware store on the handle. There was a bullet hole in the plate-glass sliding door, from the SWAT sniper's rifle. The bullet had passed through the wall on the opposite side, entering the bathroom and coming to rest inside the shower stall, shattering a tile.

"Go ahead and continue," Diane said, looking over at Lee, who nodded. "If you find anything of interest other than the machete, let *me* know." She looked at each person in the room, waiting until they had all nodded or replied before stepping back out into the hall with Lee.

"Officer Johnston. The door to the victim's room was closed when you arrived?" Diane asked.

"Yes, ma'am. But there was a key card on the carpet, right there." She pointed to a white card on the floor. "That's my business card. I gave the key card to Detective Shannon, who had me sign off on it before he put it in an evidence pouch."

"You had to use the card to get in, didn't you?" Diane asked.

"Yes. I know . . . fingerprints. But I held it by the edges as much as possible."

Lee nodded, then turned to Diane. "Where did Tanner get the right card for *this* door? The front desk?"

"Unless it was a passkey used by someone on staff, like housekeeping," Diane suggested.

Officer Johnston's eyebrows went up. "I didn't think of that. Maybe we have another victim."

"What's the number for the front desk?" Diane asked the officer, who was already checking her clipboard.

Lee was already running down the hall, looking for the closest linen closet or housekeeping location.

There was a door beside the stairwell with a sign that said "ICE." Lee stepped inside. A Pepsi machine was against a wall, and beside it a big stainless-steel icemaker. On top of the icemaker was a big wad of white sheets and a blanket. The bedding moved slightly, and he heard a noise, like someone mumbling.

Lee stood on tiptoes and reached up, moving the bedding aside. A young woman was on her side, a pillowcase tied around her mouth, serving as a gag. He couldn't see her arms, but assumed they'd been tied behind her back. The woman's pale blue eyes were full of tears, and when she tried to speak all Lee heard was "mig mife. Eee as mmm mig mife."

"It was a machete. But don't worry, he's gone. Hang on to me, ma'am, and I'll lift you down." Lee slid his arms under the woman, who couldn't have been more than nineteen and probably weighed around a hundred pounds, and lifted her off the ice machine.

"Nod if you can stand up," Lee asked, cradling her in his arms, her head up. She was so entangled in the sheets and blanket he didn't know how to try and unwrap her.

She nodded, so Lee eased her to the floor feet first, holding on to her so she wouldn't topple over. Fifteen seconds later the sheets and blanket were on the floor and the woman, dressed in a short-sleeved blouse and slacks, was standing on her own.

Lee grabbed his commando knife from the boot holster and cut the sheet holding her feet together, then slit the pillowcase that bound her wrists. Somewhere during the unwrapping, a folded piece of paper had appeared and fallen to the floor. Lee scooped it up by the edges and stuck it into his jacket pocket.

Her hands went to her gag at the same time as his. "Thank God you found me," the woman cried, putting her arms around Lee.

"Uh huh. I give you five minutes alone . . ."

Lee recognized Diane's voice and turned his head. She was standing in the doorway.

"Uh, this young lady is from housekeeping, right?" Lee stepped back as the girl, suddenly embarrassed, released him.

"Your husband rescued me, that's all, ma'am. This crazy man with a big knife—machete—tied me up and stole my key card. I work for the hotel . . . really. My name is Regina Kalugin."

"He's not my husband, Regina. I'm an agent with the FBI, and your hero is with the state police. Tell us exactly what happened."

F ive minutes later, the young woman was out in the hall answering questions fired at her from Detective Shannon—the shorter officer, as it turned out. The housekeeping supervisor was standing close by, but was not part of the interview.

Lee motioned to Diane, who scowled, then went with him back into the ICE room, which was not much bigger than a walk-in closet. "Want a Pepsi?"

Lee put three quarters into the machine and pushed a button. Bringing out one can he handed it to her, then bought himself another one.

Diane was sipping the Pepsi, her thoughts elsewhere, and after studying her expression, Lee said, "Hey, the girl hugged me. It wasn't my idea."

"That's not what's bothering me."

"Then what is?"

"I'm not that old. I don't look over thirty, do I?"

"Of course not. You could be the housekeeper's sister."

"Right. Blue eyes—blond—skinny. That's me."

"Okay, so what got you thinking you look old?"

"Everyone calls me ma'am—like I'm their mother. Even the old guys."

"I think it's just a show of respect. And it rolls off the tongue a lot faster than Special Agent Diane Lopez. You should be used to it."

"Yeah, well, I'm not." She took a deep swig of the cool drink, then raised an eyebrow at Lee. "You didn't bring me in here alone just to ply me with drinks. Does this have something to do with the note I saw you sneak a look at a minute ago?"

He brought out the folded piece of paper, opened it by the edges, and held it out for her to read. On the piece of hotel stationary, in pen, were the words:

"Take my life, I'll take yours."
—Pale Death

"He's got a flair for the dramatic. Pale Death. That's what some of the Navajos are calling him. We knew Tanner was taking time to read the newspapers," Diane said. "That's also how he found out about this judicial conference—and Judge Baca."

"I wasn't sure this particular message should reach anyone else's eyes," Lee said. "Tanner's trying to generate fear—and not just among law enforcement officers. He isn't even trying to hide the fact that he's a vampire. Kicked open that other door as a show of strength even though he had a key card that would do it for him." Lee brought out a small evidence bag, placed the note inside, and handed it to her. "This is your call."

Diane took the note and held it in her hand for a moment. "We'll need all the help we can get to stop Tanner, and this may motivate someone to come forward. The man's hiding somewhere in the community during the daytime, and we need to root him out. The more people looking, the better our chances."

"You're probably right," Lee answered. "Let's get back on the hunt, then."

Diane gave the note to Detective Shannon, mentioning that it had been found among the bedding used to bind up the housekeeper. The young woman, Regina, was standing with her supervisor a short distance down the hall, drinking from a water bottle.

Diane suggested that Shannon use care in divulging its contents, and when he read the note himself, the FPD detective nodded.

"He read me that note," Regina said. "I was so scared I'd forgotten all about it. I thought he meant me."

"Did he say anything else, maybe even something that sounded strange or silly at the time?" Lee asked immediately.

"You're right, there was something like that. He said that the government was out to get him because he was a vampire. I'm telling you, the man is *seriously* insane. Scary too."

"Vampires. What a nut job," Detective Shannon muttered, shaking his head slowly.

"All the more reason to bring him in," Diane added. "Let me know if you find *anything* that even hints at Tanner's next target, okay?"

"Of course, ma'am."

Diane sighed, then glanced at Lee, who was about to crack a smile. "Ready to go vampire hunting?"

Lee grinned, knowing it was the safest response to make at the moment.

After convincing the Farmington police to maintain a high level of security at the hotel, Diane contacted SAC Logan in Albuquerque to see if they had anything new on Stewart Tanner's background, hoping it would direct them to someone Tanner might try to contact. Tanner didn't have any family in the area, and a search through the local public schools hadn't turned up his name. There were several private schools, but none of their calls had been productive so far.

Nothing the metro agents had managed to find seemed particularly useful at the moment, though she pressed them again to track down Tanner's friends and business associates. She wanted to know the extent of his hunting skills, preferably from someone who might have hunted with Tanner.

Diane finally hung up, frustrated by the lack of information. "He was an orphan, adopted when he was in his early teens. But those records are sealed, even his birth certificate, and his Albuquerque foster parents are long dead. In short, we've got nothing new."

"Let's go harass Victor Wayne. He knows more than he's admitting about Tanner. Victor should be able to tell us what Tanner knew about his captors, and the people behind his imprisonment, not to mention the person who originally ratted him out. That'll give us a real good idea of who Tanner's potential targets are."

"Okay, but first let me talk to my SAC again. Maybe he can get someone higher up than the Bureau to lean on Dr. Wayne from another direction. Maybe Homeland Security. So far, with the exception of the lawyer, Tanner's been killing federal employees, so that might get their attention. Maybe they can classify Tanner as a terrorist."

Lee led the way out of the hotel to their unit while Diane spoke on her cell phone to SAC Logan. There were law enforcement officers from several agencies around the hotel and across the street at the brick office building. Looking up on the roof he saw the sniper was still there, but this time he had a second officer with him as a spotter. The military had known for years that sniper teams were much more effective, and despite their limited manpower, the local cops were covering all their bases—finally.

Still on the phone, Diane tossed him the keys and Lee started the engine. A moment later she closed up the phone. "Logan says he's going to find Dr. Wayne's supervisor. Wayne will be getting a call shortly. SAC Logan can apply pressure better than anyone else I know. Think we should hang around here and wait for confirmation?"

"Waste of time. Tanner won't be coming back here tonight, Diane. There's just too much firepower, and he barely escaped being shot when he stood in front of the window to taunt us after killing the judge."

"Okay. You're driving. Shall we go lean on Victor and not wait for Logan?"

"That's what I was thinking. And if he holds back again, I vote we press him until he tells us who he thinks Tanner's next target might be."

"I'm with you on that, Lee, though I think the doctor has already figured it out for himself. That's why he has his own small army of federal marshals."

"If that's what *they* really are," Lee added quietly.

CHAPTER 8

Lee and Diane found a parking place in the now very brightly illuminated parking lot next to the research lab. Before reaching the site they had already gone through two checkpoints manned by heavily armed Navajo police officers.

"You must have made a positive impact with the tribal cops the other day. They're even carrying knives. That big blade the chubby cop had, what was it, a bowie knife?"

"One thing for sure, if they ever take Tanner down, vampire or not, he won't be getting up again," Lee said, climbing out of the car. For the moment he wished he had his old .30-30 Winchester, but that had disappeared back in '45 and he'd never picked up another. He did have a department-issue shotgun, but had decided to leave it in Diane's loaner car and rely on his 9mm Beretta with the big pre-'95 legislation magazine capacity. For real close work, his big commando knife, honed to a razor's edge, would serve. Every vampire Lee had ever known carried an edged weapon.

Victor Wayne was inside the office area, seated before the late Dr. Prescott's computer terminal when they brushed past the two shotgun-brandishing "federal marshals" and entered the room.

"Good evening, Diane and Officer Hawk," he said without turning to look. "My people said you'd arrived. What's new on the Judge Baca killing?"

Lee glanced at the computer monitor just before Victor closed the software window, leaving just a desktop image of Ship Rock and a few icons. Yet that brief look had revealed text that referred to Stewart Tanner by name, something Lee and Diane had been unable to find on their earlier search through computer files.

"Tanner left a note," Diane began, then told him what it said and where it had been found. She also let him know what Tanner had told the housekeeper.

"The man is a homicidal maniac, but at least he spared that young woman," Dr. Wayne said. "Unfortunately he obviously bears a grudge against his doctors and the agency responsible for his care."

"Care? Quit jerking us around, Victor. We know that Tanner was taken into custody probably on some trumped-up charge—essentially kidnapped—and was being held against his will and experimented upon like in some mad scientist novel. Exactly *which* agency is behind all this, and how did Tanner get their attention?" Diane was barely keeping her temper under restraint, and Lee wondered how much of it—if any—was an act.

"Where would you get such outrageous ideas? Certainly not from anything you found in this office." Victor looked at her as if she was deranged, then stood. He was at least a foot taller than Diane, and a few inches more than Lee.

Maybe I should bounce him off the wall a few times, Lee thought, but instead he just smiled at Victor. Diane would take him off at the knees all by herself.

She stepped up within inches of the tall man, and the look in her eyes was definitely unenticing. "You wanna play mine is bigger than yours, mister Vienna sausage? These murders are all part of *my* investigation, so unless you want to read all about obstruction of justice charges from your communal jail cell, you'd better tell us everything you know—now. We already suspect that Tanner reads the papers, so what do you think he'd do if he found out who's *really* responsible for his treatment? Keep in mind that Judge Baca had half the county protecting him."

"You're asking for classified information, Lopez. Information you don't need to know, and information I'm not authorized to tell you."

"Authorize this!" Diane reached over and grabbed one of the wooden stakes. "Why does Stewart Tanner continue to portray himself as a vampire, and what were these doing here if nobody was humoring his story?"

Diane's cell phone rang. She flipped it open, listened for a few seconds, then handed the device to Victor Wayne. "It's for you."

"This is Dr. Victor Wayne," he said into the speaker.

The conversation that followed seemed very one-sided. Victor said "Yes sir" several times, and "No sir" once.

Lee enjoyed watching the man struggle to retain his air of superiority—and fail. Diane was probably enjoying it as well, but her expression didn't change. If looks could have inflicted bodily harm, right now Victor would have been scrunched up on the floor in the fetal position, screaming his head off.

Finally the call ended. Victor looked beaten, but not defeated. He stepped away, reaching for a cup of coffee on the desk.

"My phone, please?" Diane asked, holding out her hand.

Victor handed it to her, then sat down in his chair and swiveled around to face them. He leaned back, feigning a relaxed attitude, then finally spoke. "All right. What do you want to know?"

A half hour passed. Lee and Diane learned what they already suspected. Tanner had been ambushed by a mugger faking an injury late at night in front of the Albuquerque federal building, and been stabbed repeatedly. He'd gone down, bleeding, and the mugger had taken off with his wallet. Everything had been captured on a building security video, including Tanner's quick recovery and departure and, equally important, his vehicle tag.

"I work for the Department of Defense, and one of our agency's contacts saw the video and called our office. My people immediately saw the implications a miraculous healing ability could have for the military, and Tanner was taken into custody, bypassing local authorities. A research lab was established to study his unique physical characteristics and their possible use in developing new treatments for trauma injuries, especially battle wounds. I was appointed to oversee the project because of my medical background. But Tanner's ability to heal himself hasn't kept him from going crazy."

"What makes you say that?" Lee asked.

"Tanner actually believes he's a vampire. He said that he was attacked while on a hunting trip to Europe. He claims that he fought the vampire, but during the struggle their blood mingled."

Victor shot Diane a level gaze. "So either Tanner was lying and hoping to unnerve the people around him, or he's insane. Your choice."

Diane considered what he said, then finally nodded. "Okay, we can all agree on two things. First of all, Stewart Tanner believes he's a vampire. Secondly, we know there are no such creatures. But the fact remains that Tanner is a very skilled killer and needs to be stopped."

"Which brings up a topic we haven't discussed yet," Lee said. "Do you have any reason to believe that Stewart Tanner hunted more than animals—that he was a killer—before he was discovered by your people?"

"There's nothing about that in any agency file, anywhere. The only thing we had on Stewart Tanner were a few speeding and parking tickets. If he killed someone before the incidents here, we have no knowledge of it."

Diane looked at her watch. "It should be daylight now, and we haven't received any calls about Tanner. That means we have until sunset tonight to track him down, or the killing will continue."

"Oh, come on, we know he's not a vampire. He could be out

there right now, looking for victims," Victor said, his voice becoming perilously close to a whine.

"He *thinks* he's a vampire," Lee said. "That means he'll hole up inside somewhere and rest. He's not going anywhere now," Lee pointed out, unwilling to go into an explanation of sunblock and UV rays.

"Oh? And where's his coffin and Transylvanian soil? A church basement? Or better yet, a castle?" Victor said with a sneer.

"Hell, there's not even a White Castle in this county, is there?" Lee countered.

"Let's just assume he's staying indoors, okay, boys?" Diane said, standing. "Shall we go, Lee? I've got an idea or two I'd like to follow up on."

Lee nodded. He wasn't going to ask what that was in front of Victor, though, admittedly, the doctor didn't seem particularly interested.

"We'll be seeing you again soon, Victor," Diane said as she turned toward the door.

"Count on it," the man replied without expression.

Lee and Diane left without another word, and didn't speak until they'd passed the last cluster of Navajo police at the main highway. A big silver SUV was parked away from the department units, across the road, and Lee took a glance at the driver as they passed the vehicle. "Isn't that . . . ?"

"Charles Alderete." Diane nodded. "Thought Charles was going back to Albuquerque. I wonder how long he's been out here—in what looks like a rented vehicle?"

"I'll ask." Lee picked up the vehicle radio, and within a few minutes reached the Navajo sergeant in charge of the highway detail they'd just passed.

After a brief conversation, Lee racked the mike. "Charles showed up just after we did, apparently. The officers checked him out, and once they learned he was the brother of one of those who'd died at the river, they let him stay. The officer I spoke to said Charles has a shotgun in his car—and a wicked-looking knife."

"Not including his handgun. So Victor Wayne isn't the only person who's been lying to us recently. Charles has passed up his trip home for a hunting expedition. How long do you suppose he's been following us?"

"At least from the hotel. His showing up just after we arrived . . . I don't believe in coincidences."

"Neither do I. But is he going to try and follow us now?" Diane was driving, and she took a long look in the rearview mirror. "I don't see him, but there are several cars on the road behind us. He could be back there, somewhere. With basically just one route to Farmington, it won't be hard to stay with us."

"We could always take the southern route."

She looked at him. "Gallup?"

"No. You're not familiar with the roads around here, but there's a route farther east, closer to the old power plant, that goes all the way into Farmington. Not the main road, but it's good, new, and paved. We'll have to go slow through a residential area, but there are some good open stretches, and we'll be able to see him if he follows."

"Just show me where to turn."

Thirty minutes later, they were waiting in a hangar near the Farmington terminal while a state police helicopter was being fueled. They were going to fly to Albuquerque to interview anyone they could find who'd known Stewart Tanner. Other Bureau agents had done some of the groundwork, but Lee and Diane had specific questions to ask—those related to vampirelike activities previous to Tanner's "disappearance."

By using the helicopter, which was on standby anyway because of the search for Tanner, they also ensured that nobody would be able to follow them easily. Unless Charles chartered an airplane, they'd be hours away from his location soon.

It was midafternoon when they returned once again to Farmington. They hadn't been able to discover much more about Tanner than they'd already known. Tanner had been adopted and had taken on the name of his new parents, though they still hadn't been able to learn the identity of his biological parents nor the state where Tanner was born. As with many investigations, they knew a lot that didn't seem to matter, and maybe never would. But still they had to sift through everything, just in case some apparent trivia proved otherwise.

Though he'd never talked about his childhood prior to his adoption, they'd managed to confirm that Stewart had indeed grown up in New Mexico—at least since his early teens—attended a local college for a few years, then taken culinary classes and become a chef. After his foster parents died he'd inherited their money and used it to open his own restaurant. The competition was tough, but he'd been successful enough to stay in the black and build a steady trade.

Diane had managed to sleep on the trip back, but she was still groggy, so Lee drove their borrowed vehicle as they left the airport. There was going to be a strategy session of local law enforcement at a warehouse on the west side of town, so they didn't have far to go.

"We know that Stewart Tanner shifted his business hours four years ago to cater to the late-night crowd after returning from his last big hunting trip, so that's probably just after he'd become a vampire," Diane said, then yawned. "Is that your guess?"

Lee nodded. "Yeah, and that's when he quit dating regularly and stopped seeing most of his old friends. Too many complications from relationships when you have a secret like that."

"But he didn't become a total hermit, or change his name and disappear."

"Like me?"

Diane may have nodded, or maybe it was just a shrug. She was the only person in his life right now that held anything resembling a relationship with him, and they were taking it very slow. As far as Lee had been able to determine, Diane didn't have any close friends in her own life right now—except for him and her parents, whom she rarely saw except during holidays because of her demanding career. Of course, if they parted someday, she'd have an easier time finding friends. In his life, secrecy was a staple and that one quality made it difficult for him to make lasting connections.

Diane interrupted his thoughts. "Unlike you, Tanner was a lot more . . . public."

"Yeah, and look where it got him," he muttered.

"To continue . . . according to the people we met today, Stewart greeted and spoke with his customers and supported many charities. Tanner chose to remain in the public eye. He was never really close to anyone, according to those we interviewed, but Tanner still enjoyed the night life and partied a lot in the company of more than one group. Even when he finally lost his lifelong tan, he explained away his pale complexion with a running joke."

"He must have rehearsed it. Nearly everyone we spoke to remembered it the same—'Nothing fun ever happened until after dark.' And there's that one weird bit of information we got from that sporting goods dealer."

Diane nodded. "Tanner was an expert marksman, yet he sold all his hunting weapons and started buying knives. You think that's because he started killing people instead of animals?"

"There's nothing in the case files that points to any increase in homicides with edged weapons," Lee said. "And nobody remembers him taking more than two or three days off at a time, especially after the restaurant opened. So it wasn't like those two-week-long expeditions he liked to go on before that time. But where was he going, and why?"

"He may have been randomly killing locals or people passing through, and found an effective way to hide the bodies. There are a lot of missing people cases," she said.

"With his vampire abilities, maybe hunting animals just wasn't 'sporting' anymore for him. And, in this state, game hunting at night is basically illegal," Lee said.

"But none of this means he'd taken up hunting people. Maybe he started stalking game at night, like deer, bears, and big cats. That would be a challenge, with just a knife. And with his healing abilities, unless he got very unlucky, any wounds would quickly heal and nobody would be the wiser. He bought a van, remember? He could have lived out of it and nobody would have noticed."

"Right. Well, we're here."

They passed through a gate after stopping at a small security building where their IDs were checked, then looked for a parking place. Ahead, Lee noticed several armed officers walking toward a heavy metal door in the big, hangarlike warehouse, which also housed a package delivery service. The flat-roofed two-story building had been selected because it was isolated somewhat from adjacent structures and, with a well-lighted parking lot at night, easily guarded.

"Sure you've got enough sunblock on? Even though sunset can't be far off, the parking lot is still pretty bright."

He nodded. "Another reason why you asked for a place like this to meet. I'm sure that Victor Wayne approved."

"Lee, with people so focused on vampire behavior, I'm still worried that you'll end up giving yourself away somehow." Diane got out of the car.

"That's been on my mind too," Lee said, following her lead and exiting the vehicle. "Fortunately, being half vampire, I can load up on sunblock and spend some time outdoors. That'll discourage any theories based on conventional vampire lore."

"Then make sure you don't get hurt. Healing up in front of everyone's eyes is something to see, and it'll put you real high on Dr. Wayne's 'to do' list," Diane said in a whisper-soft voice, seeing another officer heading toward the same doorway.

"One problem at a time."

Their conference setting was limited to folding chairs placed around four long tables that had been arranged in a square. The spot had been centered beneath an array of lights out on the concrete floor of a storage area the size of a small hangar. Conveyor belt systems, sorting areas, scales, and two loading docks more or less occupied the perimeter and half the square footage of the facility, but no workers were present, only armed officers.

The sun was low in the horizon now and Lee knew time was getting critical again. Diane, the agent officially in charge of the investigation, made sure there was little time for chitchat. The only amenities were urns of coffee and plenty of cups to go around. Most of the officers, like her and Lee, hadn't had much sleep the past twenty-four hours.

A half hour later the essential information had been exchanged between the fifteen or so agency representatives present. Quick, informal reports were made that included the areas searched and scheduled to be covered, all available information on Stewart Tanner's background—minus the exact nature of the lab research and his observed abilities—and a quick chronology on his activities and known crimes.

Although Diane had been overseeing the general focus of the operation, she refused to confine herself to an office and micromanage the ongoing manhunt from there. Each agency had been given its general areas of responsibility, which basically delineated their search activities and any required actions that would take place within their respective jurisdiction. All information and leads went to a central Dispatch, and from there disseminated via radio and cell phones to each agency leader. Communication and cooperation was paramount.

Dr. Wayne spoke only briefly concerning the specifics of the killings themselves, pointing out that the murders had been brutal and straightforward, and Tanner had made no attempt to conceal his identity.

"Before Officer Hawk offers his strategy tips," Diane said, "I'd like to ask Dr. Wayne to discuss the implications of Tanner's delusions, and how his mental state and possible motivations may be useful in running him down."

Victor Wayne nodded, then stood. "Mr. Tanner's mental condition—his belief that he's a vampire—directly impacts both the nature of the crimes he's committed and how they were carried out. We need to use that knowledge to predict his behavior and stop him. For example, Tanner will avoid sunlight and only go outside at night. But once it's dark he's going to be very bold, believing himself to be invulnerable."

"He thinks he's a vampire. So, is he drinking the blood of his victims too?" one of the sheriff's deputies asked.

Dr. Wayne looked over at the OMI man and the investigator shrugged. "Not that we've been able to determine."

"But keep in mind that crazy or not, this isn't an ordinary criminal," Victor added. "This guy has extraordinary night vision and demonstrates incredible strength and ability."

"If any of the officers get a clear shot, they need to take it," Lee said. "Extreme measures will be needed to bring Tanner down. He may be constantly high on something, or maybe his abilities and delusions enhance one another. I don't know, I'm not a shrink," Lee said. "But I strongly recommend that if anyone manages to incapacitate Tanner, they make damn sure he stays down. If he gets back up, he'll take someone else out."

Lee made eye contact with those seated around the tables,

and noticed more than one officer nodding. Tanner had killed several people already, and nobody in the room seemed inclined to risk their own lives just to try and take Tanner alive.

"That's all we have for you at this point," Diane said, concluding. "It's probably getting dark outside, so be *very* careful out there. Tanner has been targeting authority figures, and you all fit that definition. We know what we have to do, so let's go get it done."

Suddenly the lights went out.

CHAPTER 9

W hat the hell?" someone grumbled, then several dim emergency battery lights came on along the walls and above the exit.

Lee glanced around, the diminished light posing no problem for him. The cavernous interior was ringed in a faint glow, and he figured the others around him would have to wait for their eyes to adjust before they could make it safely to the main door. The batteries should have been replaced long ago, obviously.

The murmur of voices grew as nearly everyone stood, anxious under the circumstances. It was darkest where their tables were set up. A couple of the folding chairs fell over, making a racket on the concrete floor.

Lee had heard a thump outside just before the big warehouse went dark. Suspecting sabotage, he stood on his chair so he could look over the tallest people, then turned to see if anyone was taking advantage of the momentary confusion to close in on them. The guards at the door had their backs to the wall, and their weapons out, but Lee knew he was the only one who could see into the deep shadows.

"Everyone remain where you are," Diane called out. "If Tanner is responsible for this loss of power, he's still going to have to cross the room to reach us, and we'll be able to see him coming. Stand back to back and cover your neighbor, but don't shoot unless you've made a positive ID."

Lee saw that Diane was alone at the podium. She'd crouched down, her weapon out. "Diane, I'm coming over," he said, walking slowly in her direction and watching to see if anyone was approaching.

There were no overhead emergency lights, only those by the exits, and the ceiling was unfinished, a mass of structural members and metal framework. As Lee looked up, he spotted a black figure crouched upon a girder. The intruder, most likely Tanner, had a coiled rope in his hands, and a sheathed knife at his waist. Diane was the closest officer below him.

"Diane. Move! Tanner's above you on a girder."

Lee drew his pistol, trying to get a clear shot at Tanner through the metal framework, but the vampire reacted immediately, throwing a knife. It was like avoiding a Nolan Ryan beanball—except for the sharp point. Tanner was fast, but the distance of the throw gave Lee just enough time to dodge. The throwing knife clanged off the concrete floor, shooting sparks and stinging him with small chunks of debris.

Lee fired. The bullet hit the ceiling somewhere behind the vampire, who was still off balance from the knife throw. Recovering quickly, Tanner whirled around, and ran across the girder toward the closest wall.

Lee shot again, hitting the girder this time. The bullet ricocheted away with a whine. The angle was wrong, and the metal was protecting Tanner. Lee stepped back and managed to get a sight picture again.

Tanner had reached the fifty-foot-high wall, where a ventilation window just below the roof was wide open. The man was climbing through the opening when Lee squeezed off a final shot with his Beretta.

Tanner flinched, but continued through the opening and disappeared. "I know what you are!" the vampire yelled back, his voice fading.

Lee ran toward the main door, hearing other footsteps close

behind him. By the time he reached the entrance, the two guards there had already opened it.

Lee brushed past them, and saw a black van hurtling away from the warehouse and across the parking lot. He snapped off three shots, but he missed the tires. The vehicle crashed through the closed chain-link gate and roared down the street. Lee glanced away, spotting a shape on the ground beside the guardhouse that was probably a downed officer. There would be more. Hearing a rush of footsteps, Lee turned his head. Several officials that had been inside were rushing to their vehicles.

"Officers are down all around the perimeter," Diane called to him, sprinting toward their unit. "They need help now. I'm going after the van and will call for backup!"

Lee was already behind the wheel when she arrived. She jumped in and handed him the keys. By the time she had her seat belt on, they were closing in on the gate. Diane was on the unit's radio as they passed the bloody bodies of two guards.

"I hit Tanner, Diane, but not enough to slow him down. Unless we catch up to him soon, he'll be as good as new." Lee raced to the first intersection, then, thinking he saw a bit of dust in the road to the right, turned down that street, which led in the direction of downtown Farmington.

"He must have followed one of the honchos to the meeting. It wasn't publicized."

"Tanner's got balls, that's for sure, coming into the lion's den like that. But I think he was after you this time, Diane."

"Good. That provides a reason for him sticking around town, and it also means he still doesn't know that Victor Wayne is the one he should be after—if he's out to settle a score, like we've been assuming."

"I'm not so sure I like your reasoning, woman. He's managed to get everyone he's gone after, so far."

"Until now. With you covering my ass, I've got the odds in my favor."

"As much as I like the thought of covering *your* ass, Diane, remember Tanner's stronger and faster than I am. He's a full vampire."

"Yes, but is he smarter than you and me together? I don't think so."

"We've been unstoppable—so far. But Tanner now knows what *I* am," Lee said.

"Yeah. I caught that. Do you suppose anyone else suspects what he meant? Like Victor Wayne?"

"Screw Victor Wayne."

"Leave that to Tanner. But if we're lucky—or very unlucky, depending on your point of view—the vampire will be coming after us—more specifically you, Lee. You're the biggest threat to him because you can counter his moves. He may start packing a gun."

"Which will make him doubly dangerous. Why don't you put out a call for all sporting goods stores to be on the alert tonight."

Diane nodded. "Will do, but in the Four Corners he's just as likely to hit a residence. My guess is that over half of the citizens own at least one weapon, and many have several. All he has to do is find a house with an NRA sticker on the four-wheel-drive pickup in the driveway."

"Good point. Let's just hope we find out about this early on instead of in the morning when somebody finds a body," Lee replied. He noticed a vehicle ahead of them that looked familiar. "Check out the silver SUV ahead. He's hauling ass, and I recognize that rental sticker on the bumper."

"You've got good eyes, I can barely tell the make of vehicle at this distance. It's not Charles, is it?"

"Yeah, it sure is, and I'm going to stick with him for a while. It's no coincidence seeing him racing around like this. You don't suppose he somehow spotted Tanner passing by in the van?"

"I suppose it's possible."

Lee stayed with the SUV, which slowed at the next intersection, hesitated, then finally turned left at the last minute. Lee had to run the light to keep up, but he'd checked and made the turn without risking a collision.

When the SUV slowed, and turned left again, Diane looked at Lee. "He's circling around . . ."

". . . like he's doubling back," Lee said, finishing her thought. They kept up with the sport utility, but didn't narrow the distance until five minutes later when the vehicle finally pulled over to the side of the street and stopped.

"Let's find out what the hell he's doing," Diane said.

Lee parked a few car lengths down the street. By the time they came to a stop, Diane was already out.

"Hello, Charles," Diane said, resting her arm on his open window. "Let me take a wild guess. You're after Tanner, aren't you?"

By then, Lee was beside her. From where they were standing they could see the passenger's seat. It was empty except for a .45 Colt Combat Commander semi-auto, two extra clips, the ten-inch blade hunting knife, and what looked like an infrared night scope. There was a big Remington pump shotgun on the floor-board, leaned up against the passenger door.

"Naw, I'm just returning some books to the library," he said, then stared at her. A second pistol bulged out from his shoulder holster. "Of course I'm looking for Tanner! The bastard killed Lynette—you remember her—she was your friend." He was agitated, his face rough with a day-old beard, and he had a wild-eyed look about him.

"Mr. Alderete, you were near the warehouse a while ago, weren't you? There were shots fired, and a black van drove away at high speed," Lee said, watching the man carefully.

"Hell, yes I was there. I've been following Dr. Wayne all day. I'd parked across the street earlier, but a cop came over and told me to leave the area so I did—for a while. I came back just as a black van came flying out the gate. I heard the shots too, so I tried to follow the van, but I lost it just a while ago. Was it Tanner?"

Diane nodded.

"Who'd he try to kill *this* time?"

Lee and Diane exchanged glances.

"You, Diane? I'm glad the bastard finally missed," Charles said, reading them correctly. "But you're never going to get Tanner, Diane. It'll take someone with the balls to blow him away—literally. No mercy. I'm the right man for this. Believe it!"

"Charles, go home. You're not in the army now, and if you don't get arrested first, you're going to get yourself or somebody else killed."

And give Stewart Tanner an arsenal, Lee thought. But maybe they could redirect his energy and save a life or two.

"You've been following Victor Wayne, hoping Tanner will target him next and give you the chance to blow him away. That your plan, Charles?" Lee said.

"Something like that. I got close tonight, and might have been able to stop Tanner if that cop hadn't run me off just before things got hot."

Diane shook her head. "You'd be dead or injured, like the guards he attacked when he broke into the place. You have no idea what you're dealing with."

"*You* are the ones who don't have a clue. Tanner is capable of . . . almost anything."

"You buying that vampire story too?" Diane said.

Charles thought about it for a moment. "Vampire? That's a crock."

Lee could tell from the drop in Charles's pupil size and shift in gaze that he was lying. Lynette must have convinced him that Tanner *was* special.

"But Tanner *is* a hunter," Charles continued. "A killer who knows how to stalk and bring down his prey just like a SEAL, Ranger, or someone from Special Forces. I've had that kind of training—have you?"

"You'd be surprised what we've been through, Charles. But if you insist on pursuing this, be aware of the danger and the consequences," Diane said finally.

"But it's not a bad idea for Charles to stick close to Dr. Wayne," Lee said. "He's already met and spoken with you, right?"

Seeing Charles nod, Lee continued. "Better let him and his people know you're there, though, or you might just get shot by one of his bodyguards. They have more than one reason to be a little jumpy."

Charles shrugged. "We all have. But if I meet up with Tanner first, he's going through a meat grinder before I'm done with him."

"Go for it," Diane said. "Just don't get yourself killed, okay? Losing Lynette was a big enough price for your parents to pay."

"And don't get caught waving those weapons around," Lee added. "If a cop sees those toys, he's liable to shoot first, then check for ID later."

Charles nodded. "I'll keep the shotgun and .45 out of sight, and my jacket closed. The toad sticker stays within reach."

"Okay," Diane said. "Good luck."

Lee and Diane returned to their car, and as they climbed inside, Charles drove by, then disappeared down a side street.

"I'm not sure it was a good idea to suggest he keep trailing Victor Wayne," Diane said.

"You want him following us instead?"

"I see your point," Diane said. "But I'm going to tell Dr. Wayne about Charles so none of the doctor's guards gets trigger-happy." She reached for her cell phone.

"It won't hurt, but Charles hasn't exactly been subtle about his intentions, so Victor probably already knows what Charles has in mind." He started the engine and eased back out onto the street.

Diane reached Victor Wayne immediately, spoke for a few moments, then ended the call. "Victor knows what Charles is doing.

His people spotted him yesterday, apparently. As a licensed gun dealer—and with a concealed handgun permit, there isn't much they can do as long as Charles keeps his distance."

Lee nodded. "And it might create some publicity Victor doesn't need right now if he confronts Charles and the press catches wind. If Tanner knew the extent of Dr. Wayne's association with the people who'd held him prisoner . . ."

"Victor knows he needs all the protection he can get," Diane said, then yawned. "Sorry, I'm getting a little sleepy. So, do we assume that you and I are at the top of Tanner's list?"

"We have to, after what happened earlier tonight. You might want to contact the other agencies and advise them to stay on high alert. Tanner might decide to stake out their offices, hoping we'll show up," he said, then after a pause, added, "And you might consider lowering your profile."

"I've already decided to remain in the field instead of directing this operation from behind a desk. I won't hide out, Lee. This is my case."

"All right, so I'll continue to cover your back. Right now, I'm going to make absolutely certain we're not being followed. If Tanner spotted Charles, he might have followed him to us."

Lee checked in the rearview mirror. It was nearly eight-thirty by now and there was less traffic, so he could keep a closer watch. He could also see details, images in the dark, that anyone other than a vampire would miss. "I gathered from your side of the conversation that Victor wanted to know our location, and I noticed you were somewhat imprecise with your answer. You picking up some vibes from the good doctor?"

"I don't trust him."

"Me neither." He drove into a residential area, an older neighborhood in Farmington containing mostly flat-topped stucco homes dating back to the seventies and earlier. Then Lee made a quick turn into an alley. Someone following would have had to give themselves away, or circle around and catch him coming out the next street over. But Lee didn't go to the end of the block, only down two houses.

As they waited, engine off and lights out, Lee checked the backyards of the houses. A few were pristine, with manicured lawns, flower beds, and even a vegetable garden in one. The yard just to his right was run-down, though, with tumbleweeds nearly man-high. Fortunately for his acute sense of smell, there were no overfilled trash bags.

"At least we haven't encountered any dogs or curious neighbors. This alley looks well traveled," Diane commented in a low tone.

"We don't want to generate police calls and attract attention, so we'd better get moving before somebody glances out a back window." Lee started the engine and slowly backed out the direction they'd come. The streets appeared empty.

"So now what? Even though it's getting closer to nine, there are nearly that many more hours to go before sunup. Random cruising isn't very effective, and there are a lot of cops out on the street searching for Tanner. He's probably ditched the van and acquired a new vehicle too, or may have taken off on foot and just holed up for a while in a garage or empty house. Or perhaps he's shopping for a gun?"

"Let's leave the search patterns to the other agencies. It's time to get inside Tanner's head. Where would he go?" Lee asked.

"He's sticking around Farmington for a reason. Maybe he lived here before he was adopted. If that's true, then in his current frame of mind maybe he feels safer here. We know how old he's supposed to be, so maybe we can get someone to search area high school records—yearbooks and such—and turn up a photo or an old classmate who recognizes him. It would be great to find the name on his birth certificate too." Diane made the call while Lee drove.

"Let's get a Farmington phone book," Lee suggested when she put away her cell phone. "We need to scout out some gun shops and sporting goods stores. Burglary would be a piece of cake for Tanner."

They drove to the coffee shop at the motel where Lee was staying, and borrowed a phone book from a waitress while they had pie and coffee. It was after dinner now, and only a few customers remained.

Lee studied the phone book listings. "If I were looking for a place to hit, I'd choose something like this place on Main Street. But it's downtown and too many people would be going through the area. There are several bars and restaurants that stay open 'til late."

Diane glanced over at the listings, then pointed to a large ad in the Yellow Pages. "Jake's Fire Control advertises new and used rifles, shotguns . . . the works. It's not too far from here either. Let's give it a try first."

They picked two more gun shops in case the first one didn't pan out, then left the coffee shop. Diane was just moving away from the curb when they got a call over the radio. An alarm had just been tripped at the Animas Sporting Goods store west of their current location.

"That's the second one on our list," Lee said as Diane accelerated down the street. It took less than ten minutes for them to reach the store, located beside two other unrelated businesses in a tiny strip mall, a block south of Main Street.

"Damn, talk about a break-in," Diane muttered, taking in the chaotic scene.

CHAPTER 10

Three police units, emergency lights flashing, had all but surrounded the building. A big yellow Hummer had run over the concrete parking barriers and rammed into the front entrance, taking out the steel door and several dozen cinder blocks.

"You could haul a cannon out of that opening," Lee commented as Diane parked the unit. A big FPD cop came out of the wrecked store just then, and Lee recognized him immediately. It was Sergeant Braun from the hotel.

The officer noticed Diane and came toward them. "He's not in the store, ma'am. There's a broken rifle rack and several smashed cabinets containing pistols and ammunition. A video camera looks like it was operating, so we've probably got the perp's photo. Dispatch said the shop owner is on his way over. He should be able to tell us what's missing. The civilian who owns the Hummer has already been called."

Lee, ever watchful, turned around slowly. Several civilians had pulled their vehicles over to the curb and were rubbernecking. There weren't enough officers on the scene to set up a perimeter, and it would probably be pointless to block off the street.

"Smash and grab, messy but effective," Lee said. "Was the Hummer hotwired?" Lee asked the sergeant.

Sergeant Braun shook his head. "Owner kept a set of spare

keys under the sun visor. Guy has a GPS hidden somewhere on the chassis, so he wasn't too worried, apparently. Vehicle looks brand-new—or did until it became a battering ram." The sergeant looked down at Diane. "You want to check out the shop, ma'am?"

"Yes. When the owner arrives, bring him to me, okay?" Diane turned to Lee. "You coming?"

Lee shook his head. "Tanner seems to have the habit of returning to the scene of the crime. I'll wait outside in case he shows up."

Sergeant Braun looked at him strangely. "You're joking."

Lee smiled, then moved over beside the police unit that was parked closest to the street. From there he could watch the scene and check out any passing vehicles. If Tanner was responsible, he'd know Diane and her Navajo vampire partner would be showing up to check it out.

Diane and the sergeant moved toward the wrecked entrance, and Lee heard Braun call one of the other uniforms over. He motioned toward the gathering of curious civilians and said something Lee couldn't hear. The officer checked the shotgun he was carrying, then walked down the length of the building, disappearing around the corner.

Within a few minutes, a large, chromed-up pickup with oversize tires roared into the remaining parking slot. An angry-looking man wearing an NRA cap climbed out so fast he almost fell. "Punk bastards. Friggin' wrecked my shop," he cursed. The man was short and built like a sumo wrestler.

As the proprietor stepped past the massive vehicle astride the sidewalk of his business, he punched the side of the door. The door wouldn't dent, but it seemed to rock just a little. It must have hurt, though, because the man flinched despite his bulk. As he looked around to see if anybody had noticed his stupidity, Lee managed to keep a serious expression, giving a sympathetic nod.

Turning back to the street, Lee saw two more vehicles cruise slowly by, drivers and passengers gawking. Lee could see their faces, and even noted that the driver in the second vehicle had an open beer bottle in his hand. Seeing Lee watching him, weapon on his belt, the man lowered the bottle a bit more and continued past the building.

Diane came out about five minutes later and walked in his direction. "He took a .30-06 Remington 700—open sights—no scope, a Browning Hi-Power with an extra magazine, and about a hundred rounds for each weapon. That's all that's missing. The owner played the video back for us. It was Tanner. He waved at the camera. Cocky bastard."

"Well, we knew that already." Lee, now standing beside one of the police cruisers, turned and watched another vehicle, a battered-looking station wagon, cruise by slowly. The driver was a sleepy-looking blonde in her early thirties, with four excited children pointing and shouting back and forth. They'd have something to talk about at school tomorrow.

"I made a quick call to FPD, and a bulletin is being sent to every agency. I've also got my SAC trying to round up more night-vision goggles." Diane took a quick look around, making certain they couldn't be overheard. "A vampire operating as a sniper raises the bar almost out of reach for the rest of us. Anyone without a night scope and a guardian angel is a sitting duck."

"But he's remained within the community, at least so far. We should be grateful Tanner hasn't gone to Albuquerque. It would be hell catching him there."

"I still wonder *why* he's sticking around? He's got to know Albuquerque and the Rio Grande Valley better than the Four Corners. Is it just his thirst for . . . revenge?"

Lee shrugged. "Gotta be more than that. Perhaps one of the locals *will* remember him—if he *has* lived here before. Remember hearing that Tanner was taking days off, and nobody had any idea where he was going? Maybe he came here—it's less than a four-hour drive."

Diane checked the street, still wary after all that had happened already tonight. "I can search for old charge card information on Tanner before he disappeared, targeting those times he was known to be out of town. If we track some of the purchases to this area, particularly Farmington, that will tell us something about where he was going on his days off. It might take a while, though. I'll have to pull some people away from the Internet or their TVs."

"Come on, Diane, you *enjoy* yanking people out of their recliners and yelling 'FBI.'"

She couldn't help but laugh as she brought out her cell phone. After a moment, she cursed. "Crap. Battery's nearly gone. I'll have to get a backup from the car."

Lee watched Diane as she walked to the vehicle, appreciating the view from this direction, though he didn't think of himself as a lecher. Then he thought about the label—obsolete, like himself—and looked away, focusing on a red Mustang as it cruised slowly past the crime scene. The driver had his left hand up to the side of his face, concealing his identity, and that raised Lee's antenna.

"Tanner! In the red car!" Lee yelled. Tanner moved his hand and brought up a pistol, extending it out the open driver's window.

Diane flattened to the pavement as shots rang out.

The bullets were meant for Lee, and struck the asphalt where he'd have been if he'd also hit the ground. But Lee had jumped up instead, pulling out his own pistol as he landed atop the police vehicle, then stepped off the other side, behind cover. More shots whined overhead, but Tanner had reacted too slowly to track him effectively.

Lee heard a shotgun blast from behind him somewhere. Braun or one of the other officers was firing back. Lee took a quick look over the hood and saw a pattern of holes just behind the driver's door. Tanner had ducked instinctively, but rose up again, firing blindly at Lee, ignoring the other cop.

Lee dove back to the pavement as bullets struck the hood right above him. The shotgun roared again, along with another weapon, probably Diane firing her pistol.

Tires squealed, and by the time Lee brought his weapon up, the Mustang was racing away, leaving rubber. Diane rose to one knee, squeezing off another shot, and Lee fired twice. The rear window of the Mustang shattered.

"Shit. Antique piece of crap!" Lee heard Braun's voice, and out of the corner of his eye saw the sergeant trying to clear a jammed round from his shotgun.

"After him!" Diane yelled, and nearly beat Lee to their unit. He started the engine and backed out into the street, his heart pumping overtime.

"Make the call!" Diane yelled to Sergeant Braun just as another officer ran out of the wrecked gun shop.

She fastened her shoulder harness by feel as she squinted ahead, trying to track the taillights of the Mustang. "He's sticking to this street," she pointed, not taking her eyes off the road.

"Yeah. Can't miss the missing window. Wonder if one of us hit him?"

"Not hard enough." She grabbed the radio mike and updated their location and the direction Tanner was heading. When she was finished, she looked over and nodded.

Lee switched on the emergency lights and siren, forcing him to raise his voice to be heard, even by Diane. "I tried for a head shot, but he was really rolling by then, and the plate glass can deflect a bullet, especially at an angle. Wish I'd have had a few armor-piercing rounds in my weapon."

"Hey, we didn't know he'd be in a car. Hollow points are better vampire stoppers anyway. At least Braun and I were able to keep him ducking. Let's just catch up to the bastard," Diane said.

"Where in the hell did he get a backup vehicle so quickly?" Lee wondered out loud, his eyes constantly checking ahead for vehicles or pedestrians who might stray into his path. "And a fast one at that."

"You don't suppose he has a partner now?" she asked.

"I didn't see anyone inside the car except for him," Lee pointed out.

"They could have been staying low. Non-vampires tend to do that when the shooting starts."

"Hell, half vampires do it too," Lee said. "I'm just glad I decided to jump instead of duck."

"Yeah, I would too if I had your legs."

"Ugh. I can't imagine that, not even for a second. You've seen my legs—and I've seen yours."

Diane managed a smile, but didn't say anything. Instead, she reached for her cell phone and managed to switch batteries in spite of their high-speed maneuvers.

The Mustang was quick and agile, a good choice for a getaway vehicle—except that it was red and flashy, Lee reminded himself as he took the next corner at the highest speed he could risk. His reflexes were superhuman, but their vehicle wasn't designed for racing, and slid, barely missing a vehicle parked against the far curb.

"Whoa," Diane yelled, the g-force whipping her back and forth as Lee maneuvered the vehicle into the center of the street and accelerated. "We're gaining—slowly. Tanner has quicker reflexes, but not as much experience with pursuit driving."

"Otherwise he'd eat us for lunch in that Mustang. He seems to know the streets pretty well for an Albuquerque boy. Any chance of getting a roadblock set up?" he asked.

Diane switched to a local tactical frequency on the radio and sent out their current location and direction.

Closing in as they neared a large grocery store and restaurant, Lee could see the Mustang still had the dealer's sticker, but he couldn't read the business name. Abruptly the Mustang swerved into the parking lot, skidding and throwing up a cloud of smoke and dust in the dangerous maneuver. The small red car hurtled past the store, then made another ninety-degree turn and disappeared.

Lee cut across the front of the parking lot to intercept the vehicle as it came out from behind the store, but it never arrived. Skillfully he executed a bootlegger's 180-degree turn and headed behind the store. There was a loading dock, but a glance to the right revealed a narrow gap in the big cinder-block wall that ran parallel to the alley.

Lee pulled cautiously into the alley, then out of the corner of his eye he could see the Mustang hurtling directly at them from the passenger side.

"Hang on!" He stomped on the gas and prayed.

Diane gasped and pressed back into the seat.

Their sedan took a rear glancing blow, throwing the nose of the vehicle to the right as metal and plastic crunched behind them. Lee corrected the wheel and slammed on the brakes at the same time, bringing the vehicle to a screeching halt at the far curb of the next street over. Beyond was a sidewalk, then another six-foot-high block wall.

Putting the vehicle into reverse, Lee swung back out into the lane, then raced down the street in the direction Tanner was heading. By the time he reached the intersection and glanced toward the alley, the Mustang had disappeared.

"He either continued down the alley, or turned left," Diane said quickly. "Your choice."

He chose left, on a hunch, thinking Tanner might be circling the area. Two blocks farther, he saw the Mustang parked in another alley on the right, just off the street. The shiny two-door, now accessorized with buckshot holes and matching front and rear shattered glass, looked unoccupied, but they couldn't take any chances. "Call for backup," he told Diane, pulling in behind the Mustang to block the exit. The big V-8 in the Mustang was still running, and even at idle the power of the vehicle was barely contained.

"It could be an ambush," Diane whispered. "Wait for me before you move in."

Lee nodded. "You're right." He stepped out of the driver's side, keeping the door between him and the Mustang. His Beretta was ready.

Twenty seconds later, Diane was off the radio and out on her side, also armed. "Okay," she whispered, "I'll cover you."

Lee came up to the vehicle slowly, his weapon directed to where he was looking. "Nothing in the backseat. Front either."

Diane came up, looked inside, then stepped back toward the rear of the vehicle. "Pop the trunk, Lee."

He reached in and turned off the engine, then pulled the trunk release.

"Nothing but new car smell. Whatever weapons he had went with him."

Lee realized he was illuminated by their headlights, not that it would make any difference to Tanner. And with a long-range hunting rifle, the vampire could shoot from hundreds of yards and take them down.

"He's got a rifle now, Lee. We're sitting—make that standing—ducks."

CHAPTER 11

Diane moved back toward their vehicle, turning around and trying to see through the darkness. Lee checked the flat roofs. Most of the houses on this street offered handy parapets for a sniper to rest his weapon. "Get in the car and circle the neighborhood. I'll do a foot search."

The roar of an engine and flashing red and blue lights heralded the arrival of a Farmington police car. "The officer and I can check the yards. Go ahead and get in," he said to Diane. "No sense in giving him an extra target."

"You're probably his priority now, Lee, but let's make him choose." Diane turned her back to him and stepped out to the curb to greet the arriving officer.

"Stubborn woman," Lee said under his breath, then took another quick three-sixty look at the area. A resident was peeking out from behind the window curtain across the street, and a black cat with one white paw was slinking across a porch two houses down.

Lee didn't speak cat, so he decided to visit the person who'd been looking out the window. "Police officer. I need to speak with you a moment," Lee announced, his eyes searching up and down the street as he stepped up to the porch.

"You looking for the man who was driving the red car?" A strong woman's voice came from the other side of the door.

"Yes, I am," Lee replied. "What did you see?"

The porch light went on, there was a pause, then the door opened a crack. There was a brass security chain across the opening, a good idea in any neighborhood. He could see reddish auburn hair, a brown eye, and enough face and mouth to determine the woman was Anglo or Hispanic and in her early forties. A hand with bright red fingernails held an unbuttoned robe clenched together in the center. Lee could hear music from a TV commercial.

"Want to come in?" the woman asked, then closed the door slightly and unhooked the chain.

"Yes, ma'am, if you don't mind." Lee had already considered the possibility that Tanner had taken the woman hostage and was behind the door, ready to blow him away. But the woman, tall and reasonably attractive, didn't seem nervous at all. More curious— even nosy, perhaps. Every community had a snoop, even back in the thirties when he'd been a teenager. At this hour, a lot of people would be settled in their recliners watching the ten o'clock news or letting the dog out one more time. But there was always a snoopy one.

Lee held out his ID for the woman to view as he stepped in, but her curious eyes were focused on his face. Maybe she'd never invited an Navajo with a gun into her home before.

"You're a policeman, right? I'm Rosanna Luna." She reached over to turn off the TV, fiddling as she searched for the right button. Finally she found it.

"I'm Leo Hawk—state police officer, ma'am. What can you tell me about the man who was driving the Mustang—the red car."

"He isn't the one who killed that judge, is he?"

"I think so. What did you see outside? Where did he go?" Lee noticed that the woman was barely holding her robe together with one hand while straightening out her rumpled hair with the other. He kept his eyes directed toward her face, wishing she'd spend more energy keeping her garment closed.

"My God, officer. And he was right out in front of my house."
Her mouth fell open, and she stopped primping. Looking down,
she saw she was showing too much and hastily started buttoning
her robe.

Lee turned away, giving her more privacy and taking the opportunity to glance into the next room—the kitchen. From what
he could tell, it was unoccupied. "Did you see which way he went,
Ms. Luna?"

"He jumped out of the Mustang, ran over here, and climbed
into the other car. Then they took off around the corner to the
left. I was thinking of calling the police when you and that woman
officer showed up."

"They? Someone was here waiting for him?"

"Sure looked like it. The other car, the big green sedan, was
parked right in front of my house for several minutes. I couldn't
get a good look at the driver and I didn't want to turn on my porch
light and create attention. It didn't look like one of those—you
know—carjackings."

"Was the man carrying something, like a rifle or pistol?"

"He was carrying something in one hand, but not anything
long, like a rifle."

"You're very observant, Rosanna. Did you notice anything at
all about the driver? A man or woman, long or short hair, what
they were wearing? Anything?"

Rosanna thought about that a moment, yawned, then smiled,
embarrassed. "Sorry, Officer Hawk. I had a long day."

"I know, ma'am." Lee smiled. "But I need to leave soon and
go after them. Do you remember something about the driver?"

"Yeah, the driver was short and had long hair. Blond."

"Maybe a woman?"

"Yes, I think it was a woman. I didn't see her face, but she
kept looking around."

"What make of car was it?"

"Big, long, green—not a Cadillac, I know those. And not a

Mercedes, though it had a front grille kind of like that. My sister has a Mercedes, so I know it was close. I think it was a Ford or Chevrolet. Four-door, luxury model. If I saw a picture, I might be sure."

"Good. Did you notice a license plate or bumper sticker?"

"It looked like a New Mexico plate, but I couldn't see what it said before it pulled away. Would you like some coffee, officer?"

"Thank you, ma'am. But I've got to use the information you've given me while it's still fresh. Here's my card, if you think of anything else." Lee handed it to her, then turned and reached for the doorknob.

"Good night, Officer Hawk," Ms. Luna called as Lee stepped outside.

"You too, ma'am." Lee walked away quickly, anxious to get away. The woman made him uncomfortable for some reason, but now they had a new lead. His eyes watching everywhere at once, Lee noted that another police car had arrived, this one a county sheriff's unit. Diane was talking on her cell phone while the deputy checked out the Mustang. The other cop, the Farmington patrol-man, was at the door of an adjacent home, speaking to a resident.

Diane looked up, shaking her head as soon as she spotted Lee, then ended the call. "Anything from the resident?"

"Tanner met someone else here and they drove away in a green sedan. From what the witness said, it sounded like a Ford Crown Victoria to me. It had New Mexico plates, but the woman couldn't get the letters or numbers."

Lee looked over at the sticker on the Mustang. "Valley Motors. Let's have someone check with the dealership—and call your people in Albuquerque. We need to verify if Tanner knew anyone in this community. Someone with long hair, blond, and probably a woman."

"A woman? That's an interesting complication. Maybe an old girlfriend?"

"Officer Hawk?"

Lee turned and saw Ms. Luna, standing beneath the porch light, waving at him.

"Your witness?" Diane asked. "She's barely dressed. Got guts coming out like that."

Lee shrugged, then turned and walked back to the porch. "You remembered something else, Ms. Luna?"

"A purse. There was a purse on the seat beside the driver. I remember it now, because she reached for it, then turned her dome light on and started messing with her nails. That confirms it was a woman, right?"

"Thank you so much, ma'am. You've been a big help. If you think of anything else after I leave, just tell one of the officers, or call the number on the card."

"I will, Officer Hawk. I will."

Lee excused himself and walked back to Diane, who was on the cell phone again. She gestured toward the vehicle, and he went around to the driver's side as she climbed in, still talking to someone.

They were a block away when Diane finally hung up. "My SAC managed to crack open some records at a small private high school in Albuquerque, then did a follow-up. Stewart Tanner's original last name was Bowen. He grew up in Farmington, an only child. At the age of fifteen he landed in a foster home after both parents were killed in a traffic accident while high on drugs. They were meth dealers, apparently. Bowen was adopted within six months by an older couple in Albuquerque, and took their name to avoid the publicity."

"So Tanner knew and probably still knows someone in this community, right?" Lee said. "Can we get in touch with some of them?"

"I have FPD rousting some local school administrators. They're going to track down any of his old teachers, check yearbooks and such, and get some names. Once somebody remembers him, we'll be notified."

"Check on old girlfriends—or female classmates that may have been close to him. My witness remembers seeing a purse in the car. Tanner's chauffeur was a female, according to Ms. Luna."

"Interesting. I also checked the key in the Mustang. It looks like it came right from the dealer. Oh, and another goodie. My SAC is sending us faxes of Tanner's old credit card statements. It was easy to get a court order after what happened to Judge Baca, apparently."

"Things are definitely starting to come together. Let's get in contact with the locals again and have them run down that Ford dealer, and check on any stolen green sedans. Two parties lost their cars tonight, and if Tanner got some extra keys at the dealership, he might have taken a third, or have plans to steal one later."

Diane hung up the telephone in Lee's motel room and turned as he came through the door holding two big paper bags. "Breakfast— thank God, Lee. I'm almost as hungry as I am sleepy. At least we know Tanner and his woman friend have probably gone into hiding for the day."

"Unless he decides to surprise us again. What did you get on the phone?" Lee handed Diane a bag so he could lock the door, then stepped over to the small hotel desk. Together they brought out the foam containers holding coffee and the breakfast specials.

"Valley Ford confirmed the loss of the Mustang sometime after closing time at nine P.M. The vehicle wasn't missed until a vehicle count at six A.M., just as the auto shop personnel arrived to handle early-morning drop-off customers on their way to work."

"No all-night security?"

"They have a service, but the rent-a-cops didn't spot the loss during their last pass, which was at three-fifteen A.M. But a dealer key was found in the Mustang."

"What about the dealership office? The key must have come from there."

Diane pulled up one of the room chairs and sat down in front of a plate of steaming hot pancakes, smearing pads of butter on them with a plastic knife. "The office manager said that one of their doors showed signs of being forced, but the alarm hadn't gone off, for some reason. The key was missing from a cabinet, but it appeared to be the only one missing, according to a quick inventory."

"Tanner hasn't been subtle, so far. How did he pull this off?"

"Maybe he lifted the key earlier when the business was open, then jammed the door later to cover what he'd done."

"Or maybe he had someone on the inside."

Diane nodded. "Like a blond woman. We need to follow up on that." She reached for the phone.

Lee reached out, stopping her. "Eat first. Let Farmington PD watch the dealership employees for a while. You need to get some sleep. You look exhausted."

Diane yawned. "Maybe a little nap . . ."

"Eat first—have some juice."

"One more thing. No new green cars like a Crown Victoria have been reported missing within the past few days. So that's still a mystery," Diane said.

"It had to come from somewhere. We'll be hearing about it before too long," Lee replied. Then he ate like a pig, polishing off scrambled eggs, four slices of bacon, two glasses of OJ, and eight pancakes smothered in syrup. Diane had about half that, then lay down on the bed and was asleep within three minutes.

He sat alone at the desk, sipping coffee and going over the past few days in his mind. Tanner was the target, but Lee couldn't help but feel some sympathy for the guy. He'd obviously been put through the ringer by the likes of Victor Wayne and his people. The same could have happened to him, or to the one other vampire he knew—a young woman he'd come across in

Albuquerque last year—if Dr. Wayne ever managed to find out about them. He decided to talk about this to Diane when she woke up.

Meanwhile, because he needed very little sleep as long as he was well fed, he'd monitor any calls coming in. Diane's calls had been forwarded to his cell phone, which was set on vibrate. Barely ten minutes had gone by before the phone began to twitch. He moved into the bathroom silently and closed the door before answering the call.

Five minutes later, Lee ended the conversation and walked back into the room. He heard movement and turned to watch Diane sit up and yawn. She looked good no matter where she was, and had gotten used to his appreciative scrutiny. Whenever she caught him watching her, she usually just smiled.

"Thanks for letting me sleep, Lee. I'm back among the living now, but I sure could use a shower. Could you hand me my travel bag?"

He nodded, then stood and retrieved her black ballistic cloth "suitcase" from where it rested against the wall. "We got some news I think you'll want to hear first." He then told her about the phone call.

"You think this Marci Walker, the woman who owns the Valley Ford dealership, could be Tanner's contact?" Diane asked.

"Considering Marci was Tanner's girlfriend before he moved away? It's a good bet, assuming that the information the detectives were able to get from an old Farmington High School classmate of Tanner's is correct. Go ahead and take your shower, then I'll tell you about a plan I just set into motion."

"Okay. Room service should be available by now, so would you order some fresh coffee for me? Strong," Diane asked, taking the bag. "I'll be out in ten, then you can tell me what you have in mind."

He picked up the phone and dialed room service to order some black coffee, then glanced over to the bottle of sunblock on the nightstand. He'd have to reanoint himself in case he ended up having to spend a significant amount of time outside. It was almost nine A.M., and the morning light already indicated it was going to be another bright New Mexico day.

A while later they were on their way to rendezvous with two Farmington detectives, the same officers they'd encountered at the hotel where the judge had died. They arrived at an old brick building at the east end of downtown Farmington. Going inside quickly from a parking area in the alley, they entered the storeroom of a small printing shop. The detectives were waiting.

Everyone seemed more upbeat due to the positive news, and handshakes were finally exchanged, even with Lee, and Detective Shannon introduced his partner, Detective Esterbrook. The FPD officers also offered them cups of coffee, which Lee and Diane accepted immediately.

Esterbrook, who was tall and physically similar to Tanner, spoke first. "We've got two uniforms watching from unmarked units. Mrs. Walker, first name Marci, arrived at the dealership, greeted some of her employees, then went into her private office—alone. She's tall, good-looking, brown or reddish brown hair, and built like a . . . well, you get the idea."

Esterbrook had carefully avoided looking directly at Diane while giving the description. He cleared his throat, finally nodded to Diane, then continued. "We're trying to track down a photo of the woman right now, ma'am. There's an officer at the newspaper office checking to see if Mrs. Walker ever made the society page. Worse-case scenario, one of our men will snap a digital photo next time she comes out."

"You tailed her from her home, right?" Lee asked.

"Yeah," Shannon said. "A big ole two-story job in a fancy neighborhood. Her late husband—he was quite a bit older than she is—has one of the biggest auto dealerships in the state. Must be a millionaire now, the woman, I mean. There were no children, so I suppose she got it all."

"All this background from the former classmate?" Diane asked.

Esterbrook nodded. "He's an ex-cop who owns a bar on East Main. Saw Tanner's photo in the newspaper, remembered the guy, called the department. Owner's name is Macky. He says that Tanner—well, Stewart Bowen then—and Marci were very close before he left town. And, chew on this, Macky remembers seeing them together not long ago—at his bar—making out like bandits in one of those dark corner booths. And this was *before* her husband died."

"That certainly reinforces the notion that Marci Walker has been working with Tanner," Diane said, "and maybe giving him a place to hide out. Does Tanner know Macky saw him and Marci together? Macky could become a target if he did."

"Macky didn't think so, and he never approached them. Thought it might be embarrassing, considering that Mrs. Walker was sucking tongue with someone other than her husband at the time."

"May have saved his life. Any idea how many buildings around the county Marci Walker owns or controls?" Lee asked both detectives.

"We're working on that. As we speak, county deputies are on route to check out the Walker cabin up near Navajo Lake," Shannon said, finally smiling. "Mrs. Walker's also got a separate garage on her main property. Then, there's the dealership, with two buildings on the lot. We don't know what other holdings she may have, though we've got a search in progress down at the county offices."

Diane nodded, then spoke. "What can you tell us about that home garage? The late Mr. Walker must have owned more than one car, being a dealer."

"It's a big four-door building with a second floor and maybe an upstairs office," the detective answered. "The estate has only two exits, one at the end of the sidewalk and the other the driveway, and gates at each spot. There's an eight-foot wall around the property."

"How many officers are watching the property?" Lee asked.

"Two. But we're hoping to get a third officer free to join them. Tanner's been known to go up and down walls like a lizard."

Diane looked over at Lee. "We'll check out the home."

Lee nodded, noticing a large, rolled-up piece of drafting paper on a nearby table. "And unless I miss my guess, those are blueprints of the Walker place."

"Good eye, Officer Hawk." Detective Esterbrook reached over and grabbed the roll. "Let's take a look."

CHAPTER 12

You plan on breaking in, don't you?" Diane said as they parked beside the curb next to a small, tree-filled public park. She'd been driving so that he could do touch-up work with the sunblock. "That's why you asked Shannon and Esterbrook to relieve the officer watching the front of the property. You gave them a heads-up so they wouldn't shoot first and ask questions later."

"Let's just say my argument was good and they agreed to look the other way," Lee said. "To go in legally we'd need a search warrant and it's possible someone would tip them off."

"You think he's really there?"

"Why not? Her home is convenient, and with her status in the community, she's got resources. The fact that he's had no problem finding transportation suggests that Marci Walker is already involved. Good thing they weren't more careful with the dealer sticker and the fact that they were having an affair."

"Reporting the thefts would have worked too, if we hadn't already been looking for a connection and had some good luck and an alert ex-cop identify Tanner. But amateur criminals make mistakes, no matter how bright they are. Too many things to consider at once," she said. "Besides, there must be strong emotions involved—and not only Tanner's need for revenge. The two were obviously having an affair before her husband died. Then Tanner disappeared, and suddenly shows up months later—a killer on the run with remarkable abilities. Mrs. Walker must have gone through the entire range of emotions—including accepting a killer into her home. No wonder they've made a mistake. They'll make more."

"We hope. And we can probably rule out that cabin. It's too far away from the action."

"We should hear soon enough. The deputies are due there about now." She looked at her watch. "Ready to go?"

They stepped out of the unmarked vehicle and walked down the sidewalk, strolling hand-in-hand like a couple on a morning walk. Lee had on a broad-brimmed hat to conceal his face, and carried a folded-up newspaper. Diane had an oversized purse.

The neighborhood was upper class, for New Mexico, and each home covered an acre or more. The houses, most of them brick or stone, were set back from the street, well landscaped with huge trees, spacious lawns, and colorful flower beds. The Walker estate was surrounded by a four-foot-high brown block wall topped with another four feet of wrought-iron fencing terminating with fleur-de-lis points. The gates were wrought iron, and the driveway entrance, double-gated, opened electrically after entering a pass code in a keypad.

Continuing on past the driveway, which led to the garage another hundred feet away, Lee glanced casually over at the two detectives, now wearing coveralls identifying them as city workers. The officers were raking leaves on the tree-covered median.

One of the detectives started whistling an old seventies tune, the signal that Marci Walker was still back at her dealership and they were clear to make a move.

As they neared the corner of the block, Lee noted a concrete-lined drainage ditch across the street that carried rainwater downhill across a large, tree-covered park. Beneath the road and sidewalk was a culvert, and it terminated to their right, where a three-foot-deep collecting basin gathered water from the Walker estate that passed through a large iron grate at the foot of the wall.

Traffic was virtually nonexistent, but Diane still kept watch while Lee jumped down into the basin. He examined the grate.

"It's pretty solid, so you'd better hand me the crowbar to make it look good," Lee said.

Diane brought the tool out of her big purse and handed it down to him. He crouched down, inserted the tool between the grate and one of the large bolts that attached it to the wall, and pushed. The bolt popped out with a creak.

He grabbed the other side of the grate and yanked, popping the bolt loose. "Didn't need the crowbar, but I don't want to look *too* strong to these detectives."

"Yeah, especially after seeing what kind of treatment vampires get up here in the Four Corners," Diane answered. She looked over at the closest detective, thirty yards away. He nodded.

"All clear, let's move," she said.

Lee pulled the grate away from the opening, set it to one side, then ducked beneath and slithered through the damp grass into the Walker property, holding on to his hat so it wouldn't get knocked off. Diane followed.

They remained still for a moment, watching the house. Ceiling-high windows at the closest end of the house revealed what they knew to be a den or living room, according to the plans they'd examined. The curtains were open, but no living creature was visible, and they'd already confirmed that the Walkers apparently had no dogs or cats. No housekeeper had been seen arriving, and no vehicles were visible on the property, so if Tanner was there, chances were he was alone.

"If Tanner's in there, he isn't going to stand in front of the open window and risk being seen by someone from the pedestrian or driveway gate. Though he could be keeping watch from behind a curtain in another room." Lee was trying to watch several of the other windows of the house at once.

"Well, even if he spots us, he can't very well come outside during the daytime—not for more than a few seconds—right?"

"But he has a rifle, so let's move." Lee rose to a low crouch, then ran for cover behind a tree farther down the wall and toward the closest side of the building. He paused, selected another tree farther ahead, then continued on again.

Diane followed, one hiding place back each move, until they were both side by side. Their backs were against the wall at an inside corner of the west wing of the roughly five-thousand-square-foot main building. They'd moved carefully as they'd approached, making sure that they couldn't be seen from the big garage at the rear of the property.

Lee motioned with an upward look. "There's a window open a few inches on the second floor. I'm going in through there."

"What if it's a trap and he blows your head off as you're climbing in?"

"Then don't let me fall on you," Lee whispered back. "Don't worry. He can't know we found out about Marci."

"What'll I do while you're sneaking around inside?"

"Work your way to the corner so you can keep an eye on that garage. If you see any movement, just call me on the cell." He'd already set the phone from ring to vibrate.

"How about opening this when you get inside so I can join you?" She pointed to the closest ground-floor window.

"Well, okay." Lee nodded. "I can use the extra set of eyes and ears anyway."

"Be careful."

Lee nodded.

"Wait a second, Lee," Diane whispered, then reached down and grabbed her cell phone. She looked at the number, then flipped the device open to take the call.

She spoke very softly, mostly listening, then finally ended the call. Lee could see from her expression it was bad news.

"Another body has been found, a piece of wood from a broken kitchen chair driven through her heart. It's Rosanna Luna, according to FPD. Wasn't she your witness last night?"

Lee nodded. "I guess Tanner must have seen her watching, then came back after all the officers cleared out. Or maybe he was hiding in her garage or house all the time. That vampire is really starting to piss me off. Let's nail the bastard."

He took a step back from the wall, crouched, then leaped up, grabbing the sill of the window on the second floor. His feet bounced against the wall, but it was brick, so it was unlikely anyone could hear.

Still angry at the unnecessary death of the woman, Lee struggled to place his emotions aside and concentrate. If he didn't pay attention now, he might fall on Diane and break her neck. Feeling the power flowing through his body and into his fingertips, Lee brought his chin up to the sill and peeked into the room through the open window.

A cool breeze blew across his face, along with a faint scent of lemon he associated with furniture polish. Pulling himself up higher, he saw the shiny wooden surface of a dresser or credenza against the inside of the window. The room was either a library or a home office.

Holding on with his right hand, Lee pushed the window up several inches, then he grabbed hold again and pulled himself up and through the window. It was awkward coming in head first across the flat service, and if anyone had been waiting for him, he wouldn't have had a chance. But the office was unoccupied, and the door leading out was closed.

He turned around and slipped off what he discovered was a big wooden file cabinet. Using his sleeve, he wiped off the scuff marks of his passage as well as he could, then crept over to the door to listen.

Deep, loud voices came from somewhere in the house, but after only a few seconds Lee realized it was from an expensive sound system set to a local radio station. The commentator was from one of those call-in shows, and he was talking politics. Turning around slowly, Lee looked for signs of recent activity, but found none. The computer was off, no papers or correspondence were on any surfaces, and the room looked and smelled like it had been cleaned recently.

The radio could mean that Tanner or a housekeeper was around, or else Marci Walker left the thing on to make anyone approaching the home believe it was occupied. He hadn't seen any sign of a burglar alarm, but maybe there was something on the ground floor that would set off an alarm.

He decided to open the door. Catching a particularly loud commercial for a local restaurant, Lee took advantage of the covering noise. He pulled the door open slowly and peered out into the hall. There were two rooms to his left, and to the right, a large stained-glass window at the end of the hall above a wide staircase.

He listened, noting that the radio came from below. Inching to his left, he walked to the stair railing and looked down. A spacious den or living room, the same room with the big picture windows he'd seen from the outside, was tastefully decorated with black leather chairs and a large maroon sectional sofa. The light fixtures and lamps were black and gold, with more touches of maroon to match the sofa. All of the furnishings rested upon a beautiful grayish white stone floor, probably marble. He'd have to walk quietly down there, but with the radio so loud, he probably couldn't even be heard upstairs.

Lee proceeded slowly, waiting at times to look around, including checking back upstairs. Once on the ground floor he'd find the room, on the west end, where Diane was waiting outside, and let her in—after he confirmed that no one was actually listening to the radio, like the housekeeper. Together they could sweep the house, their activity covered by the amplified program. If Tanner was inside, they'd have the advantage with two pistols to his one. The rifle would be a tactical disadvantage at close quarters despite its potential firepower.

Lee already knew what he'd do if they managed to incapacitate the vampire. He could see a bright patio outside through one of the windows, and already had selected a particularly hot spot.

At the foot of the stairs, Lee paused, looked into the living room, and saw one of those Bose radios beside a lamp. That's where all the noise was coming from. He waited, looking toward a wide door that led into a formal dining room.

The more he thought about it, the more Lee doubted that Tanner was in the house. He'd have kept the radio off, using his sensitive ears to listen for intruders. If there was a housekeeper, the only way she'd discover Lee would be by actually spotting him. He thought about making a quick sweep of the ground floor before letting in Diane, but decided she'd been outside, more exposed than he, long enough.

He turned to find the door beneath the stairs that led into the right room, but a large painting on the wall stopped him in his tracks. A man and woman were depicted in the flattering portrait—apparently one of the late Mr. Walker and his wife done years ago. The man was a tall, blond, blue-eyed Anglo in his fifties. The buxom woman, except for the hair color, could have been a younger version of Rosanna Luna!

Lee grabbed his phone as he walked quickly toward the glass door leading out into the patio. "I'm letting you in through a door in the room with the big glass windows," he said to Diane as soon as she answered. "You've got to see this."

Diane stood before the painting. "It certainly looks like the woman on the porch," she had to whisper loudly to be heard over the radio.

"I never checked her ID or questioned who she was. If she really was Marci Walker, Tanner was probably in the next room, laughing his head off. And Ms. Luna was already dead elsewhere in the house."

"You're lucky he didn't make a move on you right then. With the woman there they could have played you right into the grave," Diane said.

"Tanner wasn't ready to kill me yet, I guess, though the woman did invite me into the kitchen. She played it cool, suckering me like that. I should have realized she didn't belong there when she couldn't figure out how to turn off the TV set."

"What about the green sedan, then? She must have made that up too. But then how did they get away from the Luna house after the officers left the area?" Diane asked.

Lee made a quick call, and confirmed his hunch. "There was no green Crown Victoria. Ms. Luna had a gold Toyota Corolla, and that's missing. Marci Walker knows about cars, so those misleading details would have been easy for her to make up."

"So, do we still search this place for Tanner? He must have been here at one time, and neither one knows we're on to them, not yet, or she wouldn't have gone into work this morning."

"Maybe they're too cocky for their own good, but are we sure she's still at the dealership? The officers watching her are supposed to let us know if she leaves the premises," Lee said.

"I'll double-check." Diane brought out her cell phone.

"I'll keep watch." Lee stood, pistol ready, watching the stairs and the exits from the large room. He ignored the patio door for obvious reasons.

"Business as usual," Diane said a moment later, ending the call. "Mrs. Walker has been making the rounds with her employees, talking to customers, and basically doing what she apparently does at work, according to the officers watching her."

"I wish I knew for sure . . ."

". . . if she's really the person who said she was Rosanna Luna last night?" Diane finished his sentence. "One of the officers managed to get an advertising brochure which shows the woman and her late husband. The image is being faxed to the detectives keeping watch on the grounds. Wanna take a look?"

"Let's finish our search first. Tanner's got to be somewhere inside. Why not this place?"

Covering each other as they worked, Lee and Diane went through every room in the main house, checking closets and any hiding places large enough to hide an adult. Even the attic was examined. Few private homes in the Southwest had basements today, and this house was no exception, so they decided the garage would be next. Going upstairs, they found a window where they could examine the separate building while deciding on the best approach.

"Okay, Lee, we have one door and four windows big enough to crawl through. The curtains in the apartment or office upstairs are all open, so anyone inside will see us coming. The grounds around the garage are wide open for a good fifty feet or more, minimum. Even if we circle around, we'd still be exposed once we make a move for a window."

Lee shrugged. "He could pick us off with a rifle, and unfortunately, Tanner knows what we look like. Posing as a delivery person just wouldn't work either."

He watched the window for several seconds and for a moment thought he saw movement farther back in the room. "I just saw someone, or something, move. And it makes sense—it's a guy thing."

"Cars, tools, studly stuff? That what you mean?"

"Yeah. It would be the last place any honest visitor or delivery person would go, so he'd have more freedom to move around. The windows are smaller too, so any inside movement is less conspicuous. Plus, he's probably got a car in there for a quick exit."

"Maybe even that gold Toyota. You could be right. So, how do we handle it?"

"Let's overwhelm him. Get the FPD detectives to divert his attention by making a move on the garage from the side facing

the house. We'll come in the front, through one of the bay doors.
He can't confront us physically there, at least not close-up, without the risk of being fried. The doors face east, and right now the
sun will be shining into the garage several feet."

"Good idea, Lee. And if Tanner believes you're a vampire, like
him, he won't be expecting you to approach from a sunlit location.
You think you can pop open the garage door with your . . ."

"Vampire strength? Sounds Hollywood, doesn't it?" he said
with a wry smile.

"Hey, it's a good thing, like the household diva says." Diane
smiled, patted him on the arm, then motioned toward the door.
"Let's make hay while the sun is shining."

Diane made the calls while Lee watched the garage. At first, the
detectives were reluctant to move in without the necessary war-
rants, but after she pointed out that Mrs. Walker was probably
involved in a criminal conspiracy with the killer of a federal official, and that Lee believed he'd spotted Tanner, they knew they'd
be off the hook.

While they were waiting for the detectives to get set up, Diane made a call and got a warrant issued. Several provisions of
the Patriot Act came into play here, especially the sneak and peek
rule that gave them permission to search, and Diane was used to
dealing with all the legal aspects.

A half hour later they moved into position. Lee waited at the
corner of the big house, hidden from the garage by a large white
trellis containing a wall of climbing roses at least ten feet high.
The blossoms were in full bloom, and the scent was much more
satisfying than with nursery roses, which tended to sacrifice
aroma for longevity and appearance.

Diane was right beside him, cell phone in hand. Once the
detectives began to move in on the garage from the west side of
the house, she and Lee would run around to the big front doors.

They'd found a spare garage remote in the kitchen, so breaking in wasn't likely to be an issue after all. The iron gates set in the property wall that gave vehicles access to the driveway and the garage were closed, though it could be activated from a wall unit in the kitchen, which looked out toward the driveway.

There was probably another control panel in the garage, but the Farmington detectives had arranged for another officer to block the gate with a department vehicle once they moved in. Tanner wouldn't be able to escape in a car, not one inside the garage, at least.

Lee saw Diane react, then look at the phone, which was apparently vibrating. "They're moving in," she said.

To his left Lee heard running footsteps. He stepped out from behind the trellis, less than twenty feet from the corner of the garage, and pressed the remote button that, according to the label, would open the closest garage door.

The sound of a powerful engine outside in the street nearly broke his focus, and he fought to keep his attention on the garage. But when the ground shook as something heavy crashed into the iron gates, he finally turned to look.

The gates burst open at the center, almost coming off their hinges as a big black SUV with an oversized bumper came skidding onto the driveway.

"What the hell? That wasn't the plan," Diane yelled, coming up beside him.

Three big men in black clothes, flak jackets, and raid caps jumped out of the SUV, then sprinted toward the rising garage doors carrying big, strange-looking pistols. They were Dr. Wayne's people.

"No! It won't be enough!" Lee yelled, realizing that the men were planning on using sleeping darts to take Stewart Tanner alive.

"Idiots. Cover them, Lee," Diane yelled, moving forward, her pistol out. Lee quickly caught up, reaching the half-open bay door just as the first two raiders ducked into the garage.

Two powerful blasts rang out, less than three seconds apart, and someone screamed. Lee crouched low, peering inside, and saw a rifle swinging in his direction. He ducked back just as a chunk of wood erupted where he'd been a second ago and another round went off.

Diane crouched, fired a shot, then jumped up again and dove for the side of the garage as an odd-shaped, flaming stick flew out the bay door. "Cover!" she yelled.

In the back of his mind, Lee recognized the flare attached to a glass jar just before it hit the concrete. The makeshift bomb exploded with a brilliant flash of light and heat, and he turned his head away. The blast wave threw him to the ground, knocking away his pistol. Pieces of glass and debris whistled by at high speed, and Lee stayed low, groping for his weapon.

There was another gunshot, then the whine of a motorcycle engine made him turn to look. Someone wearing coveralls and a big, tinted helmet shot out of the garage on a big red Honda cycle, slipping through the opening between the ruined gate and the SUV and out into the street. Diane was already sitting up, but she turned too slowly to bring her pistol to bear.

"That's Tanner. We need to get after him," she yelled, scrambling to her feet.

Lee grabbed his pistol, noting offhand that the gasoline bomb had already burned out except for a section of lawn. He ran into the garage, putting away his handgun and whipping out his cell phone. One of the three men from the SUV was on his knees, trying to stem the blood from a chest wound one of his companions had suffered. "Call an ambulance," the man pleaded.

Lee was already punching out the number, so he nodded. As he asked for an emergency team, Lee turned and saw the third man on Dr. Wayne's team. The back of his head was a mass of ravaged red and grayish white tissue, and a jagged hole the size of a dime in the middle of his forehead was dripping a dwindling stream of blood. Even if he'd been a vampire, the deputy marshal probably wouldn't have made it.

With the detectives joining the survivors of Wayne's team, giving first aid and awaiting the EMTs, Lee and Diane ran toward their vehicle. Lee had thought for a second to take the SUV, but saw that one of the tires had been ripped open by the collision with the gate. The garage was empty of vehicles now except for a riding mower.

"Wait here. I'll be faster, and you can check on Marci Walker. If Tanner has a cell phone, she may already be getting a call," Lee yelled.

Diane nodded and came to a stop, bringing out her cell phone again as Lee ran at Olympic sprinter's speed to their unit. He was reluctant to move any faster, realizing that in this neighborhood, shots would most certainly bring people to their windows. It was a tough choice, sometimes, holding back like this in order to preserve his own identity.

Less than thirty seconds later Lee braked hard, slid to a stop, and Diane jumped in.

"Wouldn't you know it? Marci's given them the slip! The officer lost sight of her when she went into a rest room, and when he sent someone in to check, she was gone, out a small window and into the alley, apparently."

"How long has it been?" Lee asked, speeding down the street toward the location of the dealership.

"Only about ten minutes."

"Only? She could be blocks away, even if she stayed on foot. And there's still that missing Corolla."

Diane nodded. "Officers are sweeping the area, and at the same time, watching for Tanner and the red motorcycle."

"Marci knows she's got to get off the streets. Call FPD and have them start checking out the commercial buildings within walking distance, and find out if there are any businesses or rentals that the Walkers owned. If she'd been able to contact Tanner, they're probably going to meet up somewhere. He can't risk staying out much longer. Just a rip in those coveralls or an exposed section of wrist where his gloves meet his sleeve and he's going to burst into flames."

"At least she's not a vampire."

"Not yet, obviously. But now that they've been discovered, all that may change. She's obviously become part of this."

Diane shook her head. "Just what we need. Two killer vampires on the loose."

She frowned. "I just sounded like someone from one of those old movies I used to watch on Sunday afternoon *Horror Theater*."

"Yeah. Who'd have ever thunk it? Your worst nightmare is now providing your backup."

Diane smiled at Lee, then had to grab hold as he made a screeching turn onto a major avenue, slipping expertly in between two fast-moving vehicles. "You're much more than just a B-movie monster to me, Lee."

They both started laughing then.

CHAPTER 13

D iane was speaking to the Farmington officers who'd been assigned to watch Marci Walker at the auto showroom. Speaking was probably the wrong term—reaming out was more descriptive of the true nature of the one-sided conversation.

Lee had spoken to a few of the dealership employees, and clarified that Marci Walker had spent several minutes outside in the sun, checking the inventory, so that confirmed she wasn't a vampire yet.

Marci had also been recently interested, according to one of the salesmen, in a big pickup-camper combination they were offering in an upcoming hunting season promotion. Marci had driven the vehicle off the lot yesterday morning, saying she had a potential buyer who wanted it brought to him for a test drive.

The vehicle wasn't at the main residence, Lee knew, so where had it gone? It was something to mention to Diane once she finished with the Farmington officers. He knew it wouldn't take long, because Diane tended to come right to the point, then move on.

Lee was standing inside the showroom, safely in the shade, when he noticed a familiar-looking vehicle near the service department where auto shop customers parked their vehicles. As he focused on the silver SUV the driver ducked down.

As Lee walked purposefully out the door, Diane glanced his

way curiously, but Lee didn't have time to explain. Charles Alderete had raised up again, and this time they made eye contact.

Charles cursed, then reached down and started the engine.

"Don't even think about it, Alderete. We need to talk." By then, Lee was ten feet from the vehicle and Charles had the common sense to raise his empty hands up so Lee could see them.

"What's going on, Officer Hawk?"

"I think you know already, Charles. You've been following us again, haven't you?"

"Kind of. Actually I was watching Dr. Wayne's plush rental apartment, like you suggested," Charles said. "When his men took off in their raid gear, I followed them into that upper-crust neighborhood. But I hung back too far and lost them. By the time I relocated their vehicle, you and Diane were already racing away, so I went after you. But I noticed the name 'Walker' on the mailbox as I was taking off. Does Walker own this business, and how is he connected to Tanner?"

"Can't say, not right now." Lee looked at the man's eyes, but couldn't sense any deception. "Did you happen to notice a man on a motorcycle racing through that neighborhood while you were looking for Wayne's men?"

"A big red one?"

Lee nodded.

"Can't say, not right now."

"How'd you like to spend the next few days in a cell?"

"You wanna trade information, or you wanna lean on me?"

"You tell me where the motorcycle went, and I'll back off."

"Okay. I'm guessing it was Tanner on the motorcycle?"

"Right. Now, where did he go?"

"Down the street, heading east. Which would tend to suggest he wasn't coming here. So, it looks like you guessed wrong." Charles shook his head, then cursed. "Wish I'd have followed him instead of you. That helmet he was wearing sure covered him up. That, and the overalls. Even the gloves weren't that out of place. I should have caught on."

"Because a vampire needs to stay covered up during the daytime?"

"Something like that." Charles looked at him very closely, but Lee's sunglasses hid his pupil size, if he was counting on reading Lee. "You know a lot about vampires."

"Hey, I watch movies. TV too."

"Okay, Officer Hawk. Now I've done *my* part. Why did you guys come here, and why is Diane ragging those Farmington cops?"

"Tanner stole a red Mustang from this dealership after getting a key from inside one of the offices, so we were guessing he might be coming back."

"Gotta be more to it than that." Charles reached over and opened his glove compartment, revealing a scanner. "Officers are looking for a woman named Marci *Walker*. No coincidence that this is the same last name as on the mailbox at that fancy house that Dr. Wayne's people raided. Did Tanner kidnap one of the Walkers?"

"Mr. Walker, the former owner of this dealership, died months ago. His wife disappeared from here earlier today and we're trying to find her. That's pretty much it."

Charles looked at him for a while. "That's all you're going to say? There's got to be more."

Lee shrugged. "I've already told you more than I should because you know Agent Lopez, and because you lost your sister. But one word of advice, Charles. Be careful, stay out of the way, and try to stay alive."

Lee turned and walked toward Diane, who was alone now, watching. She nodded to Charles, then accompanied Lee to their vehicle without speaking.

"I found out about the missing pickup with the camper shell while you were talking to Charles. How'd he find us, anyway?"

Lee explained about Wayne, and told Diane what he'd said to Charles. She picked up the radio mike, and gave instructions to Dispatch to keep a lookout for the motorcycle and the camper, then she called Dr. Wayne. A few minutes later she hung up.

Lee started the engine. "Back to the Walker home?"

She nodded. "We'll meet Victor there. He screwed us royally trying to take Tanner like that right in front of our noses, but that cost him two more men. The guy shot in the chest just died. Maybe now Victor will come clean with us about Tanner."

The return trip to the Walker estate took less than ten minutes. Farmington was now sprawled out wide on both sides of the river, but the roads were pretty good and it wasn't even close to the size of Albuquerque.

When they arrived, they immediately noticed an empty white SUV parked beside the curb just past the damaged gate. A yellow crime-scene tape was stretched across the driveway entrance, and an OMI van was backed up almost even with it. An ambulance was alongside, and as they parked across the street, a body bag on a gurney was being loaded into the ambulance by two attendants. Another body was already inside the vehicle.

Lee and Diane ducked under the tape, showed their IDs to the uniformed officer, then walked into the still-open garage. The two Farmington detectives, Shannon and Esterbrook, were processing the scene. Seeing who had arrived, Shannon looked up, the obvious question in his eyes.

"Tanner's still on the loose, but without the rifle now." Lee noticed the Remington on the garage floor. "He may have met up with Mrs. Walker, then taken off in a pickup with a camper shell. There's a bulletin out now on the pickup and motorcycle."

Detective Shannon stood. "So Tanner *did* have a woman helping out. Maybe now that she's been identified, it'll drive him into hiding and slow the body count."

"Maybe. Where's Dr. Wayne?" They hadn't seen the federal man outside, and he wasn't in the garage, at least downstairs.

Detective Esterbrook pointed toward the narrow metal stairs. "Up there. There's a small apartmentlike workshop, and it looks like that's where Tanner was spending his daytime hours. Oh, and Tanner may have taken a bullet as he broke out of the garage. We're going to be checking for a blood trail once we process this area."

"Got gloves?" Detective Shannon added.

Lee nodded, pulling a pair of latex gloves from his jacket pocket and handing them to Diane. He then brought out two more for himself.

"Try not to touch the handrails," Esterbrook said. "They need dusting."

"We'll be careful," Diane said as she put on the second glove. Leading the way, she climbed up the metal steps to the second floor of the garage. The structure had been completely finished and painted even on the inside, and was pleasant and clean— except for the two bloody spots on the floor below.

When they reached the small office-workshop, the surviving federal marshal from the earlier raid was using a flashlight to search beneath a metal futon, which was still laid out in bed mode. The rumpled condition of the blankets and the indented pillow suggested that Tanner had been resting there.

Dr. Wayne was standing beside a big metal desk, examining pages of the local newspaper spread across its surface. He turned and nodded to them, no expression at all showing on his face. "Special Agent Lopez, Officer Hawk."

Diane ignored the doctor and turned to catch the attention of Dr. Wayne's man, who'd stopped what he was doing and had risen to his knees to see who the visitors were.

"The detectives downstairs can use your help—right now," Diane announced.

The man, who'd probably aged ten years already today, got the message from her tone but still looked at Victor before answering. "Yes, ma'am," he replied at last, getting a nod, then climbed down the stairs slowly, careful not to touch the handrails.

Diane's voice was low, but lethal. "Your tactics suck, Dr. Wayne, and the deaths of those two men are on your head. What in the hell were you thinking? No, forget that—you obviously *weren't* thinking. Do you have *any* tactical experience?" Diane's voice had turned to ice, and though Victor was a head taller, she was in his face.

Lee hadn't seen her that pissed off in a long time. She was right, of course, but he wondered if venting her frustration out at the federal man would do any good. Victor Wayne had obviously sat back while Diane and the locals did his legwork, then moved in at the last minute to try and take Tanner from under their noses.

"Officer Hawk, if Dr. Wayne doesn't tell us *everything* he knows right now, would you mind throwing him down the stairs for me?"

Victor smiled, but Lee knew she wasn't kidding. And it wasn't difficult matching the coldness in Diane's words. After all, Victor Wayne's hirelings had tortured Tanner for months simply because Tanner was a vampire. "No problem. Head first okay?"

Victor's mouth dropped open and his veneer of arrogance lost a layer before he could recover. "You really think you can muscle me around, Hawk?"

Lee reached out before Victor's next heartbeat, grabbed him by the belt, and lifted the two-hundred-pound man off the floor at least eight inches. "Ever felt *real* pain, Victor?"

The big man clenched his fists for a second, then decided it was a bad idea and almost immediately held them out in submission. "Okay, okay, I'm not a fighter. Set me down and we'll talk."

"No, Victor. *You'll* talk. Got it?" Diane said.

Victor nodded, squirming slightly as he dangled in the air.

Diane turned to Lee. "Sorry. I know you would have enjoyed doing it. Maybe later."

Lee lowered Victor slowly, then let go of his belt, stepping back a foot, but still within easy reach.

Victor cleared his throat, then managed a weak smile. "You wouldn't have really . . ."

Diane raised an eyebrow.

"Sideways. Head first would have been too easy," Lee spoke softly without inflection.

Victor's smile faded and he tried to step back, adjusting his trousers, but he bumped into the desk and nearly fell. Once he regained his balance, he cleared his throat again and looked back and forth between Diane and Lee nervously. "I feel really bad about what happened to my people. They were good men. I was just trying to take Tanner alive. His . . . biology could have helped balance out the loss of life. The strength and speed he's shown, and his fear of sunlight, all remarkable. Did you know my man is sure he shot him in the thigh, yet Tanner drove off without even flinching? Stewart Tanner is extraordinary. We need to bring him back under our control so we can study what he really is."

"Quit running off at the mouth, and don't tell me you're beginning to believe that vampire crap. If you'd have let us do our job, a lot of lives could have been saved," Diane argued.

Lee was wondering now how close Victor was getting to the truth. Belief in vampires among people like him was dangerous. Lee knew he had to subvert those thoughts. "Did one of the detectives downstairs tip you off about our plans?" Lee asked. He suspected it had probably been the patrolman assigned to block the gate, but he wanted to hear it from Victor.

"It was Officer Wrightmeyer, the patrolman watching the gate, but the news didn't give us much time to come up with a better plan. I realize now that I should have coordinated the assault with you and the detectives."

"You knew all along that Tanner grew up in Farmington, didn't you, Victor? Yet you still missed the part about his affair with Marci Walker. You and your people are sloppy." Diane was fishing, but on the right track, obviously.

"Victor didn't care about Tanner's past—once he had his guinea pig," Lee reminded Diane in a disgusted voice.

"Okay, all true," Victor admitted reluctantly. "We need to move past that and concentrate on finding Tanner. His hiding place has been compromised, and we know about his girlfriend. He's going to have to find somewhere else to lie low. The stolen rifle was left behind, so all he's got is a pistol now, right? And he's been shot." Victor was sounding more confident now that he realized he wasn't going to be beaten unconscious—or worse. He took a step in the direction of the stairs, and Lee blocked his way.

"Don't start relaxing now, Victor. You're not leaving this room on your own power until we get *all* of Tanner's history, starting from the moment you and your 'people' discovered him," Diane said.

"It'll take a while." Victor pulled out the desk chair and sat down, facing them.

For the next ten minutes, Dr. Wayne essentially verified what they already knew from the documents and secret files they'd seen, and added details surrounding Tanner's initial discovery and incarceration. Finally Victor stood. "Can we get back to work now?"

Lee and Diane exchanged glances. "Okay," she finally said. "But if you get any information we should have—and don't tell us immediately—it's going straight to my boss and in the first line of every report I file—not to mention the press."

"I'll do much worse than that, Victor. I'll make sure that Tanner finds out *you're* the man responsible for all the misery in his life. Give him a focal point for his hatred, so to speak," Lee said flatly.

Diane nodded her approval. "Sounds fair. Now let's find Tanner and Marci Walker before they leave New Mexico and disappear completely."

CHAPTER 14

The surviving member of Victor's "team" was now near the gate, beside the black SUV, pointing to something on the ground when Lee and Diane walked up. Victor crouched to scrape a sample of the gray powder into an evidence pouch.

"I know I hit him, he grabbed his thigh and almost wiped out the bike. You can't take a bullet in the leg without bleeding."

Lee noted the biological ash where the vampire blood had burned away, leaving just a residue. He'd seen it before. Unfortunately, so had Victor Wayne.

"Looks like the same residue from where that CIA man died over in Albuquerque. And near where you two encountered those terrorists a few months earlier," Victor looked up at Diane to confirm.

"Doesn't look like it came from blood, but, hey, I'm not the forensics expert here," she said, *not* looking at Lee.

"Suppose this scorch mark originated from that gasoline bomb, or the flare Tanner used to set it off?" Lee said, turning to point toward the burned section of grass and the fragments of glass, paper, and residue scattered around the garage and backyard of the Walker residence. "It'll take hours to find every piece of that bomb."

"The local crime-lab people will be here soon to check it out. They've been working overtime, and hoped to be able to catch up on Tanner's work from last night," one of the Farmington detectives—Esterbrook—said as he came up. He handed Diane his cell phone. "Ma'am, you wanna take the call? It's from Dispatch."

Diane took the receiver, then, after a moment, gave the cell phone back to the detective and turned to Lee. "A patrolman thinks he's found the motorcycle Tanner took from here. It's in the parking lot of a flower shop. The officer is interviewing the shop owner now."

Lee looked at Victor. "You may want to go over the house very carefully. There may be a clue that'll point to Tanner's future targets."

Victor nodded. "We'll be in touch."

With a nod, Diane turned and walked toward the gate. Lee followed.

Once they were in the car, Diane spoke again. "Once Victor realizes that the ash on the driveway is oxidized vampire blood, he'll know that the man who died in Albuquerque was a vampire, and that the terrorists who died over by Fort Wingate were vampires too."

"Unfortunately, you and I are connected to all three incidents in one way or the other. That's going to place us on the slides of Dr. Wayne's biggest microscope," Lee responded—a touch of fear for himself and her—clawing into him. He wasn't at all sure how long he could endure what Tanner had gone through without losing his own sanity. And although they couldn't do much to Diane, they could use her to control him.

"Well, at least you're only half vampire, which means you'll be able to mislead him about the sunlight thing. With sunblock on you can stay outside, at least for a while."

"I still want to avoid Victor as much as possible. The man has really gotten under my skin. I'd have loved to throw him down the stairs, you know. Tanner was a person with a secret before the experiments started. Victor turned him angry . . . and into a killer."

"Dr. Wayne's a bigot, in his own way. People like that are hard to take no matter how noble they try and make their bias sound. Tanner was singled out because he was different, and nobody has the right to experiment on another person like that. Lynette was my friend, but what she and the others did to Tanner was cold and cruel and unconscionable."

"In my youth it was the Nazis who treated prisoners like lab rats. Then in the fifties, the CIA experimented with mind control and slipped LSD and other drugs into subjects without their knowledge, just to see what would happen. Other countries have done much worse to their own citizens. And now Dr. Wayne has singled out vampires."

"Obviously only a few people know about it, though. But things have a way of balancing out. Victor will get his payback someday."

"You're right. If I were more like him, I'd provide the payback myself."

"But you're not, Lee. I've seen what you go through killing a skinwalker, no matter how evil they've become. You know that they were regular people before their affliction made them into animal predators."

"Thank God we don't have to deal with that now. Vampires are enough to worry about. Let's just get to Tanner and his lady before they kill anyone else. Once he's dead and she's been locked up, Dr. Wayne and his unfortunate followers will be moving on."

"You think Tanner will allow himself to be taken alive, after what he's been subjected to and done in retaliation?"

"No. But maybe we can save Mrs. Walker—if that'll make any difference to her."

They arrived at the flower shop within minutes. A police officer was crouched beside the parked motorcycle, taking notes on a clipboard. A young woman in a yellow apron was standing in the shade of the shop's awning on a concrete step, watching.

Lee felt his face and neck, checking for the presence of sunblock. They'd switched seats and Diane had driven the rest of the distance while he added extra protection for his skin. The latex gloves he'd had on before had caused his hands to sweat, and once he took them off, he'd noticed that he was losing his coverage.

It was still too warm in the year to wear leather gloves without being conspicuous, and he didn't want that now, with everyone thinking about vampires.

Diane must have had it on her mind. "Gloves, partner?" She called, tossing him a pair of latex gloves. With the motorcycle to examine, they could justify the use without raising eyebrows.

"Thanks." Lee nodded to the officer, named Benally, according to the tag above his uniform pocket.

"I spoke briefly with the shop owner"—Benally gestured with his lips, Navajo style, toward the woman—"and she said the motorcycle driver pulled up beside a pickup, one with a camper shell. It had been parked there since yesterday. Somebody opened the door, and they drove off together."

Lee looked over at Diane, who had continued on and was speaking to the woman on the porch. "Did the flower-shop woman notice another woman hanging around the pickup earlier?"

"That Walker woman we're looking for? No, I asked her that. But the woman doesn't get a chance to look outside her shop much, being by herself a lot of the time. She only noticed the motorcycle because of the distinctive engine sound."

"Was the motorcycle driver holding his leg, like he's been hurt?"

Benally nodded. "How'd you know?"

"The guy on the motorcycle killed two federal marshals just before he got here. It was Stewart Tanner, the guy we're *all* trying to stop."

"Pale Death? That's what the *Dineh* are calling him."

Lee nodded. "I've heard that. Anything else?"

Officer Benally pointed to the ground. "Just some gray ash on the side of the bike and there on the ground. Does Tanner smoke?"

"Sometimes," Lee said, checking the scorched blood on the ground and bike without touching it. "We were hoping for a lot more," he muttered.

Benally looked at him with narrowed eyes. "I don't follow you, Officer Hawk."

"Ignore me, Officer Benally, I was making a bad joke. Just remember that if you happen to meet up with Tanner, don't try to take him prisoner or listen to any of his bullshit. Take action as quickly as you can. Shoot him several times, and make it in the heart and head. The guy can't feel any pain, apparently, so you're going to have to destroy him from the inside out. Never take your eyes off him, either, even if he looks dead."

"Ah, my cousin warned me about that. He's the sergeant you spoke to at the Fruitland roadblock the other day. He's been spreading the word about Tanner to all the *Dineh*."

"Good for your cousin. Believe him."

Diane came back just then, nodded to Benally, then motioned Lee toward their vehicle, tossing him the keys. "You drive. I guess we know where Marci went when she left the dealership. You notice this shop is less than a mile from there." Diane pointed toward a narrow alley just fifty feet away. "I bet she ran down the alley, all the way. The pickup was here right where she'd left it."

"Wait for the detectives, officer. They'll be sending someone," Diane yelled to Benally. When the patrolman nodded, Diane moved around to the passenger's side of the vehicle, and Lee climbed in behind the wheel.

"The pickup and camper should be easier to track down, Lee," Diane said as they got under way, heading toward the center of town.

"Think they're planning on leaving Farmington? Tanner can stay inside that camper during the daytime, and they may have provisions for days." Lee pulled out a map of the area, already considering possible escape routes.

"Roadblocks are still up on the major routes, but there are just too many possibilities to cover every dirt track and gas and oil well service road, though. Let me check on the air cover." Diane checked her cell phone, looked down at the portable charger they had keeping fresh batteries available, then dialed.

"They've been good planners so far. What if they only had a short distance to go, like a barn or warehouse somewhere?" Lee pointed out. "We still don't have a complete list of every place Walker owned, do we?"

Diane shook her head. "Not yet, but FPD is supposed to be putting together that information. I'll give them another call. Meanwhile, let's check the obvious, circling the neighborhood around the flower shop for a place big enough to hide a pickup with a camper. Most garages will be too small for a high-profile vehicle like that."

"Maybe a commercial garage. Let's check them all, and hope that Mrs. Walker doesn't own property out of the county. That wouldn't show up in local records. Now here's where we can use some of your federal juice, and maybe Dr. Wayne's contacts. The Walkers had to pay taxes on all their holdings. Can you get someone to grab their accountant-bookkeeper-tax man, whoever? They must have had a lawyer or financial advisor."

"Do you suppose Dr. Wayne will get ethical on me if I ask him to find a hacker to check out the Walkers' home computer?" Diane asked.

"Ethical, him? Ask if you want, but don't make it a request that he could use against you someday. Victor's probably way ahead of us on anything illegal already."

Diane looked over at him. "You're right. Maybe I shouldn't

have left him alone in that house. If he manages to discover where Tanner and Mrs. Walker are hiding first . . ."

"He's running too low on personnel for a move like that, isn't he?" Lee shot back. "And he doesn't have the balls to try it on his own."

"Yeah. But if he's really part of some defense agency, more goons are already on the way."

Diane remained quiet for a while, and Lee didn't interrupt the silence between them. The importance of giving others time to think was a trait valued by those of his tribe. Instant answers weren't necessarily a sign of intelligence, only speed. Yet, in today's world, with speed being the criteria, people who took their time before they answered were considered hicks, slow, stupid, or worse.

"Let's rely on information the locals can provide," Diane said at last, "but I'll ask Victor to check it out anyway. We can give him some time—maybe for his reinforcements to arrive—then pull a Charles and watch his moves. If Marci and Stewart Tanner have a particular hiding place in mind, Dr. Wayne's people may lead us to it."

"Might work. And with all the other local law enforcement people blanketing the area, everything we can think of is already covered. There's one more thing we might consider, though."

"What's that?"

"Those camper shells can be lifted off and left in a garage. With Tanner's strength, he could do it alone, and Marci must know more than the average person about automobiles and trucks. It's her business."

"Right. We need to look for a pickup without a camper as well. I'm also going to have the dealer employees verify that no other vehicles are missing from their inventory, and that the Walkers didn't own any other vehicles that we haven't heard about yet."

"I can find out immediately. I have friends in the motor vehicle department," Lee said. They both brought out their cell phones and began making calls while Lee cruised slowly down a street close by the flower shop. Every Ford pickup of the right color and model with a camper shell would be checked and ruled out, and every potential hiding place logged and checked.

Diane was on the phone longer, but finally ended her calls and turned to Lee. "We've got Victor Wayne pegged. He'd already started browsing through the Walker computer. Marci Walker apparently has her taxes done by an accountant, but her late husband liked to be on top of things. A lot of their investment records are on the computer and Victor is wading through them. There are some properties bought and sold, apparently, but he hasn't found them all yet. There are hundreds of files, and he's having to look through them all."

"I've got an idea. Any idea where Victor Wayne is staying— his rental—a plush apartment, according to Charles?"

Diane looked at him suspiciously. "I can find out. Why?"

"Just find out."

Fifteen minutes later they were walking along the sidewalk in front of an exclusive, ten-suite rental apartment complex almost hidden within the shade of dozens of skillfully placed ponderosa pines of all sizes. The back and sides of the complex were secured by a tall, textured block wall, and the grounds were landscaped with more evergreens, thick hedges, and seemingly random plots of perfectly manicured grass.

A high brick and wrought-iron fence along the front of the structure prevented street-side access to the luxury apartments. Guests and visitors gained access through a wide gate in the center and down a flagstone walk. At the gate stood a uniformed guard.

"I wonder if the taxpayers are footing the bill for this palatial retreat? I'm lucky if the Bureau puts me up in a place where the cockroaches are too small to carry away my handgun during the night."

"You know there's a pecking order in federal agencies."

"We already knew Victor was a real pecker. No surprise there." She smiled, then yawned. "Did I sleep last night?"

"Your eyes were closed from time to time. Does that mean anything?"

"I'll let you know next shootout. By the way, how do you plan to gain access to Dr. Wayne's suite? There are high walls, gates, guards, and probably land mines."

"Well, assuming you're kidding about the mines, I've got a plan." As they strolled down the sidewalk, Lee nodded toward a covered parking garage across the street. "Those are the vehicles belonging to the tenants, don't you think?"

"Let's see. Mercedes, Land Rover, Lincoln, Lexus. Of course these vehicles belong to the guests. What's your point?"

"Well, I noticed that a gray-haired gentleman and his two sexily dressed female companions just exited the maroon Mercedes, and instead of crossing the street to the complex the three lovebirds went into that small, solidly built room." He glanced in that direction.

"The one with a security guard just outside? I get it. He must be a doorman for the entrance to a stairwell."

Lee nodded. "Exactly. My guess is there's a tunnel beneath the street that leads from there to the complex. Wouldn't want the paying guests to get their thousand-dollar suits all dusty or rained on?"

"Sounds about right. So, how do you plan to con our way past the parking garage security?"

"Not us. You. The guy's probably not my type, but your feminine attributes and charm will do the trick."

"You're kidding."

Lee shook his head. "Face it, you're a hottie even in a business suit."

Diane rolled her eyes. "If I do this, you definitely owe me one. Make that two."

"Whatever I have is yours. Just get us past the guy without having to ID ourselves. We don't want Victor to discover we've been going through his drawers."

"Rephrase that, will ya?" she said with a groan. "I feel crappy enough having to flirt with a security guard."

"Okay. Not drawers—closets. But maybe I can make it easier on both of us. I'll call in the vehicle tag on that Mercedes—it's a NM plate—and once we have a name . . ."

"We'll know whose name to use to get in the door. Cool."

Five minutes later they climbed up the below-ground stairs onto a covered gazebo-type platform inside the upscale facility. "Did you notice all the celebrity names on the 'they stayed here' list back at the desk? So this is where ex-vice presidents reside when they descend upon the Four Corners to give speeches," Diane whispered, looking around but seeing nothing but tasteful potted plants and flagstone walkways leading in several directions. Polished brass signs indicated apartment numbers for each path.

"My guess is that William Melton has less inspirational motives for staying here. Great idea saying we're part of the entertainment for his 'party.' And that wink you gave the security guard really helped, Diane."

"What helped even more is keeping our weapons and handcuffs out of sight."

"Who knows?" Lee whispered, putting on latex gloves as they walked down the stone walk that led to Victor Wayne's rented apartment, actually a small cottage. "Mr. Melton might consider handcuffs party favors."

The lock on Victor's door was expensive but mechanical, and it took Lee about the same time it took Diane to don her own gloves to pick the lock with the special tools he always carried.

"No alarms," Diane whispered as they stood there looking around the spacious living room/office of the luxury rental quarters.

"No need," Lee reminded. "The place is secure—right?"

"I noticed that Victor carries an expensive PDA. He's bound to have a notebook or laptop computer too. I wonder where it is?" Diane looked around, spotting an Internet port located at the rear of the cherry-wood desk in the corner, beside a big armchair.

"Forget the drawers, but maybe there's a safe in the closet." Lee checked. "It's here, but too small for even a notebook computer," he added a few seconds later.

"How about the traditional hiding place?" She pointed toward the next room, where Lee could see a king-sized bed.

"Might be." He followed her into the bedroom and lifted up the mattress. At one end of the foundation was a thin, expensive laptop computer. There was a cable attached to the device that enabled the Internet connection.

"Bingo." Diane picked up the computer, stepped back, and Lee eased the mattress back down. "He's even got wireless capability," she added, placing the device on the desk and opening it up to expose the keyboard and screen.

"He's bound to have password protection. Know how to get past it?" Lee asked.

"I picked up a few tips at a Homeland Security workshop given by a former hacker. But it may take a while. Do we have time?"

Lee started to speak, then he held up his hand. "We've got company," he whispered.

Diane looked over at the door just as the sound of light footsteps on stone reached her ears. Hearing someone fiddling with the lock mechanism, she grabbed the laptop, then motioned Lee toward the bedroom. He followed noiselessly, closing the door nearly shut behind them.

Diane was right beside him, holding her breath, as a minute, then two passed, and the faint scraping sound in the lock continued. Finally they heard the apartment door open. "Gotcha," someone said softly. Then the door closed.

Lee and Diane made eye contact, then she smiled, a relieved look on her face. "Charles," she whispered. "I'm so going to kick his ass."

"Anybody home?" Charles called in a normal voice, obviously hoping it was a rhetorical question.

Diane stepped around Lee and swung the bedroom door open. "Charles, you're such an idiot!"

Lee, two steps behind her, saw the stunned look on Alderete's face. He held the handle of a bulging gym bag in one gloved hand, and some kind of electronic box in the other.

"Uh . . . what are you two doing in my room?" Charles managed, struggling to save himself.

"Weak, really weak. You know this is Victor Wayne's home away from home. That's why you're here," Diane said.

"So what? That's why you're here too, right?"

"Right," Lee said, trying to get Diane's attention as well. "And if you want to stay out of jail, Charles, you're going to help us with this black bag job."

Diane quickly saw the logic of the situation, and they all got to work. Charles had brought some hacking software he insisted he'd traded for discounts on legal gun purchases, so he and Diane began to work on getting through Wayne's passwords.

Lee searched the rest of the apartment, and soon discovered a manila envelope in the pocket of a comfortable-looking old denim jacket that Wayne might have worn while off the clock. The envelope, folded into thirds, was one of those legal-sized ones that normally sealed with glue and a metal butterfly clip, but Victor had used a paper clip instead. The outside of the envelope had two stamped markings—"U.S. Air Force" and the other "Classified"—in red ink.

Lee had set the envelope aside while continuing his search, but finally, after running out of likely hiding places, he sat down in the middle of the carpet and slipped off the paper clip.

Inside was a black-and-white photo of a woman with Asian features who appeared to be in her early twenties, and two yellowed typed pages that appeared to be some kind of medical report. The report was dated April 24, 1955, and all names and agencies had been blacked out. After skimming a few paragraphs, Lee felt a wave of sadness for the woman in the photo. Then, as he continued to read, anger began to rise in his throat. "Shit. Patient Alpha."

Charles was busy at the laptop keyboard, but Diane, who'd been watching the computer display from over the man's shoulders, turned to look.

"What?" she asked.

Lee shook his head and held up his hand. This information wasn't for Charles. He continued reading the report, considered keeping it for a moment, then reluctantly put it back inside the envelope, then back into the jacket pocket where he'd found it.

After checking a few more places, but finding nothing, Lee came over to stand beside Charles. He and Diane were browsing through file names, trying to guess which ones to display on-screen.

"I got in. Officer Hawk," Charles said with a grin. "According to my source, this program can penetrate security programs and read the passwords directly. If you're feeling particularly hostile, you can even change the password so the owner won't be able to access his own files. The program capitalizes on a bug that nobody talks about because it can't be patched. You'd have to upgrade to the next generation operating system—which is still in beta testing and not available yet. Damned handy."

Diane kept her eyes on the screen. "Go to the L's. I saw a file that looks promising."

"Okay," Charles said, scrolling up the screen.

Lee saw one that caught his eye. "Lazarus?"

"Yeah." Diane nodded.

A minute later they were all silently reading a report that filled in more details about the experiments they'd run on Stewart Tanner.

"Dr. Wayne is responsible for all that?" Charles said with a growl as the information appeared on the computer screen.

"We've known he was directing the operation," Diane confirmed. "And we'd suspected he'd come into the picture early on. But now we have written confirmation that Victor Wayne initiated the experimentation on Tanner. He secured the funding, established the lab, and hired all three researchers, including Lynette."

"Wayne's also responsible for the security. All this time he's tried to make us believe he was just keeping an eye on the place. But apparently it was his baby from the beginning," Lee concluded.

"He really believes in vampires, then. He knows the truth," Charles said, his voice low.

"What truth are you talking about, Charles?" Diane asked.

There was a noise outside and everyone froze. Lee walked silently over to the window and glanced out from behind a curtain. "It's just the older gentleman with his lady friends. But we'd better take this conversation up somewhere else. No telling when Victor and his people will be coming back." Lee looked at his watch.

"And we don't want to meet them on the way out." Diane looked down at the computer display. "Or have our presence here compromised. Can you make copies of this stuff?"

"I can do better than that," Charles said with a smile. He reached down into his gym bag and brought out a small device that Lee recognized as an external hard drive. "I can make a copy of everything on his computer within a few minutes."

"Why in the hell didn't you do that in the first place?" Diane grumbled, poking him on the shoulder.

"With you guys being here, I forgot about it."

"Unforget, make the copy, and let's clear out," Lee replied. He looked over at Diane. "While he's working, you and I need to remove any evidence that we were here."

By the time they'd put everything back where they'd found it, Charles was finished backing up the hard drive. They returned the computer to its hiding place under the mattress, then straightened out the bed so it looked undisturbed.

"Wait a second," Diane said, then walked over and sat down on the bed. "He'd sat on the bed and left a mark, I just remembered."

"Nice touch. Glad you're on my side," Lee whispered.

"But is the butt width still the same?" Charles snickered as he checked his gym bag, then put the chair back in place before the desk.

"Dangerous words, Chuck. She carries a gun," Lee cautioned.

Diane shot daggers at Charles, then looked out the window. "Clear."

Then Lee held up a hand. "Wait. Charles, you're going to have to go out the way you came in, and not with us. What'd you do, climb the wall?"

"Sort of. I found a blind spot where the guards can't see, and parked my rental SUV there. I stepped across from the roof. There's a fake gardener's business sign on the door and tools in the back."

"But you're on the inside now," Diane pointed out.

"I found a tree branch. I'll just climb the tree, walk out, then use a rope I brought to slide down. I've picked up a few skills along the way."

"We're meeting at the coffee shop I told you about," Diane said to Charles. "Be there."

Charles nodded. "Count on it. There's something you both need to know about Stewart Tanner. The truth." Without waiting for a response, their companion opened the door and walked out, heading in the opposite direction they'd be going.

"What do you suppose he meant by that?" Diane asked as they stepped out onto the small porch.

Lee pulled the door shut, checked to verify that it was locked, then quickly pulled off his latex gloves and shoved them into a pocket. "I guess we're going to find out," he said as they walked quickly down the flagstone walk toward the gazebo.

CHAPTER 15

Diane stepped out the stairwell door into the parking garage, and Lee followed. "Where's the security—"

There was a blur, then her voice was cut off by a forearm across her throat. Tanner stepped from around the corner, pulling Diane against him with his other arm.

"Thanks for the appetizer, Hawk," the vampire whispered harshly, removing his hand from Diane's throat as he felt for the handle of a big hunting knife at his belt.

Lee knew he was fast, but Tanner already had the long blade up to Diane's throat when he fired. Lee wasn't interested in any of that "shoot the knife out of the hand" crap either. He'd aimed for Tanner's knuckles.

The force of the 9mm slug shattered Tanner's right hand and he yelped in pain, losing his grip. As the knife fell Diane suddenly went limp, collapsing to the concrete and giving Lee a shot at the vampire's torso.

But Tanner reacted instantly. He kicked out at Lee's gun, knocking it up and away, then reached for the pistol he'd jammed into his belt.

Diane pulled her pistol out of its holster and fired immediately without aiming, striking Tanner in the thigh. He grunted again, spun around, and dove for the open door. Diane fired again, twice, her second bullet hitting the metal door with a thud as the vampire pulled it shut.

Lee had his backup .45 out now. "Cover the door!" Without waiting for a response he ran out of the garage. Across the street, he saw the security guard at the property gate crouched down low, yelling into his radio and looking in their direction.

"I'm a cop!" Lee yelled as he jogged across the pavement. "A man with a gun is going through the tunnel to your side. Call the police."

Lee heard a gunshot, then another, and knew Tanner had been seen. Unfortunately, it was probably someone else who'd just been shot. The guard fumbled with his keys to open the gate for Lee, but there was no time. Lee hurtled the five-foot-high entrance, then realized that Tanner wouldn't be able to run around in the apartment compound for more than a few seconds at a time. The vampire would be trapped within because of the light. His only escape would be by vehicle—the shaded garage.

Knowing he'd been faked out, Lee stopped and turned. "Diane, he's got to come your way!"

There was a loud thud, then gunfire—several shots. Lee ran back through the now open gate, brushing past the confused guard, then across the street as fast as he could go. Ahead, he heard a hollow thump, shattering glass, then squealing tires and two more shots. A gold Toyota raced out the other side of the parking structure.

His stomach fell, but Lee continued into the structure. "Diane?"

"Shit, shit, shit! The bastard's getting away again," Diane yelled, stepping around from behind a tall SUV, disheveled and obviously very pissed off as she shoved a fresh clip into her pistol.

"At least you're okay, woman." Lee picked up his lost Beretta, checked to make sure it hadn't been damaged, then returned it to the holster.

"Barely. Tanner ripped the damned door off the hinges and used it as a shield. Then he threw it at me! Knocked me down."

Lee saw where she was pointing. A red Mercedes had three feet of metal door sticking out of its windshield. "Guy's rough on cars."

"I'll get some city units looking for the gold Corolla," Diane reached for her cell phone. She took a few deep breaths. "You'd better see if he's hurt anyone else—like the security guard."

Lee turned toward the small structure that sheltered the tunnel entrance and noticed an arm dangling down from the flat-topped roof. "Call the EMTs. We've got at least one victim."

The attack on them had been costly for bystanders. The security guard was dead from a broken neck and a woman employee at the other end of the tunnel had been shot in the leg as she tried to crawl beneath her desk. But they had Tanner on the run again now, and he'd have to find shelter or another vehicle quickly.

Lee wasn't worried that Dr. Wayne would know they'd been up to something once he learned where the incident had taken place. The bigger concern was that Marci Walker would be meeting up with Tanner soon to provide him with even more re-sources and another hiding place.

They were now waiting for Charles to arrive at the coffee shop where they'd stopped for a fast lunch. Diane had called him a half hour ago, mentioning that they'd been delayed, but now it was Charles who was late.

"You've been fidgeting ever since we arrived, Lee. What's bugging you?" Diane asked. "We know Tanner must have fol-lowed us from the dealership, or the flower shop. Don't blame yourself for not spotting the tail. I didn't see it coming either."

Lee's fist clenched, then unclenched. If he didn't find a way to deal with his anger, it would probably eat him up inside a little bit at a time for the rest of his life—which would be considerably long, if he had any say about it. "Sure we screwed up, but now we know Tanner can and will attack us in the daytime. We'll be ready next time. But, no, that's not it. I'm just really pissed off at Victor and the whole system he represents."

"Okay. Could it be that old envelope you found in his apartment? I thought I saw a photo in there along with the papers you were reading. And if I remember correctly, you said something about Patient Alpha," Diane pressed gently.

"Yeah. Just as we suspected, Stewart Tanner wasn't the first vampire the government turned into a lab rat. Before, back in 1955, it was a young Korean woman named June—no last name was given. She was the wife of a U.S. Air Force pilot."

"You're kidding. The government has known about vampires all this time?" She lowered her voice automatically, though none of the other diners seemed to be listening.

"According to the report I read it was just that one instance. June was in an accident outside a remote air force base in Nevada. Her husband was killed outright, and all she remembered was the accident, and passing out while trapped in the wrecked vehicle. Airmen apparently found June later, outside the wreck, dazed but unhurt despite having bled all over her clothes."

"She was injured, but rehealed? That does sound like a vampire."

"Yeah, but there's more to it. The accident was at night, and the airmen who came across the accident site saw someone running away in the dark as they approached the scene. Marks indicate that whoever it was had pulled June from the wreck."

"A vampire, perhaps? A man or woman who used their blood to save—and turn her? That wasn't you, was it?"

"No. Vampires have no right to turn anyone else into what we are. It's a curse, not a blessing. I wouldn't do something like that to anyone."

"You did it to me," she whispered.

"That was different." He looked her in the eyes. "You know that, don't you?"

"Yes. I also know you saved me from the consequences, you and John Buck. Unfortunately, this Korean woman didn't have a Navajo medicine man down the road to bring her back from that . . . 'curse.'" Diane smiled. "Still, it must have been a tough call for you. All I know is that I'm glad to be alive and sitting here now."

"So am I. For you, that is."

"So tell me the rest of June's story."

"Well, she certainly wasn't a vampire *before* that night—according to her and neighbors who said she'd been real outdoorsy. But when doctors discovered she was vulnerable to light, and self-healing—the whole vampire thing—they confined her and called in their superiors. June was isolated in a wing of the hospital and studied for several weeks. By then, she was 'classified.' This was the Cold War, and June was suddenly an asset."

Diane sighed. "That sounds like what I remember from history. Was it really that bad then, Lee? The fifties and sixties?"

He shook his head. "It's true that some people *were* paranoid about the Communists, especially those in government and in the military. A few even dug fallout shelters, but most of the civilians took it all in stride and got on with their lives. Me, I had my own version of paranoia to keep me busy."

"So what eventually happened to June? Did it say?"

"After several months of tests she committed suicide. Jumped out a window in midafternoon. The research ended and the ashes were stored in a sealed container. Dr. Wayne must have tracked these records down."

"So the son of a bitch lied to us once again. You *should* have thrown him down the stairs," Diane said, reaching for a french fry now that she'd finished her green chile cheeseburger.

"Hey, don't blame me. I *wanted* to. He's a genuine asshole."
He looked toward the door. "Speaking of . . ."

Diane sat up straight. "Victor Wayne is here?"

"No. The other asshole. The kind-of-good one."

Charles Alderete stepped into the foyer, spotted them, then
walked over to their table. He was carrying a small briefcase, and
his leather jacket concealed his pistol to the casual observer.

"Get tired of waiting for me, guys?" Charles said jokingly,
then sat down at one of the extra seats.

"You obviously stopped by your motel to change clothes and
strap on your arsenal," Diane commented. "Want some coffee?"
She waved toward the waitress and pointed to her cup.

"Been living on that stuff lately, that and whatever burgers
I can grab," he said, yawning.

Diane yawned back. "Don't start with that. Nobody is sleeping since this business began."

"Can't afford to waste the time," Lee added. "Charles, you
mentioned something about Tanner—and the truth. What were
you talking about? Is it something your sister told you in confidence?"

"Good hunch, Officer Hawk. But you aren't going to like, or
believe, what Lynette said."

"Try us," Diane urged. "We've seen a lot lately that's been
hard to believe."

"Lynette *wasn't* crazy, though she used to love playing tricks
on us when we were kids. Remember Halloween, Diane?"

She nodded. "But we're adults now. What did she tell you,
Charles?"

He leaned back, trying to appear casual, but his expression
changed and he was obviously struggling with the words. Charles
finally leaned forward and held their gaze. "Tanner *really* is a vampire," he whispered. "Vampires *are* real."

Diane rolled her eyes. "And Victor Wayne is really Victor
Frankenstein?"

"Damn it, Diane, I'm not kidding—not now. Maybe he isn't a blood-sucking undead demon with hypnotic eyes, but Tanner isn't natural. Haven't you noticed?"

Lee cleared his throat. "Okay, we've all noticed, and we've been reading in the paper that Tanner *believes* or at least claims he's a vampire—of sorts. What did your sister say to make you believe it's not just a madman talking?"

"The guy starts to smoke—his skin, not a cigarette—when he's exposed to certain wavelengths of light. You looked in the lab where they kept him, I'm assuming. Didn't you notice the lights were different? Lynette said that was to keep him under control. And, according to what I was able to scrape together, Tanner broke out when the electricity failed and the lights went out. And, he *broke* out, physically. The guy's too strong for someone his size and weight for it to just be good muscle tone. And he heals almost instantly. Lynette said they cut his skin on purpose, then watched it heal right back within seconds. That isn't natural."

"Or believable, Charles. I know Lynette was honest and trustworthy, but where's the proof?" Diane insisted, knowing already about the camcorders and visual records.

"She told me they were forbidden to take any photos or record what they saw. Hell, they couldn't even bring a cell phone into the facility. Some of those have photo capability, and their boss—Victor Wayne, I guess—said it would compromise security." Charles leaned forward. "You don't have to believe it all, just accept that Tanner is extraordinary."

Diane and Lee exchanged glances. Either Lynette didn't know about the camcorders or, more likely, she'd lied to Charles about this important detail.

"Can Tanner see in the dark? Turn into a bat?" Lee asked.

"You really asking, or are you trying to bullshit me, Hawk? I don't know the answer to those questions. The bat thing, I seriously doubt. Can you imagine a two-hundred-pound bat? But the ability to see in the dark, who knows? Lynette didn't say anything, but maybe Tanner was able to hide that from them. Come to think of it, he did escape when the lights were out, didn't he?"

Lee shrugged. "There was emergency lighting in the lab—battery-powered, of course. He wouldn't need to have infrared vision to find his way out." Lee didn't recall seeing any such lighting, but Charles had no reason to lie to them about what Lynette had told him. Apparently the researchers, and maybe Victor Wayne, didn't know vampires could see in the dark.

"Okay. You've encountered the man and I haven't—yet. But understand something. When I finally catch up to Tanner, I'm going to shoot him, stab him, impale him, decapitate him, then burn the body up or toss it out into full sunlight. Whatever it takes to make the bastard disappear completely—for good. And don't try to stop me, either, or I'll be first in line to tell everyone about your little visit to Dr. Wayne's apartment."

Diane's eyes suddenly went cold. "I don't flinch from threats—I make them. And, vampire or not, Stewart Tanner isn't getting out of this alive. We'll see to it. It's our job—our responsibility. Just don't get in our way or you'll end up in jail. If that happens you'll be no use to anyone, and we could use your extra set of eyes. You have my cell number. If you see Tanner, or think you know where he is, call. You can't take him alone."

Diane took a sip of water, pushed her plate away, then looked over at Lee. "You think we should see what's on that hard drive of Victor's?"

"That's what you've got in the case, isn't it?" Lee said to Charles.

He nodded. "Let's do this in private, okay? I thought I was being followed earlier, so I don't want to risk anyone looking over my shoulder. Hacking is a very private pastime."

Charles went with them, leaving his SUV in the parking lot, and they checked into a motel room a few miles away. Charles got to work immediately, and using extra connectors that allowed him to access the copied hard drive, he was soon going through virtually every one of Dr. Wayne's files. Now that he had the passwords, no document was safe from their scrutiny. Unfortunately, there wasn't much more to be learned, and even Wayne's address book wasn't any help. There were no names, only initials, and the only ones they recognized were for the dead researchers.

Finally Diane, who'd been watching Charles work from a chair beside him, stood and stretched. "We've got to get going, Charles. I need to touch base with the teams out searching, then discuss our coverage for tonight. Keep reading the files, if you want, but don't get caught with that hard drive. It could put you in jail for twenty years."

Charles nodded. "Don't worry. I've got a program that's supposed to wipe the hard drive, then write over every byte with ones and zeros—makes it virtually unrecoverable even by the CIA. Once I run that, I'll melt the thing with a propane torch just to make sure."

"Stay in touch," Lee said.

Charles stood, then nodded to both of them. "I know we're not a team, but we're working in tandem on this now, so if I can help in any way, give me a call."

Diane gave Charles a hug. "We don't know who Tanner will be attacking next, so stay safe."

"You too."

Once outside Lee looked around carefully to confirm there were no obvious surveillance people, then he and Diane walked to the unit. The moment they were in the car he brought out the sunblock from his pocket and began applying the lotion freely to his neck and hands.

"You okay?" Diane said as she slipped into the passenger's side.

"Yeah. It's been a while since I touched up, and I could feel the heat as soon as I left the room. Times like this I'm glad I'm not Tanner. Though I *could* use a tall mug of pig's blood."

"We just ate a ton of food, didn't that help?"

"Yeah. Blood is more of a craving than a need." He started the car, then pulled out into traffic. "We're going to touch bases with the local honchos, right? See if they've found that gold Toyota?"

Diane nodded. "We also need to find out if anyone's got a lead on properties Marci Walker owns—anything that might work as a hideaway. If that doesn't pan out we'll check the homes of her old classmates or friends."

The drive through Farmington, with side streets dotted with fast food restaurants, mini malls, and the occasional old home remodeled into a small business, was uneventful. The mid-afternoon traffic was heavy, especially in the downtown area, which held many businesses in brick buildings that dated from the thirties and forties.

They automatically took closer looks at small gold cars and pickups of the right make and color, especially those with camper shells. Since half the vehicles on the road seemed to be big pickups, and there were quite a few metallic-colored compact cars as well, Lee and Diane were kept busy.

Diane used her cell phone again, and when she hung up, she sounded discouraged. "All of Marci's known properties have been checked out—at least those with structures on them. There are a few empty lots, and a rural property east of the city. It's an old orchard, part of a farm that had been broken up and sold to developers, according to the clerk working for FPD."

"Might be a good place to park and stay out of sight. Any officers headed in that direction?"

"No, wanna take a look?"

Lee shook his head. "How about having a county deputy drive by? If they see a vehicle, or even a tent or shelter, word can be passed along to us. I have a hunch that the vampire and his girlfriend are still within the city. All the main roads are covered, and I've seen the agency helicopters checking the open areas and along the rivers."

Diane nodded, and made the call. Lee, meanwhile, got on the radio and contacted Detectives Shannon and Esterbrook, who'd been working the Walker residence where they'd left Victor Wayne.

When Diane ended her call, Lee spoke. "Victor and his man left the Walker house about a half hour ago. According to Detective Shannon, Victor made a point of saying they hadn't found anything useful in the Walker home office or computer that might help track down Tanner's location, and he shrugged off the news of Tanner's afternoon attack on us in the parking garage."

"Dr. Wayne doesn't care about our safety. As a matter of fact, he's probably hoping Tanner finishes us off. We know too much, and we're in his way."

Lee nodded. "You're right. And apparently Victor made a show of leaving casually and unconcerned. But Esterbrook, who'd been outside, said Wayne and the federal marshal hauled ass once they were halfway down the block."

"So Victor must have found something on the computer. Any hint about where he was headed?"

"The good doctor said they were going to grab a meal, then pick up some extra help flying in from Colorado." Lee looked at his watch. "Detective Shannon checked. The next flight coming in from Colorado—Grand Junction, I think—is within the hour."

"We can switch cars, stake out Victor, then see where he heads once his reinforcements arrive."

"My thoughts exactly. But what did he discover on that computer?" Lee asked.

"I've got an idea. Let me talk to Detective Shannon again." Diane started dialing.

Twenty minutes later, sitting beside the road in a recent model pickup they'd borrowed from a local state patrolman Lee knew,

Diane got a call. From the expression on her face, Lee could tell it was good news.

Diane confirmed it immediately when she ended the phone conversation. "The detective went to the computer Victor was accessing, checked in the documents recently accessed, and got us what we need, or at least what Victor saw that got him motivated. The Walkers owned, until recently, a steak house out on East Main. Marci sold the place after her husband died. According to the detective, the place has been shut down, pending some remodeling. He gave me the address."

"You know, there's a good chance that the Walkers kept a key to the place. Even if they have to break in, Marci knows it's unoccupied and off the radar now. There's a good chance they might have decided to rendezvous there."

"So, do we go and look, or do we stick around and see what Victor has in mind?" Diane asked. "I doubt he's going to check on his own place to make sure we didn't steal anything. Catching Tanner alive is his big concern, especially if he can do it with us not around."

"Then let's get Shannon and Esterbrook involved in this. They can watch Victor and his people and we can check out the restaurant. If we can beat Victor to the target, even better. He really got in the way at the Walker home."

"If Tanner and Marci are there they'll be keeping a close watch. Although Tanner has healed back up by now, my guess is that they're going to be paranoid," Diane said. "And their vehicles are going to be well out of sight."

"If we expect to get close, undetected, we'll need to change the way we look."

"Good idea. Tanner already knows about us—a Navajo man and a Chicana. So we need to become someone else. How about if we get a child or two?"

Lee's eyebrows rose, then he realized Diane was looking at

two mannequins in the window of a clothing store. "Sounds like a plan."

You're too pretty to be a guy." Lee glanced over at Diane, who'd removed all trace of makeup, had her hair stuffed up into a cap, and was wearing a glued-on mustache.

"How do men cope? This mustache itches. Hopefully no one will get close. If they do, they'll know in a flash it comes from a Halloween makeup kit."

Lee reached back and adjusted his long ponytail. "Hey, bro. Maybe we better watch this masculine identity talk in front of the kids."

Behind them in the jump seats of the pickup were two well-behaved dummies of grade-school-aged children. They were realistically painted, articulated, and fully dressed. The talented shop owner had placed them in very natural poses—the girl dummy had on headphones, and the boy seemed to be playing a handheld game.

"I hope this isn't a waste of time." Lee adjusted the bandanna he wore. "And I hope no Indians see me. I look like a Hollywood stereotype."

"Maybe you should have kept the cowboy hat."

"Too small. One of these days, they'll come up with an adjustable model, like that baseball cap of yours."

"Okay, time to look casual, like we're talking about trucks, sports, and our ole ladies. I can see the restaurant up ahead, on the left," Diane said.

As they drove by the two-story building—a brick structure that probably had been a shop at one time—Lee noticed a sign on the front entrance that read "Reopening Soon Under New Owner," but though he could see chairs on tables beyond the café curtains, no one was visible inside. There was a small parking lot in front, but only a big trash bin occupied any space, and it didn't appear to have anything inside it. Apparently, no remodeling had taken place as yet.

"Let's try the alley. I saw a sign about more customer parking in the rear," Lee said. As they circled the block and neared the entrance to the alley, they could see a parking lot used by several businesses, judging by the number of cars there.

Diane kept going, and they were able to view the building from the rear across the parking lot. No suspicious vehicles were in the alley beside the former restaurant, but Lee, able to see into shadows and darkened rooms, spotted someone standing by an upper window.

"There's a woman in there, or else a man with long hair."

"Good! But there's no truck, gold Toyota, motorcycle, or anything," Diane said.

"They may have hidden both vehicles inside a garage close by. Ditching the car would be easier, so let's see if there's any building around tall enough to accommodate a pickup with camper."

Diane circled the block completely, but to avoid being seen passing by again so soon, she went around an adjacent block and came up from another direction. "Look—ahead on the left. Sam's Auto Clinic. They've got an oversized garage beside the main building. Big enough to hide both vehicles and then some."

As they passed by, Lee noticed that the building was a former gas station that had gone out of business. The separate garage was a large, ugly, corrugated metal building with two enormous doors.

"You wanna check it out now, or come back if we don't find anything else?" Diane asked.

"Let's circle the adjacent blocks, just in case they decided to pass up the obvious solution. From what we've seen already, I'd be surprised to find more oversized garages, but we don't want to make a move on the wrong place. If that was Marci Walker watching and she sees us creeping around the neighborhood, she and Tanner could be out of there in a hurry and we'd never see them go."

"Maybe I should keep an eye on the woman while you check out the neighborhood," Diane suggested.

"Tanner's too damned dangerous for you to risk a confrontation alone, Diane, even in the sunlight, and he's still got the pistol."

"Tanner won't be able to sneak up on me across an open area. If I find a spot where I can watch the back of the restaurant with a pair of binoculars, at least I'll know if Marci tries to leave. We can't risk losing them if there's a chance we've actually found out where they've holed up. And Dr. Wayne and his people might be coming straight from the airport. It isn't that far from here, either."

Lee thought about it for a moment, then nodded. "Okay. Let's find a spot to drop you off, but stay in touch via cell phone. Avoid the radio network because Victor could be listening in."

Diane pulled up against the curb one block south of the restaurant, took the binoculars Lee handed her from beneath the seat, and got out on the driver's side. "Be careful," Lee said, sliding over to take the wheel.

"Where are you going once you check out the neighborhood?" she asked, looking toward the restaurant.

"I'll park out of sight of the store—over there." He pointed to a spot two buildings west of Sam's Auto Clinic. "You can keep watch or join me then, whatever we decide."

She nodded, so he drove off, circling to the left now, to check the area west of the restaurant. Setting his cell phone on the seat beside him, he operated the vehicle automatically, having spent so much of his ninety-year lifetime on the road, patrolling New Mexico highways.

A few blocks away from Main Street, homes and apartments stood adjacent to businesses, like laundries and convenience stores. What he missed most these days were the mom-and-pop groceries that had been a fixture during his early years. The small stores had once been on nearly every major street in Farmington back in the fifties, but now, after having been slowly driven out of business by the big chains, were only found in the smallest of communities.

There were few multistory buildings in this area except for the apartments. He swung the pickup back to the east, taking a quick look behind him to verify that the dummies hadn't tipped to the side despite their seat belts. Having children in the vehicle, even those made of plastic, felt odd. Lee hadn't been around children since he'd been a kid back on the Reservation, and he didn't have any idea what it was like being a father. Of course, being sterile, it wasn't something he'd thought about since his wife had died.

Vampires had notoriously good memories, and his late wife Annie's image was still vividly implanted in his mind. The memory was bittersweet—along with the good, it served as a constant reminder of what a moment's carelessness could do to the ones he loved. As if on cue, the cell phone sounded. It was Diane.

"Lee, the woman in the window hasn't moved at all. I think she's related to our children."

"A mannequin? That's just too coincidental."

"Not when you notice that the store next to the restaurant is a boutique. I remember seeing women mannequins in the window."

"So either we've been misdirected, or it's just plain bad luck. Why don't we check out Sam's Auto?"

"Where are you now?"

"Two blocks to the northeast," Lee answered. "I'll keep circling and come down the street from the north. Just stay where you are."

"Okay."

Lee remained observant, not wanting to miss a single clue. He passed an auto paint shop with a large bay door, but it was open and he could see a panel truck, masked and ready for painting. Wrong make and model for their quarry.

He was half a block away when the cell phone rang again.

"The dummy moved. She may have spotted me," Diane said breathlessly.

Lee looked ahead, but Diane wasn't where he'd left her. "Where are you?"

"I'm beside the west wall of the building south of the alley, behind a tree. I'm watching the back door of the restaurant."

"Stay where you . . ."

"There she goes, Lee. It's Marci, and she's running east down the alley. I'm going after her."

"Watch out for an ambush. I'm south of your location. I'll head east at the next street and parallel you." Lee's heart was pumping overtime now. He didn't know if Marci was a diversion, leading them away from Tanner inside the restaurant, or racing to get their escape vehicle. "Diane, stop where you are now, and keep an eye on the back of that restaurant. She might be trying to lead us *away* from Tanner. I can catch Marci a lot faster, and then go back as soon as I have her. Tanner won't be coming outside in the full sun."

He stepped on the gas, screeched around the corner, then pulled up beside the curb. Sam's Auto was just two buildings down, across the street, and the big garage was right in front of him. Someone was crossing the gap between buildings, running down the alley, east.

Lee sprinted across the street toward the big metal building. "Diane, I'm heading toward Sam's garage. I didn't see any side doors, but there may be an exit in the back. Can you see it from where you are?"

There was a pause of about five seconds. "Yes, Marci just went in through a small door. Need backup?"

"Not yet. Can you move closer to the restaurant? If Tanner is still inside, he might find a way to cover himself with a tarp or something and run out the front."

"Right. I'll check the main entrance, then come around back again. You know, we could use a third set of eyes."

"You don't suppose we got lucky and Charles followed us again?" Lee had slowed his approach to the garage, wanting to make sure that Marci didn't come out the front if he went to check the back.

"I'll give him a call."

Lee hung up, then put the device on vibrate and fastened it to his belt. He brought out his pistol and stopped in the gravel driveway, watching the front of the faded green, corrugated metal structure. Closer now, he could see that the chain in front was threaded through two large eye bolts, but not padlocked. That was all there was holding the doors shut at the moment. The gap between the two doors was less than an inch at most, and he couldn't see more than a few feet inside. Lee noticed the glint of glass, or chrome, but he couldn't be sure without getting closer.

He walked over to the left side, but couldn't see anyone, so he crossed back to the right. Still alone, Lee stood in front of the doors and listened. Faint footsteps crunched in the gravel inside the garage. No surprise, he already knew Marci was there. Lee holstered his pistol and stepped to the left, wanting to make sure she couldn't peek out between the doors and see him.

A car door slammed inside the garage, and the engine started up with a roar. Uncertain whether to run to the side or step back, Lee hesitated a second too long. The doors burst open and a large pickup with two people inside sent sheet metal and wood flying in all directions, catching Lee in the right shoulder as he dove to the left.

The impact knocked him sideways even more. He ducked his left shoulder and head, rolling over and coming to his feet, but the momentum propelled him farther, into a forced run he couldn't control for another ten feet. Finally, Lee managed to come to a stop and turn around.

The pickup, camper shell atop, was roaring up the street, heading east. The sound of another racing vehicle, coming up from the west, made Lee spin around.

Reinforcements. Charles Alderete, in his SUV, roared past Lee at high speed. The man looked in his direction a split second, but didn't slow down. He continued in pursuit of Tanner.

"Wait for us!" Diane yelled from behind the garage, running up from the north side. She stopped beside Lee, and they watched Charles skid around the corner in hot pursuit of the pickup.

"Crap!" Diane exclaimed. "We figured Tanner was in the restaurant, not the garage. All we would have needed was a few more minutes and we might have had them both."

Lee felt moisture on his shoulder, which, he realized, was also warming up. He looked down and saw his jacket had been torn open, revealing a jagged cut oozing blood. It was starting to steam.

"Get inside!" Diane grabbed his other arm and pulled him toward the open garage.

Lee cooperated. In a few more seconds the skin would have begun to burn. Sunblock didn't work where flesh was exposed like that. Now, in the shade, the burning sensation stopped. "I'll be okay in a few minutes. Get somebody besides Charles onto Tanner's trail." He turned and noticed the gold Toyota Corolla in the back of the big garage. Beside it was a motorcycle, an old Harley atop a canvas drop cloth. An open box of mechanic's tools was sitting within reach of the Harley, and Lee saw a blue and white plastic cooler on the ground against the wall. A Coors beer bottle was atop it, open and half empty. That was a bad sign. Nobody he knew left beer behind.

Diane already had her cell out, but while she spoke she didn't take her eyes off Lee. Soon, the bleeding stopped and his wound began to close. He reached into his pocket, found his plastic bottle of sunblock, and started to apply it to the new skin.

"I'll get the pickup," she said. "Keys?"

"In my left jacket pocket."

She reached in, feeling around, her hand shaking slightly. "Quit almost getting killed, Lee. That scares the hell out of me."

"I apologize. Don't want you to get upset."

"Don't patronize me, you jerk!" She located the keys, jabbed him in the ribs, then ran off to retrieve the truck.

Lee walked over to take a closer look at the Toyota and the rear of the garage, an uneasy feeling in the pit of his stomach that had remained since spotting the unfinished beer. Inside the Toyota, sprawled across the backseat, was a big black man in jeans and a bloody T-shirt. He'd been stabbed in the chest and, from the angle of his head, had his neck broken before being stuffed into the little car. A medical examiner would be able to tell what had killed the guy, but there was no doubt *who'd* killed him. Lee made the call while waiting for Diane.

CHAPTER 16

Where *was* Charles?" Lee asked as he drove east. They'd just received a radio call from FPD Dispatch reporting Charles's vehicle in pursuit of Tanner's, racing through a nearby neighborhood.

Diane—who'd unhooked the mannequins and placed them on the floorboards in back, their usefulness ended—had insisted Lee drive so she could use the cell phone and radio more effectively. The emotion she'd shown earlier had quickly been replaced by the coolness she always reserved for crisis situations. "Charles said he lost us earlier on East Main, so he was circling, trying to track us down. I gave him our location."

"He could get killed, chasing them like that. The body count is continuing to rise. Tanner has nothing to lose."

"I'm not so sure, not with Marci in the truck with him. He might have a death wish, but I doubt he'd want to take his childhood sweetheart with him. She was probably around when he killed the Harley owner, but notice, Lee, how he left her out of the parking garage ambush."

He nodded. "The chilling life of a vampire . . . and the woman who loves him. Do you remember an old TV soap opera called *Dark Shadows*?" Lee said with a wry smile.

"I was a little kid then, but, sure, I sneaked a few shows when my mom wasn't around. It came on after school. I'm surprised to hear you ever watched soap operas, Lee."

"Not macho enough? Hey, a vampire, even a half vampire, doesn't normally have much to do during the daytime. It was a slow, difficult time for me. Annie had died, I'd tracked down and killed the skinwalkers who'd done it, then I was forced to change my identity again and go into hiding. TV gave me an escape mechanism for several years. I even followed a game show or two."

Diane sat there awhile, quiet, but searching, as he was, for any indication where Charles or Tanner may have gone. After a while, she looked over. "You kid around so you won't have to take your life too seriously, don't you?"

"Yeah, being a cop, *you* do a lot of that too," he said. "We get to see the worst of human nature on a daily basis. It'll eat you up inside if you don't find a way to let off steam. We need humor just to get by."

"One day at a time, partner. And right now we have to find Tanner and his lady friend *before* they kill someone else—which might be Charles, if he doesn't have an accident first."

Diane's cell phone rang. "Charles? Oh, Victor." She turned to look at Lee.

"Yes, we were converging on that garage a short time ago and almost got run down when Tanner and the woman crashed through the doors in that pickup. They killed another civilian, but you've probably heard about that already. We're trying to find Tanner now before they ditch the truck."

Lee knew they'd been correct about Victor Wayne. He'd been forced to wait for his reinforcements before going to the old Walker restaurant and they'd beaten him to the punch. If they'd all been able to work together Tanner might be out of circulation by now. Lee listened to Diane, who told Victor which area they were searching, but nothing else, and she didn't mention Charles Alderete at all. After another minute, she ended the call.

"I got the gist of the conversation. You think Dr. Wayne and his people will search the same area?"

Diane shrugged. "He was vague about that. He's kinda pissed right now. Probably angry that something hinky went down at the apartment complex where he's staying, *and* that we didn't tell him we knew about the restaurant. But, hey, he didn't tell us *he* knew."

Lee nodded. "You need to keep trying to reach Charles," he said, and saw her dialing. "Is it ringing?"

Diane nodded. "Yeah, but I can't get him to answer."

"He's not used to high-speed pursuit, and he may not want to risk taking his eyes off the road. Or the phone may be out of his reach—like it slid across the seat in a sharp turn. Just keep trying."

Lee stayed in touch with the other agencies via radio. Local officers had lost track of Tanner and Charles, but were able to tell him what direction they'd been headed. He picked up the pace.

Several minutes went by, then Diane cursed and put away her cell phone. "Just got through. Charles lost him, Lee. Tanner apparently turned onto a side road during a few moments when Charles had to slow for traffic. He's circling around, trying to pick up the trail again."

Lee drove to the area she mentioned to help in the search. After fifteen minutes of driving up and down paved and graveled roads in the newly developed upper-middle-class residential area, checking down alleys and scrutinizing pickups with camper shells, Diane finally motioned for Lee to pull over.

"Let's get some local officers to continue working the area. I'm going to set up a meet with Charles," Diane said.

After removing their disguises and switching back to an unmarked Bureau sedan—minus the mannequins now—they found Charles parked at a gas station, checking under the hood of his rented SUV while refueling. When he saw them pull up, he looked over, shaking his head. "I thought I could get close enough to do something, but he was able to maintain at least a quarter-mile lead. I had some hairy moments running stoplights and stuff, and finally lost him. If I'd have had your car instead of this top-heavy monster, I could have had a shot. Now, if we'd been out in the sticks . . ."

"Charles, you lost him. Leave it at that." Diane got out of the car and walked around to the front of Charles's big vehicle. Lee exited as well and stood in the shade of the pump island, a few steps from their car.

"I should have stayed on your tail like I did at the beginning. If I hadn't lost track of you guys earlier, I'd have been there to back you up when you found Tanner and that woman. Who is she, anyway?"

Diane ignored the question.

Charles looked over at Lee for an answer.

"Elvira?" Lee offered, straight-faced.

Diane barely avoided a chuckle while Lee strolled casually toward Charles's open driver's side window.

"Our first priority is getting Tanner, and we appreciate what you've done so far. But you're going to get killed if you keep it up. Go home, Charles," Diane said quietly.

"You know I can't do that."

"Yeah, I know," Diane replied with a sigh. Lee walked back toward their car, and nodded that it was time to leave.

"Where you going now?" Charles called out.

"We've got two killers to track down," Diane said. She climbed into the car, Lee started the engine, and they drove away.

A half mile down the road, Diane turned to Lee. "You grabbed his keys, right?"

"Not permanently. I put them in his ashtray," Lee said. He slowed, then made a right turn. At the next block, he turned right again.

"Were you making sure we'd be able to ditch him?"

"Not exactly. I want to turn the tables and follow *him* for a while."

"Why?"

"I think he knows where Tanner went. You notice that thing he does when he's lying? With his eyes?"

"Yeah," Diane replied. "You're right. But if he knows where Tanner is, why didn't he just move in and try to take him out before dark? Or have us do it for him?"

"I believe Charles will let us know what he's got planned—eventually. My guess is that he wants to see Victor get a little justice of his own too, and he's waiting things out. But we need to make him think he's free to set it all up. We'll follow, but as far back as possible. Get those binoculars, the gas station is just around the corner. I hope he hasn't found the keys already."

Lee stopped as soon as he saw Charles's rented sport utility vehicle, still beside the pump. The man was at the pay window.

"Maybe he didn't find the keys yet," Diane said.

They watched as Charles walked nonchalantly back to the SUV, took a cursory look around, then climbed inside. A second later he drove off.

They waited until Charles pulled out into traffic before coming up to the intersection. A light changed to their left, and oncoming vehicles kept them from coming out immediately, but fortunately Charles was still in sight when they got out into the flow again.

Diane lowered the binoculars for a moment as the road got bumpy near an intersection. "He's using his cell phone. Wonder who he's calling?"

"Well, he still has two hours and"—Lee checked his watch—"twenty minutes, approximately, until sundown. So assuming he knows where Tanner is, he's going to have to make a move soon if he wants sunshine on the side of the good guys."

"I'm going to get some FPD officers involved. We don't want to lose Charles now. Any suggestions?"

Lee nodded. "Shannon and Esterbrook. They've been working on this from the moment Tanner hit town. Just make sure they don't tip off Victor and his crew."

Diane nodded and flipped open her cell phone as Lee slowed for a four-way stop. They still had Charles well in sight, so Lee wasn't worried.

As Lee stopped, being the first vehicle at the intersection, he checked both ways. A yellow car was coming up from the right, but Lee could see the sporty Camaro starting to slow. Lee drove forward, but suddenly the Camaro accelerated, the driver honked, and the vehicle raced into the intersection.

"Shit." Lee slammed on the brakes, but it was too late. They slid and clipped the left rear fender of the Camaro as it shot by.

"What the hell?" Diane looked up, startled by the jolt.

The driver of the Camaro jumped out, along with three equally oversized companions. It took a few seconds because the vehicle was a two-door, but from the team jackets it was obvious the group was comprised of local high school athletes, either football players or wrestlers.

"You hit my car, asswipe!" the red-haired driver yelled from behind an equally flushed face. "You better be fucking insured!"

Lee took his eyes off the approaching teens. Charles's car was turning down a side street. In another few seconds, they'd lose sight of him.

"Screw it, Lee, we gotta stick with Charles," Diane said. She reached over and hit the emergency lights for just a second.

"Crap, Louie! He's a cop!" one of the teens yelled. The young men stopped in their tracks.

Lee hit the gas, whipping through the intersection. He raced to the next block, turned sharply, and stared down the empty road. "Where'd he go?"

They hurried to the next intersection and Lee slowed again. He looked left, and Diane to the right. "Not this way," she yelled, then reached down and punched out a number on her cell phone, quickly reporting the accident and location while Lee continued to search.

"Not this way either. He might be circling, or maybe he spotted us when we hit the Camaro." Lee decided to take the turn to the left, but after another block without finding Charles's sport utility vehicle, he knew they'd lost him.

Still searching as he drove, Lee looked over at Diane. "Sorry. If those kids hadn't decided to run the stop sign at the last second . . . shall we put out a bulletin on Charles?"

"Yeah." She made the call while Lee continued to cruise up and down the neighborhood. After ten minutes they arrived at a busy artery and entered traffic.

"Where we headed?" Diane watched his eyes.

"I'm thinking our best bet is to find Victor Wayne and stick with him. We've got patrols all over the city and sooner or later one of them will spot Charles, if he's sticking to the streets," Lee said.

"Okay. And we did notice Charles was calling someone on his phone. Who else do we know he's been in contact with around here besides us?"

"FPD and Victor Wayne." Lee smiled. "You may be right, lady. Maybe Victor will lead us to Charles, who'll lead us to Tanner and his woman."

"Any idea where Victor is now?"

"His apartment to see if we broke in? We're going in that general direction now."

"Yeah, and Charles knows where it is too."

Dr. Wayne and Charles were standing in the shade beneath the roof of the parking garage across from the fancy apartments, just outside the yellow crime tape still up from the previous incident. Lee and Diane had stopped a block away, around the corner, just close enough to watch the meeting without being noticed.

Diane had the binoculars, and despite the shade, Lee could see inside the covered space where four of Victor's men stood beside his white SUV.

"What do you suppose Charles is telling Victor?" Diane whispered.

"Well, if he knows exactly where Tanner and Mrs. Walker are hiding, he's not going to give out that information right now. Once Victor knew that, he wouldn't need Charles. He'd probably hand him over to FPD."

"Or bring him along to make sure there are no tricks," Diane said. Victor had motioned with his head toward his crew, and two of them, and Charles, were getting into the white SUV.

Victor and the other man walked to a second vehicle, a rental van, and climbed inside. The SUV drove out into the street, heading north. The van followed immediately.

"Here we go," Lee said, following at a safe distance. "If they're going to check out Charles's information, they'd better not take too much longer. Another hour and the sun will be setting."

"Let's go fishing for information, Lee. I'm going to call Victor and suggest a meeting for, say, within a half hour. If he makes excuses, it'll be a good way of confirming he doesn't want us around, which will, in its own way, confirm what he has in mind."

"Surprisingly, I think I understand what you just said," Lee said, then grinned.

Diane smiled back and punched out Victor's cell number. "Hi, Victor. This is Agent Lopez—Diane. We need to meet and talk strategy. Thirty minutes, at a coffee shop?"

She stuck out her tongue and made a face.

"Oh, okay. As soon as you finish up there, give me a call and we'll set up something. We need to know where to target our search once the sun goes down."

She ended the call, still watching Victor's van moving through traffic two blocks ahead. "Lying bastard said he was still working the scene at Sam's Auto Clinic."

"At least we can confirm he doesn't want us to know where he's going. And that's a good sign."

"So what's the plan when we finally get to wherever Charles is leading them?"

"Make sure they don't take Tanner alive. At least that's *my* plan." Lee reached down and tapped his hand on the butt of his pistol.

Within ten minutes they reached a bluff looking down upon a box canyon lined with recently paved roads and a few new, up-scale houses under construction. At the far end of the development, across the small valley and on the highest location, almost level with them, two rows of new homes were already completed. From the landscaping and the presence of cars in driveways, most of these houses were occupied.

Lee pulled over to the side of the road. They could watch the two vehicles below, winding around the development at slow speed, without revealing their own location. And because the entire development had only one access road that came past their current location, he knew they couldn't lose their quarry unless everyone took off on foot.

A quarter mile away, in a fenced compound, were several pieces of road equipment, including dump trucks, a road grader, and other vehicles. Several private vehicles were parked in the same general area, including a pickup with camper shell that looked very familiar.

"Check out the vehicle park," Diane said, the binoculars to her eyes again.

"That Tanner's truck?"

"Damaged front end, green paint and all," Diane said.

Lee located the SUV and van again. They were parked side by side at the end of a circular drive that ended in front of the foundation of a future home. No other vehicles were around—it was six o'clock in the afternoon and the workers had already left for the day.

Nobody got out of their vehicles, which suggested they were either planning or just watching. No buildings were close by, and there was little cover if they intended on sneaking up on anyone before dark.

"Do you suppose Tanner and the woman are still in that pickup?" Diane asked.

"Maybe. Where else would they have gone? That vehicle park doesn't have any better options, except maybe that little site trailer—the one with the name of the construction company on it."

"If Marci scouted out this backup refuge while Tanner was making his move on us in the parking garage, then they had a reason for picking this particular location."

Lee looked at the fenced-in compound, then noticed a large drainage pond, mostly dried out from a lack of rain, that fed into a concrete-lined ditch. The ditch continued down the canyon and away from the development. Above the pond were several large culverts that fed runoff from drains at curb level at various road elevations of the circling route.

"Those culverts are big enough to crawl through," Lee pointed out. "Or for a shorty like you, maybe even walk, hunched over."

She ignored the tease and followed his gaze. "Only one of the feeder pipes passes close to a building that's already been completed. That green one with the sign on the patch of lawn two levels down." She reached for the binoculars.

"The one with the big car and realtor bumper sticker parked in the driveway? It's a model home."

She put down the binoculars. "The two of them could have used that culvert to get all the way up there without the presence of a stolen vehicle to give them away. Or sunlight. They might be in the model home."

"Which means the realtor who owns that car could be in deep trouble." Lee looked down at the vehicles that had brought

Victor Wayne and his crew. "If Charles reached this point and watched them go into the tunnel, he's thought of that too."

"If Tanner sees them coming, he'll know he's trapped," Diane pointed out. "But the ball game changes in a half hour or so." She looked toward the setting sun. "Once it's dark, Tanner'll probably be able to get away on foot. The way you have to circle around the road if you're in a car, he could just go on foot uphill and escape before they could reach the next level."

"So Victor has to act now if he has any brains. But we've already seen one example of his pathetic tactical skills. He could even get himself killed this time."

"They're going to do something, Lee." The two vehicles started moving again. The SUV went left, and the van to the right.

Lee started their vehicle. "We can't beat them to the model home, and if they try to assault the place before dark, the only exit for Tanner is via the car or down the culvert. We can go up that pipe and cut him off."

"What do you think I am, a sewer rat? I'm not crawling up that thing. It must be two hundred yards or more."

"You don't have to crawl, shorty. Just creep along all hunched over."

"You're kidding."

"Of course I am. You'll need to stay outside to keep watch for me. Once inside, I'll be blind to the rest of the world."

"Think your radio will work inside that metal cylinder?"

"Just yell, the pipe will contain and focus the sound. Or fire a shot outside it—or two."

They reached the fence within three minutes. From their low elevation they could only see one vehicle, the SUV circling around clockwise. The van, which was going around to the right, was on the inside lane and the angle was wrong to view it.

There was a gap in the chain-link fence at the gate where someone, probably Tanner, wearing that helmet and gloves, had twisted it around. They slipped through and ran toward the drainage pond and the culverts running uphill from there. The connecting culverts were held in position by concrete supports spaced evenly along their length, and the drainage pond was lined with big boulders, like the bottom of an enormous aquarium.

Lee looked at the openings. The culvert that led up to the road in front of the model home was missing the big wire grate the others had bolted in place. There were rips in the metal where Tanner had pried it loose, probably with a metal bar or fence post taken from the construction site.

"Flashlight?" Diane reached into her jacket pocket.

He frowned.

"Ooops. Sorry, hawk eye. May I offer you the shotgun?"

"Yes, of course. That way, with just one shot inside that tunnel I can completely eliminate all my hearing capacity," he answered sourly.

"Okay. You're right. If I yell 'Yes,' that means Tanner or the woman has entered the tunnel. If I yell 'No,' that means they've taken a vehicle or gone in another direction. You should be able to hear my voice all the way to the top."

"If not, hit the pipe with a rock one time for yes, two for no." Lee clambered up into the culvert, which was about three feet off the ground, then started up. The structural ribs were deep enough to give him footholds, though the slope was steep. "Wish me luck."

"Better than that. *Good* luck," Diane said, then stepped back, made sure she had a big rock handy, then pulled out her binoculars and looked around. The sun was still up, but at the bottom of the box canyon they were already in shadow.

Diane continued to step back until she could see the roof of the model house toward the top of the canyon. Just the rear of the white SUV was visible a short distance from the building. Then she saw the front of the van, farther down the street, past the house. The road was blocked on both sides now. Tanner, if he was inside, couldn't use the car to drive away. Then Diane heard a gunshot, then another.

Lee hurried up the big pipe, using his hands occasionally to give himself an extra push. He wasn't crawling, it was more of a low sprint accompanied by an occasional touch in order to maintain his balance. One of the advantages of being a half vampire was that you rarely got tired. He could have done this for hours, if necessary.

The darkness inside the culvert posed no visual problem for him, and the drainage system was so new it hadn't experienced enough rainfall yet to get rusty, slippery, or muddy. There was some dust, of course, this was New Mexico, but not nearly as much as expected. And there were no reptiles or rabbits, at least this far in—so far.

He heard what sounded like a gunshot, a distant booming, twice. But it came from above, not below, so all he could do was surmise that Dr. Wayne and his goons were making a move on Tanner. They'd wasted several minutes deciding what to do, and Lee wondered if Tanner would be able to hold out in the house until dark. After that, he'd be in charge, especially if he still had that pistol and enough ammunition.

The gunshots continued, getting louder, and as Lee approached the top end of the tunnel, he heard shouts.

"Where'd he go?" It was Victor's voice. "*Somebody* was shooting at us."

"He didn't get outside. I've gone completely around the building," a man with a deep voice yelled. "Is there a basement?"

"How the hell should I know?" Victor yelled back. "I'll keep watch on the outside, you and the others clear the rooms, one at a time. Try not to shoot Tanner in the head or the heart, but put him down quickly and don't let him get back up."

"There may be a hostage. They didn't drive this car here, according to Alderete."

"Well, don't kill any hostages if you can avoid it. But if you see Tanner, take the shot. He'll do the same to you."

"What about the woman with him, Marci Walker?"

"Take her out if she resists. Besides, we don't know what Tanner's done to her. She might be just like him now."

"What the *hell* are you talking about?"

"Just do it—now—before it gets dark."

Lee remained inside the culvert, watching from the shadows. Dr. Wayne was standing on the roof, holding a riot gun, and four men, heavily armed with assault rifles and shotguns and equipped with body armor, were against a side wall, discussing their assault plans.

Lee took out his cell phone and dialed. "Diane, Victor's people were fired upon, and Tanner and the woman are apparently inside the home. There's a hostage, but Victor's pretty much written her off already. Four of his men are about to assault the place. I'm at the top end of the culvert, so Tanner can't get past me. My bet is that he'll try to hold them off until the sun goes down. It can't be much longer."

"Want me to come up?"

"No. Block the road leading out of the development and use the shotgun. If Tanner gets to a vehicle he'll still have to come your way to get out."

"And if he holds out until dark?"

"All bets are off. Just get someplace where he can't sneak up on you. At least you'll have a chance."

"What are you going to do?"

"I'll help cover the outside for Victor, and keep watch. If Tanner makes a break for it, I'm the only one who can come close to keeping up with him in the dark. Just be careful."

"Yeah, you too."

Lee hung up, then watched as the four men split into two assault teams. One pair was obviously going to break in through the front, the other via the back. The realtor's red Caddy was in the driveway, parked within inches of the garage door. Victor, on the roof, would be watching for anyone coming out a window or door.

He hated the whole thing. He had to stop a killer and he'd do what he had to, but he couldn't help but sympathize with Tanner. They made his life hell, treating him like an animal, and now were hunting him down like one. Systematic torture had driven him insane and yet there was no one to side with him . . . to uphold his rights, if he was morally entitled to them after killing at least three completely innocent people. Lee thought about the judge and the lawyer for a second, wondering how innocent they really were. But the mechanic—he made the list no matter what.

Knowing that part was out of his hands now, he focused on the job at hand. One of the assault team had mentioned Charles. Was he still in the SUV? Lee couldn't check without poking his head out of the culvert, and with Victor up on the roof with the shotgun, it was dangerous to show up unannounced. Victor was obviously jumpy, and would likely shoot first.

All Lee could do was wait. Seconds passed, and Lee could hear an occasional shout, and the sound of a door being kicked open, but no gunshots. Then Lee heard a door closing loudly. Two or three more minutes went by, then there was a thump and a flurry of gunshots, shouts, and screams. After that, it was very quiet again—a bad sign.

Lee noticed that the sun had finally set.

Victor, who'd been pacing back and forth across the roof, waving the shotgun around, went anxiously over to the edge of the roof. "Hey!" he yelled. "Report. You got him, right?"

The front door burst open, and someone ran out in a panic, tripping over a railroad tie that was part of the landscaping. Victor fired, missing and kicking up the turf beside his target.

"No, no, don't shoot. It's me, Larry. Tanner got the others. Cover me," the tall federal marshal yelled, scrambling to his feet and grabbing a pistol from his holster. Lee could see blood on the man's arm and upper chest, but it might not have been his.

"Crap," Lee mumbled. He had to do something now before Tanner got away again. "Hey, I'm Officer Hawk. Over here by the pipe." Lee waved his left hand, praying they wouldn't shoot.

"Watch for Tanner. It's getting dark and he's already taken out three of my men!" Victor yelled, trying to spot where Lee was located.

"I'm coming out of the culvert. Don't let Tanner run uphill or get past you." Lee scrambled out onto the ground. The marshal was spinning around like a top, waving his pistol around in near panic. He wouldn't be much use.

"Hey, let me out! Hawk, I'm over here!"

Lee recognized Charles Alderete's voice. The man was inside the white SUV in the driver's seat, waving an arm and yanking at something. Victor must have handcuffed him to the steering wheel.

"God, Victor, you're a real piece of work," Lee yelled, waving at Charles to let him know he'd heard. "Where's Tanner's hostage?"

Suddenly there were gunshots, and chunks of the roof flew into the air around Victor's feet. He started yelling and jumping around like a barefoot kid on an anthill. Tanner was shooting through the ceiling at the sounds of his footsteps. It would have been funny in a movie.

But this was real life, and Lee realized he was running out of trained, dependable backup except for Diane, and she was probably hundreds of yards away right now. Instead of firing into the house, the federal marshal fled toward the van. Victor leaped off the roof into a fountain, dropping his shotgun when he hit the water.

Lee glanced over at Charles. The only way he could free him quickly was by breaking the steering wheel, and then Charles would know *he* was unnaturally strong. It would also take too long.

Hearing the sound of breaking glass around the back of the

house, Lee ran forward, using the house as cover. His phone started to vibrate. He reached for the device, keeping watch as he continued to slip along the side wall.

Water was splashing, and Lee turned for a split second to look. Victor Wayne was feeling around in the small pond for his weapon, all the time looking at the house instead of where he was putting his hands. The man was terrified.

"Yeah?" Lee knew it had to be Diane calling.

"I can see someone on the hillside, climbing up the rocks. It looks like two people, one pulling the other by hand, but it's hard keeping the image in this scope." She paused a moment, then added, "It's Tanner and a woman in a dress."

"Can you get a shot at Tanner?" Lee moved forward quickly now, reaching the base of the steep slope. He could hear footsteps above, and saw shapes, but was unable to determine who it was from the viewing angle.

Headlights came on from the van below on the road, aimed up the hill, followed by a spotlight. The federal agent who'd run to the vehicle wasn't totally useless after all. The spotlight, directed up the hillside, finally landed on Tanner and a woman in a red dress. "There he is," the agent yelled, trying to keep the two fleeing climbers in the beam. "Shoot him."

"Can't risk it. I'd probably hit the woman from this angle. What about you?" Lee asked Diane over the phone.

"The light helps, but they're moving pretty fast, and it's easily four hundred yards. It would be a luck shot, and I have an equal chance of hitting the woman."

"Then hold off. Marci Walker was wearing a pants suit. This might be the hostage."

"I'm going to circle around and try to cut them off when they reach the top of the canyon," Diane said.

"Okay," he said, then stuck the phone back onto his belt.

Lee continued running uphill, leaping from rock to rock and picking his way around the brush that remained on the slope. Tanner and the woman—he still couldn't tell *who* it was—disappeared from his view. They'd reached the top.

Lee pressed on even faster, knowing that he had to get them back in sight. At the same time, he tried to recall the layout of the community just ahead—the direction Tanner was going. With darkness upon them, the vampire had an immeasurable advantage. If he and the woman made it to the river valley to the south, they'd have the opportunity to elude the search teams.

Lee scrambled up the last few feet to the curb of a paved road, then stopped, keeping low in case Tanner suspected he was being followed closely.

Tanner and the woman in the dress were running toward an older home, a farmhouse, that lay some distance from the bluff beside a small apple orchard. In front of a two-car garage was a shiny blue van—a customized Dodge, with running lights, a covered spare tire, and chromed ladder on the back doors. Beside the van was a white flatbed Ford truck. Tanner was still pulling the woman along, but she wasn't making any attempt to resist. It was Marci Walker after all, and she'd switched clothes with the realtor.

Lee reached a pile of tumbleweeds that had collected against the fence on the opposite side of the road. Just then, Tanner stopped and turned, taking aim with the assault rifle he'd taken from one of the marshals. Lee ducked down and froze.

Tanner didn't fire. He looked right past Lee, sweeping the road and cliff side. In the distance, to Lee's left, was a set of headlights coming in their direction. Maybe it was Diane.

Marci, now out of Tanner's grip, had frozen in place, looking around in a panic like a deer caught in headlights. Then she started walking down the street. In a few seconds, she started to run.

Tanner turned and sprinted, vampire speed, quickly catching up with Marci and grabbing her roughly by the arm. He slapped her so hard across the face Lee could hear it even from this distance. Then Tanner pulled her toward the house, dragging her along as he trotted at an easy pace. Lee knew he could probably hit Tanner, but with the handgun a quick put-down would be unlikely, and that wasn't a percentage strategy against a full vampire, already better armed than himself.

Within seconds Tanner and his reluctant partner reached a wooden gate, part of a low picket fence that contained a front yard lawn and tall shade trees. Tanner grabbed Marci by the shoulders, said something Lee couldn't understand at that distance, then pushed her toward the van parked in the driveway.

Jumping the fence, Tanner ran up to the door and kicked it open. Lee heard the snap of splintering wood and several dogs— small breeds based upon the tone—started yapping.

Lee sprinted forward. Hopefully Tanner was after transportation, not victims, especially after shoving Marci toward the van.

Watching the open front door, Lee almost missed Tanner and a middle-aged man in a white undershirt and jeans coming around the back of the house. Tanner held the struggling man by the neck with one hand, pushing him along.

Unwilling to risk a shot now, Lee took cover, hitting the ground beside some kind of flowering shrub. Raising himself off the ground silently, he took aim, hoping that Tanner would give him an opening for a head shot.

Tanner hauled the man to the driver's side of the van, tossed the keys to Marci, who'd rolled down the window, then crossed around to the passenger's side with his hostage, out of Lee's field of view. A few seconds went by, then the passenger's side door slammed.

Lee decided to move forward just as the engine started. The vehicle lights went on, then the van raced backward, forcing Lee to dive aside to avoid being struck. He scrambled to his feet as the vehicle spun around, then raced to catch up before the van reached the end of the short driveway.

At the last second he leaped up, catching hold of the ladder on the back left door. The van hit a bump in the road just then, sending him flying up into the air. He managed to hang on with his left arm, but the violent motion knocked the Beretta out of his hand and onto the ground.

Lee managed to swing around and grab the ladder with his right hand so that he was facing the back of the van. Feeling around with his feet he managed to find the bottom rung of the ladder. He'd lost his pistol, but at least he was securely attached to the vehicle now.

Looking to his right over the spare tire, then left as they bumped along the graveled road leading to the street, Lee couldn't see either side mirror, and the small windows in the rear doors of the van had heavy curtains. If he was careful, nobody would know he was there.

Tires squealed, and Lee hung on grimly as the van made a hard left turn onto the paved street. As the ladder creaked, Lee thought for sure that the bolts holding it to the door were about to snap loose. But they held—for the moment.

Headlights from a vehicle behind them in the distance caught his attention and he cursed silently. All he needed now was to have his presence announced to Tanner and the woman. The hostage they'd taken would be the first to die, or the driver of the vehicle behind them.

The van slowed. Marci, who was probably driving, must have been told they'd gather too much attention speeding. Then he felt his phone vibrating. "If it's a telemarketer," he muttered, "I'll kill him."

Lee reached down slowly. Unless he was very careful, he'd lose the phone, just like his pistol. At least he had the smaller .45 backup in his pocket, and the dagger in his boot. The phone, unfortunately, would be irreplaceable.

He eased the small device from his pocket very slowly with his left hand after looping his right arm through a rung on the ladder. Praying Marci wasn't about to take another fast curve, Lee held the receiver to his ear.

"What in the hell are you doing? Couldn't you find a cab?" Diane was almost yelling, probably a good thing considering the road noise and the wind whipping past him.

"They've got a male hostage in the van. And Marci doesn't seem too happy with the way things are going. Tanner had to force her to go with him."

"Say again."

Lee repeated the message, as loud as he dared. "Keep traffic away, and give us plenty of room. If you lose me, call back and I'll let you know where we are."

"You hope. I'll do what I can to keep you safe. Just hang on."

"No kidding." The call ended and Lee slipped the phone into his inner jacket pocket. It was less likely to get lost or damaged there, and he'd be sure to feel the vibration of another call. That done, he grabbed hold with his left hand again and looked around at the various passing landmarks he recognized, trying to get an idea of where they were going.

Diane slowed and fell back, then signaled and turned. About ten seconds later, he saw lights again, coming from the direction she'd gone, and recognized their vehicle. It was a smart move—turning, doing a one-eighty, then coming back out again like you were another car. It would probably fool Marci, and hopefully Tanner, unless he was keeping constant watch behind instead of in front. Fortunately, Diane's vehicle was a very common, generic-looking government sedan.

The residential area ended and they turned onto a main artery. From the signs they passed he knew they were heading east toward Bloomfield, a former farming community now dominated by natural gas and oil well businesses and their support industries.

It was probably seven o'clock by now and, fortunately, there wasn't a lot of go-home traffic around to see him hugging the back of the Dodge. If Tanner knew he was out there he'd probably start shooting from the inside. Although the bullets wouldn't kill him unless Tanner destroyed his heart or scored multiple head wounds, falling off a moving vehicle at sixty miles an hour onto the pavement would probably break several important bones and knock him unconscious. Getting run over by the first vehicle to come along would likely finish him off. He'd be roadkill for sure.

Lee hugged the ladder, read the "I heart Yorkies" sticker beside his hand for the twentieth time, and tried to keep track of their route. At least Diane was back there somewhere and knew about his situation, and the additional lights on the rear of the van made it easy to spot.

Lee wondered where they were going, or if Tanner had a plan at all, especially since Marci Walker wasn't a willing accomplice anymore. If they tried to pass through Bloomfield someone was likely to notice him attached to the van, and with more than one traffic light along the journey, another driver would undoubtedly alert Tanner or Marci. Lee could hear the radio playing inside the van. The kidnappers had apparently picked a hostage who'd installed a great sound system. Either they liked country-western music, or Tanner was hoping to catch a news broadcast of recent events—perhaps noisy firefights in local neighborhoods.

Lee put his ear close to the metal door and listened. He could hear quite well, and as long as a sudden bump didn't cause him to whack the door with his head, he could make an emergency call to Diane if things went wrong and his voice would be masked by the sounds inside.

amn." Diane set down the cell phone and put both hands on the steering wheel. According to the deputy federal marshal still at the scene, the woman realtor in the model home had been decapitated. Two of the deputy marshals were also dead, and a third, badly wounded. That raised Tanner's score to at least eight killed today, and the night was young.

She'd asked about Charles, and was told he was alive and well, still double-handcuffed to the SUV's steering wheel when reinforcements arrived.

The van that Lee was clinging to for dear life had bright orange running lights along the back—loaded with options—and she had no trouble keeping it in sight. The driver was being careful not to attract attention by speeding. At the moment the vehicle was rolling down the highway toward Bloomfield, and she knew there was a major roadblock there manned by county deputies. If the van continued on that route, there was going to be a bloody confrontation for sure, right out in the open. She'd already called ahead, and officers were at the barricade.

A sign on the right announced Salmon Ruins. Beyond the museum and Native American ruins lay the lights of Bloomfield. Her heart thumping, Diane realized she needed to close the distance between her and the van and be in a position to react instantly if something went wrong. Reaching for her radio mike, she tried not to think about how vulnerable Lee would be once the shooting started.

Just then the driver of the van slowed, signaling to make a left turn. Diane racked the mike and cut her own speed. She'd have to follow without making it obvious. The van completed the turn and Diane continued on past the intersection for just a short distance, checking traffic. Hitting the brakes and swerving at the same time, she slid around, doing a one-eighty and hoping an on-coming pickup was paying attention.

The pickup screeched to a halt, the driver honking the horn as she slid to a stop, now facing the right direction. Accelerating quickly, she whipped to the right at the corner, entering the street where the van had gone.

"Thank God Lee ended up on a custom van," she whispered to the Almighty Himself, seeing the running lights of the vehicle farther down the street. The speed limit here was twenty-five, and the van was holding true. She reached for the mike and announced the van's location to the senior officer at the Bloomfield roadblock.

The change in direction, though it hadn't been abrupt, was a surprise to Lee. He knew there was a major roadblock in Bloomfield where Highway 64 and Highway 44 met—it had been there for days now.

He thought about the tactics he'd use if Tanner and the woman tried to run the barricade, and started to reach for the cell phone to call Diane when Marci suddenly made a left turn. The street they were going down now was strictly residential, with unremarkable but homey-looking pitched-roof, ranch-style houses, white picket fences, and the mandatory barking dogs. Nearly every driveway held a pickup or SUV, and sometimes both. These people weren't rich, but they were doing okay by New Mexico standards.

As a state policeman, Lee had traveled residential streets in Bloomfield before, but without a map he had no idea where they might be going. Looking around for street signs, he spotted Diane and was relieved to discover she'd managed to stick with them.

The van continued north for about a mile, Lee estimated, then turned back to the east. After another mile, they came to a stop. To his left, Lee could see a road, big enough to be Highway 44, which continued north to the county seat of Aztec. There was a streetlight, but fortunately no vehicles close enough to see him clinging to the back of the van. Then Lee looked down on the pavement. The shadow of the vehicle created by the streetlight showed the outline of the vehicle, and his shape on the back. He thought about flattening out a bit more, trying to blend with the bulge of the spare tire, but realized a moving shadow was even more informative than one that was still. He didn't move.

Then the music inside the van stopped. An announcer came on with a special news broadcast, and Lee put his ear against the door to listen. There were voices back and forth, but from what Lee could gather, Charles Alderete had spoken to a reporter at the scene of the model home shootings and was claiming that Dr. Wayne was a fed, responsible for Stewart Tanner's murder spree.

Alderete, according to the reporter, said his sister had been required, under Wayne's orders, to conduct painful medical experiments on Tanner, and this harsh treatment had led to his criminal insanity. Charles said that a rogue government project had gone wrong, leading to Tanner's escape and the murder of innocent people.

The sound had been turned up on the radio during the bulletin, and the quick story was repeated, along with the tag line "human guinea pig"—a quote from Charles himself. Marci started cursing, there was the sound of a slap, and Tanner yelled at her to shut up. A few seconds later, however, the music started up again. The radio was turned down, and this time Lee could hear Tanner curse softly, just once.

They peeled out, crossed the highway, then slowed and continued east on the residential street. Diane, who'd stopped at least a quarter mile back while they were sitting still at the intersection, began following them again. Lee knew if they continued on east they'd go through the small community of Blanco. After that, there was only a sparsely populated rural area.

Suddenly it became clear to him that they were headed for Navajo Lake. A turn back onto Highway 64 east of Blanco, then a left onto Highway 511 confirmed it. The air was getting cool, and not just because of the time of day. They were slowly climbing into the hilly country that lined the San Juan River, which was narrow and icy at this point.

Farther ahead, just below the dam, the river widened onto what the fishermen called "quality water" and no bait, only artificial lures, were allowed for angling. Lee had fished for catfish and trout before his affliction and still missed hiking along the riverbanks under the sun without fear.

Right now, Lee felt more like cold bait himself—Velveeta cheese on a treble hook in a swift current. Or a captive worm about to be grabbed by a hungry trout.

He could see junipers and piñon trees passing by, and the river canyon on his left was getting deeper and narrower. It had been a while since he'd been up here, but Lee knew the dam wasn't too much farther. He could see headlights in the distance behind them and assumed they were from Diane's car. There was only the main road up here, so good parallel routes were unavailable. But that fact also allowed Diane to keep her distance. She hadn't called, so Lee assumed she was still on their trail.

Marci Walker couldn't know for certain that deputies had already visited her cabin, but Tanner must have figured out that if the authorities knew about the old restaurant in Farmington Marci used to own they'd also know about the cabin up by the lake. So where were Tanner and Marci going? The thought occurred to Lee that maybe their hostage had a cabin.

The phone started vibrating, and Lee wondered if Diane was considering the same problem. It took him a second or two to answer the phone because that required getting a solid anchor with just one arm looped around a ladder rung. His feet were getting sore now from crouching astride the metal bars, not designed as permanent footrests, but the alternative was to dangle.

"Yeah?"

"You still playing Spider Man?" Her voice was clearer than he'd expected. Maybe there were cell phone towers up here because of the tourism.

"Why? You just hit a big bump on the road?"

"Funny. Listen, we've got two deputies watching the Walker cabin, but Detectives Shannon and Esterbrook have learned that the Walkers often visited friends on weekends at another cabin several miles from theirs, closer to the dam. This might be the place where they're heading."

"I guess we'll know when we get there. Did you hear what Charles told the reporter?"

"How'd you know about that?"

"Tanner heard it on the radio. So did I. This van has *good* speakers."

"I can't get an officer there ahead of you, but I'm calling for backup. It'll be just you and me for a while."

"I like the odds. Marci isn't armed, and I don't think she'll fight anyway. From what I can tell, she wants out, and will desert Tanner if she gets the chance. He's been slapping her around."

"Bastard. Their friend's cabin is about five miles farther, supposedly up a dirt road. Be ready for a bumpy ride."

"Okay. And give Tanner plenty of space. I'm going to make my move as soon as they begin exiting the van, so I want him to feel secure."

"Okay." There was a long silence. "See you soon."

Lee slipped the phone back into his pocket. Diane had wanted to say more, her voice had gone real soft at the end. She hadn't wanted emotions to distract him, but experience had taught him that emotions—fear, anger, and even love—could be a source of strength. Soon he'd be dealing with a full vampire, a creature stronger and faster than himself. He needed to let his love for Diane become a positive power within him.

The temperature had gone beyond cool to cold, and if they weren't going fifty miles an hour or more, Lee could have seen his breath. It felt like they were in the mountains already.

The dam was just to his right as they turned north, and he realized how big the structure was. It wasn't concrete, like the Hoover Dam, instead it was composed of rock, earth, and whatever else the engineers had packed together, but Navajo Dam never failed to impress him.

The road wound back and forth around curves as the route skirted hills in the canyon country, so Lee had to hang on tightly. They passed a recreation area, and beyond Lee could see a lighted marina extending out into the lake, surrounded by dozens of boats tied up alongside. The cabin they were headed for, if that was indeed their current destination, couldn't be much farther ahead. He reached down to confirm that his short-range .45 was still there, along with a single backup clip. He had twelve rounds and his double-edged commando knife.

Tanner was carrying an assault rifle with an unknown amount of ammunition, and probably the pistol. Lee knew he was outgunned and at a physical disadvantage, so when he made his move it would have to be quick and deadly. Surprise would be his best weapon.

Lee focused on trying to hear what was going on inside the van. He hadn't heard the male hostage during the entire trip. Was the man alive or dead, or did he just have the common sense not to ask questions when he didn't really want to know the answers?

Lee heard the radio being switched to different stations, then, after a moment, it went silent. They were slowing down. "It's just ahead," Marci Walker said clearly. "On the left."

Lee tried to look beyond the road to get an idea of the layout he'd have to confront. Piñon and juniper trees, with stands of ponderosa pines interspersed, covered the hilly area around this part of the lake. Chances were the cabin would be hidden from the highway. That had the dual advantage of hiding someone approaching as well, so Diane might be able to close in without being detected, at least to the turnoff.

The turn signal started blinking, and the van slowed, coming to a full stop in the road. Lee's throat went dry and he reached down with his right hand for his pistol.

There was a big whoosh of air and a sudden leap in the noise level as a vehicle passed by in the other lane. Lee flinched, almost losing his grip on the ladder. They were waiting for a pickup to pass before turning. He cursed softly, disgusted with himself for being so jumpy.

Turning, they left the highway with a bump onto a gravel road. There was a rippling feel and a rumble below, and Lee's feet almost slipped off the metal rung as they crossed a cattle guard. Then the ride got real dicey.

The road they were following went from gravel to wide ruts within just a few yards, and the van rolled slightly on the uneven ground like a rowboat sideways to a storm. At least the suspension was good on the Dodge, though the trip must be a lot more comfortable inside than out.

After a few more minutes of gentle to severe rocking and a random series of hops, the sound of the road changed to gravel again, and Lee looked down. They had to be very close to the cabin.

The van swung around in a one-eighty, and as they made the turn, Lee saw the building, a simple wood-framed house with what looked like redwood siding, a pitched roof, and a big stone fireplace at one end. The structure was small but cozy-looking, with the windows covered by iron bars to cut down on break-ins when the owners were away. But those wouldn't stop a vampire.

No vehicles were in sight, and there weren't any lights on in the cabin. Chances are it was a weekend residence, which meant the owners were extremely lucky tonight.

Lee grabbed his pistol and made sure the safety was off. Gathering power from the turquoise bear hunting fetish in his pants pocket, he eased to the ground as the van came to a stop, sliding a few inches in the gravel.

Crouching very low to avoid being seen in the side mirror, Lee moved around to the passenger door, on the side opposite the cabin, praying that the first person out wouldn't be the hostage.

"Stay!" Tanner yelled. There was a thump, and someone screamed. It wasn't a woman's voice either.

Lee cursed silently. Maybe he was already too late to save the hostage, but he instantly recognized the vampire's face as he opened the door and turned to step out of the van. Lee fired three times into Tanner's chest before he realized the man was wearing a bulletproof vest.

"You!" Tanner groaned, grabbing his midsection. Then he kicked out, delivering a glancing blow to Lee's forehead, knocking him to the gravel. Marci screamed, and Lee could see her scrambling to climb out the driver's side. The vampire was fast, and the assault rifle rested against the dash within arm's reach.

Lee fired again instinctively, taking out a chunk from Tanner's throat and splattering blood everywhere, but the wound didn't slow him down much. The assault weapon came up, and Lee rolled just as Tanner fired from the hip. One of the bullets nicked him in the side, the others spit into the gravel, showering him with rocks.

Lee kept rolling to the right, the front of the van blocking Tanner's line of sight, then managed to crouch, pistol ready despite the sting of the bullet, which must have nicked a rib. The vampire had disappeared. Hearing running footsteps, Lee turned his head and saw Marci racing up the road toward the highway— alone.

There was a grunt from inside the van. Lee kept low and slipped around to the passenger side, hoping that Tanner had lost consciousness. But no such luck, despite all the blood on the seat and gravel where he'd exited the vehicle. In the backseat was the hostage, middle-aged, graying hair, and needing a shave. The man, who seemed in good physical shape, was half naked, tied to the backrest with his belt and jeans, with duct tape across his mouth. His eyes were wide-open, his blood-splattered face projecting shock as he stared at the knife jammed at least four inches into his thigh. He was alive, and would probably survive, but where was Tanner?

Lee spun around, pistol ready. The blood trail suggested the vampire had circled around the back of the van and was coming up behind him. Lee crept around, expecting an ambush, but nobody was in sight, and all the stealthy motion did was send a wave of pain down his body. Lee heard what sounded like splintering wood and looked toward the cabin, fifty feet away. A thick trail of blood led across the gravel toward the structure. Up on the porch, he saw a door closing. It was Tanner. Unless Lee acted quickly, the vampire would be healed up again and at full strength.

Lee wanted more firepower, so he ran around to the passenger side, out of view from the cabin, and took another look inside the van. The barrel of a pistol was sticking out from beneath the front passenger's seat, and Lee picked it up. It was the Browning Hi-Power taken from the gun shop, and had a full clip of 9 mm rounds. The Browning was an excellent weapon and nearly the same size and weight as his Beretta. It would do.

He stuck the Browning into his belt and turned to the wounded man, noting that the blade had apparently missed a major artery and the blood flow wasn't going to be fatal immediately. "I'm a police officer, and more help will be here soon."

Lee reached over and turned off the van's dome light, took out the commando dagger from his boot, and cut the man free from the seat. Then he reached between the opening between the front seat backs and lowered the hostage to the floorboards, hoping Tanner was still too busy healing his wounds to take a potshot right now.

"Try not to move, and stay low. Can you breathe okay?"

The Anglo man shrugged.

"Removing the tape in a hurry might take part of your lip. You might want to work on that yourself if you feel up to it. I hate to leave, but I've got to go take care of the man who did this to you before he comes back."

The man's eyes widened, then he nodded.

"Good. Hang in there, buddy," Lee said, then leaned across the passenger cushion and pulled the key from the ignition. If Tanner decided to leave, he'd have to walk or hot-wire the van.

Lee jogged to the right, deciding to circle the cabin and make sure Tanner hadn't gone out a back door. Moving quickly, eyes on the windows, Lee took out the nearly spent .45 clip and inserted the second, full one into his little backup weapon, then put the pistol into his pocket. Taking the Browning in hand, he checked the safety lever to make sure it was down—ready to fire.

Just as he reached the right front corner, now beside the wall, he was illuminated by headlight beams. He stopped, not looking at the vehicle directly in order to preserve his night vision. "Tanner's in the cabin, wounded. I'm checking for any other exits," Lee yelled. "He has an assault rifle."

The car swung left, placing the engine block between the driver and the cabin front, the headlights illuminating one side of the cabin as she parked a dozen feet from the van. "Marci's safe now," Diane yelled, climbing out. "Said Tanner is loony."

"Ya think?"

"Why don't I cover the front?"

"Good idea," Lee yelled, now able to see the rear of the cabin. "Load AP rounds or take head shots. Tanner's wearing a vest. The hostage is in the van. He's wounded, but I think he'll make it."

"Thanks. I've already added the EMTs to our backup."

Lee could see there was no back door to the cabin, and that the two windows were barred, like those in front. Tanner would have to make a lot of noise breaking out, and they'd be able to hear. Lee stood behind a pine tree, just in case Tanner had followed his movements, and looked for any openings that might provide an exit. Again, everything looked tight. Even the concrete foundation was sealed except for a crawl space blocked off by carefully stacked cinder blocks.

Then Lee came up with a strategy. He grabbed a big rock, actually more of a boulder weighing perhaps sixty pounds, then hurried around to the front, crouching low as he passed under a window. He stepped back a few feet from the door, then threw the boulder—like a basketball—into the middle of the thick wooden door. As if launched by a medieval catapult, the heavy stone crunched into the wood, caving in the center as it splintered two or three heavy planks.

Expecting a quick reaction, Lee dove toward the end of the building, barely making it to the corner as several bullets kicked up the ground at his heels. Diane fired her shotgun at the window Tanner was shooting from, shattering glass and driving him back.

Lee scrambled to his feet, sprinted around the cabin via the back too quickly for Tanner to track him, then emerged from the far end of the house. Moving as quickly as he could, he continued the near-circle, ending up on the passenger side of the van, out of sight.

Diane was less than twenty feet away, crouched low behind her own vehicle. Lee was glad to see she was wearing a bullet-resistant vest.

"Where *is* Marci?" he whispered.

"Hugging a tree farther up the road, courtesy of my handcuffs." Her gaze never left the cabin, but her words were directed to him. "Just like to throw rocks, or was that last stunt part of a plan?"

244 DAVID & AIMÉE THURLO

"I think he's only got the one clip, and I have his pistol. He can't have more than a dozen rounds left now." Lee took a quick peek into the van through the open passenger door and noted the injured man had managed to remove the tape from his mouth. "How you doing?"

"I've been better," the former hostage managed. "When you gonna pull this thing out?" He pointed to the knife still jammed in his thigh. Blood was still seeping from the wound, but no worse than before.

"I'll let the EMTs do that. The bleeding will kick up once the blade's out, and they'll have the skill to deal with it. But now I need your help. I'm going to have to get you out of there because I need to borrow your van." Lee turned to Diane. "I'm bringing him over beside you. If you see Tanner, blast him."

Lee tried to be gentle, but he had to move quickly, and the handle of the knife bumped the seat when he slid the man out onto the ground. There was a loud groan, and the man's eyes closed.

Lee dragged the man by his shoulders over behind Diane, protected by her car. "I think he passed out. You think he needs a tourniquet to slow the bleeding?"

"Keep an eye out for Tanner. I'll look him over."

Only a few minutes had gone by since Diane had arrived, but a full vampire could be healed within fifteen minutes or less, depending on the severity of his injuries. If Lee was going to make his move, it had to be soon. "What you got in the trunk?"

Diane had just reached into her vehicle and brought out a first aid kit. "Two flash bangs, tear gas canisters, one smoke grenade, ammo. Anything special in mind?"

"The flash bangs should help. Keys?"

"Here. The stuff is in the black briefcase." She looked up from the injured man and reached into her pocket, bringing out the keys. Lee grabbed them, then moved to the rear of the vehicle, all the time watching the cabin. Tanner wasn't visible, but

Lee knew he was probably just standing back, watching and waiting as his neck mended.

"How's our patient?"

"He's out to the world. Tanner's our priority now."

"We're on the same page then." Lee opened the trunk just enough to reach in for the briefcase, and saw a ballistic vest inside as well. Twenty seconds later, he was wearing the vest, and had two flash bang grenades in the pockets.

"What's the plan?" Diane asked.

"I'm going to break into the cabin and put Tanner down."

"Simple and direct. How you gonna do that and stay alive, Lee?"

"I'm taking an old travel companion with me." Lee nodded toward the van.

"Okay. It could work. But expect me to come in right behind you. He's going to be tough to deal with," Diane replied.

"Just cover my ass. And remember his assault rifle will penetrate your vest."

"And yours, Lee."

"Here goes." He passed behind her, and she reached out for his arm. He paused, gave her hand a squeeze, then hurried over to the van.

"Want covering fire?" she said, bringing the shotgun up and aiming it toward the cabin.

"Naw. Let's make it a surprise." Lee slid into the passenger's side of the van, closed the door behind him, then maneuvered over to the driver's side. He started the engine, put the vehicle in gear, then backed away slowly, as if leaving.

Lee glanced over at Diane. She had no idea exactly what he had in mind, but was self-disciplined enough to keep her eye on the cabin. Lee floored it now and, instead of heading straight for the front porch of the cabin, went to the right, parallel to the structure. When he reached the end he made a sharp left, cutting around the corner. Then he started honking the horn.

Hoping Tanner was confused about the chaos and uncertain about which side to cover, Lee continued to lean on the horn as he raced down the back wall, then turned left sharply again, nearly clipping the corner. As soon as he cleared the left front corner of the cabin, Lee cut the brakes, slid sideways across the gravel, kicking up dust, then accelerated toward the cabin at an angle, planning on ramming the nearly destroyed front door—driver's side first.

By the time Tanner realized he needed to start shooting, Lee had ducked down to the floorboard on the passenger's side. The van bounced right up the steps.

The jolt was terrific, tossing Lee around like a tennis ball in a clothes drier, but the momentum of the van carried him halfway into the building. Wood and chunks of plasterboard started falling from the wall and ceiling and the dust was terrible, but the bullets striking the driver's side of the van and the vampire's insane howl told Lee that Tanner was mobile now, though thankfully on the other side of the room—and the van.

Lee, on his belly, grabbed for the passenger's door handle, but it jammed after opening only a few inches. Punching the panel of the door with the heel of his hand, he forced it open another two feet. As Tanner's half-assed war cry vibrated in his ears, Lee felt a sharp thump across his shoulder and realized he'd been grazed by a bullet that the vest had managed to deflect.

Suddenly there was a blast from a new direction—Diane and her shotgun. Lee took the opportunity to dive out onto the floor and forward roll back to a crouching position. As Diane fired again, Lee drew the Browning and hugged the front corner of the van. When he looked around the side, pistol first, he saw Tanner stumbling back across the debris-covered floor, swatting at bloody wounds on his face as if he were under assault from wasps. His hands were empty and his screeches had become mere gasps and grunts.

Lee stood and fired, hitting Tanner under the arm where the

vest didn't cover. Tanner yelped, then fled toward a bedroom ten feet away. Lee fired again, this time trying for a head shot that sounded like a clean miss.

Diane fired twice with her pistol. Lee could see the dust kick up from the bullet impact on the back of Tanner's vest as he ducked into the bedroom. The vampire kicked the door shut behind him, and Lee's next shot was probably wasted, holing the door.

"Those should have penetrated his vest, Lee," Diane shouted, picking her way farther into the room around big pieces of the old door frame and fallen ceiling panels. "Let's finish him off."

Lee saw the assault rifle on the floor among shattered chunks of wood, sheetrock, and a half dozen or more shell casings. "He's probably unarmed, but he's still fast as hell and can grab our weapons if he gets close enough. And remember, the room has a window."

There was a small pop, then a crackle and new sounds and smells came to life. Lee stepped back just as the hood of the van blew up with a whoosh, shooting flames out six feet in all directions.

Diane was knocked back a few steps, but she'd thrown her arm up to cover her eyes and escaped being scorched. "Whoa. We've got to get out of here before the gas tank goes up."

"I'll cover the bedroom door. Once you get out, go around to the bedroom window and keep watch. If you see his face or he tries to break out . . ."

"Right." Diane picked her way past Lee and hastily around the front of the van, keeping as much distance as she could from the cooking engine compartment. The smoke was getting thick and harsh already, but she moved quickly. A few more seconds and she squeezed through the gap between the side of the vehicle and the caved-in wall, disappearing.

Lee saw the bedroom doorknob turn, so he fired three shots,

one down low, and another to either side. Tanner yelled, and the doorknob stopped moving.

Then Lee backed out of the room, stumbling twice on debris because he didn't want to take his eye off the door. The flames were rising higher now in the engine compartment, the black smoke filling the room. Feeling his way the last seven or eight feet, Lee hugged the side of the van and slipped out onto the porch.

Hoping he had at least a few more seconds, Lee stuck the Browning into his belt, then leaned against the van and pushed as hard as he could. It only rolled another three feet before the rear wheel touched the porch step and stopped, but the intrusion would increase the chances that the exploding gas took down the building quickly and completely.

Lee's cell phone began to vibrate, but he took several steps back away from the porch before answering it. "Yeah. What?"

"I had to make sure you got out, but didn't want Tanner to know," Diane said. "I've moved back some more, but I haven't seen him at the window. Think the van is going to blow soon?"

"It can't be long now."

"Lee, the foundation looks pretty solid. Suppose there's a basement?"

"Crap. Maybe. And Tanner is strong enough to rip up the floorboards if he can get something to pry with."

"Like a metal rail from the bed?"

"Better keep an eye on the crawl space. It's got some cinder blocks in the way, but Tanner will be able to push them aside without much trouble if he can get beneath the floor."

"Gotcha."

Lee noticed that the fire inside had spread to the curtains and the splintered lumber from the door and exposed wall studs. The house was going to burn down, that was certain. He turned his head slightly, trying to hear the sirens of approaching backup and rescue units, but got nothing.

Still watching the shattered entrance to the cabin, especially the gap between the van and the structure, Lee moved back farther now. He wanted to take a look at the wounded former hostage, but was still afraid to look away from the cabin for even a second in case Tanner decided to make a break for it. "Kind of strange, hoping the fire department doesn't get here soon," Lee said.

"I know what you mean, but . . ."

The van's gas tank exploded, flinging wood, metal, plastic, and glass out like a Mount St. Helens eruption—all in one direction. The heat and force of the blast knocked Lee down. He'd seen just a brief flash before the explosion, however, and was turning away when the full force arrived, so he fell facedown. Flying debris landed all around, smaller chunks whistling overhead, and there were several clanks of metal as pieces bounced off Diane's car. Hopefully the former hostage was well enough protected by the vehicle.

Somehow he'd managed to keep the cell phone in his grip. Sitting up and looking toward the raging inferno of van and cabin, which was totally engulfed now, Lee spoke. "You okay? Diane?"

He stood and began to walk quickly toward the rear of the cabin. Tanner wasn't coming out the front, that was certain. "Diane?"

"Lee, help. Tanner!" Then he heard gunshots.

He raced toward the rear of the cabin, switching the Browning to his left hand and pulling out his .45 with his right. Rounding the back corner, he saw Diane kneeling on the ground, pistol in hand, aimed toward an opening in the foundation. Several cinder blocks had been pushed or blown away.

"I'm okay. Tanner pushed the blocks out, and I managed to get enough angle to shoot him in the arm and maybe the shoulder. He ducked back inside." She stood, wiping at her eyes with a sleeve. "Got soot in my eyes, or dust from the blast. Knocked me on my butt."

"You held your own. That's a win. Why don't you take a walk around the cabin   make sure he doesn't try a walk-through-fire stunt, then chec   the wounded man and our backup. I'll make sure Tanner doesn   come out alive."

"Want my pistol? There are still three or four AP rounds in the clip." She held out the weapon, watching the house instead of him.

"Naw. Keep it and the shotgun. I just wish we had something more explosive than those flash bangs. Maybe a fragmentation grenade."

"Won't need it once the house collapses—if the heat and fumes don't get him first," Diane said. "I'd better get around to the other side." She turned and jogged away, carrying the shotgun in front of her with both hands, ready.

Lee only glanced away for a few seconds and was able to detect movement in the crawl space as Tanner sneaked a look. Six feet above, flames licked at the bedroom window, and higher, the roof was yellow-orange, shooting sparks into the sky. It was getting hot in the cabin.

Wondering what the chances were that the cloud of sparks drifting away would set off a forest fire, Lee inched toward the crawl space. Closer now, he could see floor joists and the support piers, but the vampire was hugging the foundation wall, hidden from sight.

"Come out, Tanner, you've been through enough. Let's end it. I'll make it quick," Lee yelled, getting down on one knee, inching even closer to the wall but still keeping some distance in case Tanner had found a tool or something to jab at him.

"If they can find *me*, Hawk, they'll find *you*. Think on that," Tanner said, his voice faint and hollow in the enclosed space. "Give me a way out and you'll never see me again. We're like brothers, you and me. The same, really."

"Don't include me in your family, Tanner. We're not even close to alike. You killed a lot of people who had nothing to do with your situation. Good people with families who just happened to get in your way."

"I had no choice. It was them or me. And Victor Wayne's people . . . those doctors you're defending? They set me on *fire* so they could time how long it took me to heal up again. What would you have done?"

Lee had seen several vampires explode into flames, and heard their screams cut short as they literally disintegrated. It wasn't something to talk about.

The fire and smoke were getting worse, and Tanner started a long coughing spasm. Finally he stopped. "Let me go and I'll just disappear. I'll hide it better this time." His voice was a mere whisper now.

Lee could finally hear sirens in the distance, and he was grateful. Hopefully one of the vehicles was from a fire department. If the wind picked up, a lot of forest would burn down, and he didn't want that to add to an overburdened conscience.

He'd already decided Tanner wasn't coming out alive, even if that meant he'd have to crawl inside and kill him up close. The former cook, restaurant owner, and hunter had become a mass murderer. Certifiably insane, Tanner would keep killing, as he'd shown with even the innocent.

"Time's up, Tanner. I can kill you, or let the smoke and flames do it for me. Your choice."

Hot winds generated by the swirling fire started whipping up dust and debris, and Lee thought he heard Tanner say something. Lee stepped closer, still wary.

"I'm afraid of fire, Hawk. Don't let me die like this. Give me your pistol. One shot in the heart. I'll do it myself. No guilt for you either."

"What makes you think I'd feel guilty? Just move into view. I'll have no problem. How many did you kill—today? Eight?"

Another minute went by, then Tanner spoke again. "Will you do one thing for me, then, Hawk . . . after I'm dead?"

"What's that?"

"Kill Victor Wayne. He made me what . . . I've become."

"You weren't the first vampire to end up as a guinea pig. But there are a few of us around that want to make sure you're the last. That's all I can promise you."

The noise from the sirens grew closer and Lee could hear vehicles, especially the deep rumble of a fire engine. He reached down, released the clip from the Browning, then quickly thumbed out all the rounds before inserting it back into the butt of the pistol. He tossed the pistol into the opening, then stood back, his .45 aimed at the spot. "There's still one round in the chamber, Tanner. Aim for your heart, and don't miss. I'm leaving you in there, either way."

"Fuck you very much, Hawk."

"You too, vampire." Lee took another step back. A blood-soaked hand reached out for the Browning, then disappeared from sight.

Out of the corner of his eye Lee saw Diane standing to his left, well back, looking in his direction. Her shotgun was still ready.

A few seconds went by, Lee heard what could have been a sob, then the gunshot.

Lee moved closer, his forty-five still ready in case Tanner was trying to fool him one last time. Then a low rumble started to build, the sound increasing quickly. Lee stood and stepped back in a hurry. With an enormous cracking roar, what was left of the roof came tumbling down, collapsing the weakened walls. The ground shook, and all they could see through the crawl space opening were flames and billowing smoke.

It was ten in the morning, and Lee sat in a big government SUV, reapplying sunblock. Tanner's body hadn't been found yet, but it was no surprise to him. Even a dead vampire's remains turned to ashes when the sun came up. When the forensics people and the firemen uncovered the spot where the body was, once the ruins cooled enough to sift through, it would flash into a powder. The next heavy rain, Tanner's ashes would become just another few pounds of sediment carried down to the river a quarter mile away. Or perhaps he'd end up in a landfill along with the charred remains of the cabin.

Lee didn't know if a vampire could suffocate from the smoke and toxic fumes, but he did know it was possible to hold his breath a long time. He'd made himself pass out years ago in a half-assed experiment. The reports back at the research lab on the Rez hadn't documented any respiratory experiments conducted on Stewart Tanner, so it was a question that would go unanswered. But fire was definitely a yes.

The vampire was gone now, and even if the lack of a body extended the search, it probably wouldn't last long. Lee's musings were brought to reality again when the car door opened.

"Set to take another walk through the forest to satisfy the skeptics who insist on finding Tanner's remains?" Diane asked. Her hair was tucked up into a baseball cap, she had a canteen on her waist, and she looked exhausted.

"Yeah. Beats sifting through burning rubble. But let's insist on the river this time. I'm still hot from last night."

Ten minutes later, after a climb down a steep trail, Lee stood in the shade of the cliff beside the river, looking for a cave or overhang on the opposite bank that could theoretically contain a hiding vampire. Diane had a handheld infrared scope that would detect heat. Together, they believed no living creature could escape their scrutiny, especially one as large as Stewart Tanner. Besides, he'd died beneath the cabin.

"Dr. Wayne still a no-show on the search?"

Diane lowered the scope. "While you were putting on more sun protection, I got a call on my cell. According to Farmington PD, Dr. Victor Wayne took off for Albuquerque on a chartered plane with the federal agent that was wounded at the model home fiasco. The patient is headed for the University Hospital there. At least he's going to make it."

"Doesn't seem right that Tanner and so many others paid with their lives and Victor's still alive and kicking."

"He'll get his. I have a feeling that in the mad scramble of bureaucrats out to cover their own butts, Victor'll get offered up as a sacrifice to the families of the victims. But I wonder how many people really knew what was going on with Tanner and the research? And how are the government honchos going to justify all the casualties resulting from trying to keep control of a self-proclaimed vampire?"

"That's their problem now." Lee looked down at the river, then started walking slowly upstream. "If I'd have made it to the river, I'd have gone this way."

Diane followed his gaze. "You believe Tanner faked his suicide, lasted out the fire, then somehow made it to the river before daylight?"

"No. But you're going to have a person watching Marci Walker for a while, aren't you? Just in case? She knew he was a vampire, and they were lovers—for a while."

"Yeah. And if Tanner can come back from the dead for anyone, it'll be for Marci. Crazy or not, she swears he loved her."

Lee turned to look at the beautiful woman walking beside him. "Yeah, vampires are people too."